THE BARBARIAN PRINCESS

D0879625

THE BARBARIAN PRINCESS

SKHARR DEATHEATER™ SERIES BOOK 07

MICHAEL ANDERLE

DISRUPTIVE IMAGINATION®

This book is a work of fiction. All of the characters, organizations, and events portrayed in this novel are either products of the author's imagination or are used fictitiously. Sometimes both.

Copyright © 2021 LMBPN Publishing
Cover copyright © LMBPN Publishing
A Michael Anderle Production

LMBPN Publishing supports the right to free expression and the value of copyright. The purpose of copyright is to encourage writers and artists to produce the creative works that enrich our culture.

The distribution of this book without permission is a theft of the author's intellectual property. If you would like permission to use material from the book (other than for review purposes), please contact support@lmbpn.com. Thank you for your support of the author's rights.

LMBPN Publishing
PMB 196, 2540 South Maryland Pkwy
Las Vegas, NV 89109

Version 1.00 June 2021
ebook ISBN: 978-1-64971-847-1
Paperback ISBN: 978-1-64971-848-8

THE BARBARIAN PRINCESS TEAM

Thanks to our JIT Team:

John Ashmore
Dorothy Lloyd
Diane L. Smith
Zacc Pelter
Jackey Hankard-Brodie
Kelly O'Donnell
Peter Manis
Jeff Goode
Rachel Beckford
Paul Westman

If I've missed anyone, please let me know!

Editor
SkyHunter Editing Team

To Family, Friends and
Those Who Love
To Read.
May We All Enjoy Grace
To Live The Life We Are
Called.

— Michael

CHAPTER ONE

The difference lay in the heat, she decided.

Cassandra had been around numerous fires, some of them under control and some of them not and yet, if anyone had asked her what the difference was between regular flames and dragonfire, she would have told them it was the heat.

It had an explosive element to it as well, but she was ten feet away from the green-and-blue flames and it scorched her skin even from that distance.

A massive beast—a size she was told dragons no longer attained—wandered across the rocks, which seemed to be on fire as well. She knew stone couldn't catch alight, yet the evidence to the contrary was visible and inarguable. The dragon didn't care much about this apparent contradiction, however. Instead, it slithered through the flames like a snake before it launched skyward. Its colossal wings carried it higher and fanned the fire into the paladins at the same time.

She stepped into the path of the blaze as her teammates tried to retreat. With grim determination, she called on all the power she had available to her and breathed out to stop the inexorable advance of the flames.

"Help me!"

They were the last words she heard before the conflagration overwhelmed her. The blast rumbled and roared through her senses and she realized the dragon now breathed fire on them again. She was utterly powerless and without help, she was no match for it.

The flames crawled up her arms and although she knew she screamed, she couldn't hear it. Pain whipped across her skin like it was being scraped off her with a rusty dagger.

The agony was unbearable but she would hold on as long as she could. Even if they wouldn't help her, she could keep the shield up long enough for them to remove themselves from the battlefield. They could survive and she would haunt them for the rest of their lives for being fucking hide-their-heads-up-their-asses cowards.

Darkness enveloped her suddenly and no longer constrained by her shield, Cassandra was able to move. She rolled off the bed and onto the cold stone and flailed for any sign of the shield she could use to defend herself. It seemed impossible that it had vanished without a trace. She would have felt that.

As her eyes adjusted slowly, she realized she was no longer out on the Seastones. The dragon was gone and so were her paladins. She was in her room in the temple. The tangle of sheets on the bed told her she had been asleep and from the looks of it, not particularly restfully either.

The fact that she couldn't remember the dream didn't mean she didn't know what it was about. It followed a hundred different scenarios but always ended the same with her alone and her hands outstretched to stop the dragonfire but to no avail.

Cassandra shivered gently, pulled the blanket from her bed, and wrapped it around her shoulders. An odd effect from that day was that she had an inordinate difficulty warming herself—like her body was actively sapped of heat—and she needed to be bundled in blankets and covers almost all the time.

They'd found only her alive. All the others had been turned to ash as they tried to run before the flames caught up with them. The shield had been all that saved her life long enough for the healers to help and even then, it had taken weeks for her to recover. Weeks of walking around with bandages covering most of her body like a leper.

None of the scars remained. It felt almost impossible. There should be some kind of physical sign of what happened but when she looked at her skin, she found nothing. Even the old scars she'd collected from her various battles were gone.

The only real loss was her hair, which had already begun to grow again. She liked it shorter, though. It gave her a somewhat boyish look—or it would if it didn't match the rings under her eyes.

Sleep would come, the high priest told her. He had merely neglected to mention when.

After a long moment during which she stared at nothing, she registered something happening outside her room. With a grimace, she pushed from the floor and drew her blanket tighter around her shoulders as she moved toward the door.

The shouts weren't that uncommon among the denizens of the temple. She had been around for long enough to know that their philosophical arguments often tended to get heated before too long.

And yet, when the sound of a hard fist impacting flesh echoed through the hallways, she decided she needed to involve herself. Not because she expected any of them to be hurt but in the end, it was her job to put a stop to fights when she could. Most of the academics in the temple listened to her when she told them to calm themselves.

It truly was odd how they were the ones who got worked up the easiest.

Cassandra pushed the door open, stepped into the hallway, and followed the sound of the vociferous debate. It seemed to be punctuated by more sounds of violence, which confused her somewhat. This was not how most arguments went, of course. Perhaps they were getting worked up over whether the gods were siblings or entirely unrelated. It was one of the most sensitive subjects as it involved the question of whether or not there was a father and a mother, as was implied if they were brothers and sisters.

"You cannot walk into the temple like this!" the high priest yelled. "It's simply not done!"

That meant there was someone new in the temple.

"I can wander in whenever the godsbedammed hells I want. Haven't you heard? I'm the Barbarian of Theros!"

It couldn't be. She narrowed her eyes and turned the corner.

"Barbarian of Theros or not, to invade the temple in the middle of the night—"

"If I were invading, there would be considerably more trouble involved and many more of your guards would be dead by this point."

She reached the scene of the altercation and paused to study it. Two of the guards scrambled to their feet, located their weapons, and rushed to where a tall, powerfully built human held the high priest by the collar with one hand. He dragged the man behind him while he held one of the guards by the jaw with the other.

A tall barbarian, no less, with bright red hair and scars across his exposed skin. There was no possible way to mistake Skharr DeathEater at this point and she simply waited to watch events unfold.

"Your violence disputes that." The high priest managed to regain his footing using Skharr's arm as support.

The barbarian laughed and tossed the guard into a nearby pillar, although with considerably less force than what he generally brought to combat. The other two defenders rushed closer and seemed determined to use their weapons with deadly intent.

He caught one with a swift kick to the knees before he could close the distance. The man tripped and fell heavily as the other lunged forward with his spear.

It looked like a sound thrust but to the man's astonishment, it missed. His large opponent simply swayed to the side to avoid it, kicked the spear out of his hands, and grasped him by the neck to lift his feet off the floor.

If there was ever a time to get involved, it was now or Skharr would eventually kill the men.

"Skharr," she called and clutched her blanket lest she lose it. "What in the nine hells are you doing here?"

All the men looked to where the paladin stood, although the warrior appeared to be the only one who was happy to see her. His warm brown eyes lit up and a broad grin spread across his features as he dropped both the guard and high priest like a child who had found a nicer toy to play with and decided to abandon those he already had.

"Cassandra, it's good to see you again!" he responded as he approached her. "They said you weren't available but I had a feeling that if I made enough noise, you would find me eventually."

"That is your preferred tactical approach, yes." She smiled, took his proffered hand to shake it firmly, and tried not to wince when he almost crushed her hand in his grasp. "Is that why you are assaulting the high priest and the temple guards?"

"In fairness, they attacked me first." Skharr growled his annoyance as he glanced at the group that regained their equilibrium and helped each other to stand slowly. "I could have retaliated in kind but I feel that would have escalated the situation and resulted in deaths and serious injuries. Theros would not have been pleased about that."

He had a point there, at least.

"What are you doing here?" Cassandra asked once she was assured that none of the guards would continue their attacks. She had no idea why they had tried to stop him from reaching her, but she didn't have much say on how the temple was run. They didn't question her staying there for as long as she needed to and when she asked for something, it was delivered. The high priest, however, had the final say in who was admitted.

That seemed both logical and appropriate, but from what she'd heard about what the barbarian had done, he had as much right to be in the temple as she did.

"I've come to collect you, of course." He grinned. "Horse and me. We've been told that you've been through an ordeal and it won't be resolved by hiding in your room while you barely eat and wallow in your nightmares. Frankly, I can't think of anything that does solve."

She raised her eyebrows. What had happened to her hadn't been spoken of beyond her talks with the high priest, which meant the word had been given to him by Theros. She assumed as much, at least. If the high priest had sent for him, he wouldn't have needed to brawl his way in.

Yet brawl he had and might have to continue. A handful of bruised and battered men rushed into the antechamber and looked like they were ready to continue the fight since the intruder had left them behind.

"Are you here to take her away?" the high priest asked and approached them cautiously.

"Aye. And I'm not here to deal with your ass-licking toadies— something you've forced me into and wears on my patience."

"What patience?" Cassandra asked.

"You ask that while a group of battered bastards is spread all over this fucking temple," he retorted.

"Battered!" The priest looked like he didn't quite believe his audacity.

"Your men could have been killed," she pointed out to the man and raised an eyebrow. "You do know who he is, yes?"

"Of course." The cleric adjusted his ruffled collar and straightened his long gray beard. "The Barbarian of Theros is known to us."

"Then why did you try to stop him?"

"Because he said he was here to collect you."

"And?"

"Well…it is highly questionable given your status."

The man had a point, although Skharr held a similar status to hers. As such, there wasn't any real reason why the man had any right to deny him access. Of course, she would have some say as to whether she would leave or not, but if the barbarian had been contacted by Theros, she wouldn't.

"Fuck off now," the warrior said bluntly. "And see to your men. They fought well, even if it was for an idiot."

With a wordless splutter of indignation, the high priest turned to the injured men as a handful of the temple staff came out to see what all the trouble was about. Some immediately began to attend to those who were injured.

"I think you enjoyed that a little too much," Cassandra pointed out once the man was out of earshot. "Do you honestly think Theros would be pleased that you chose to bully his high priests?"

"He knew who I was when he sent me here to find you," he answered smoothly. "If he wanted the godsbedammed god-sucker to be left with his dignity, he should have warned the bastard."

She shook her head as he began to stride down the hallway and away from where most of the guards were huddled, unsure of what to do about the barbarian who strolled calmly through the temple after he'd fought them every step of the way. In fairness, Theros should have known better but had chosen to send him without warning regardless.

"Theros sent you?"

"Aye. He appeared to me on the road once I had delivered a dwarf to his family and said you'd had a run-in with a dragon that left you scarred."

Cassandra looked at her arms as a tingle of sensation traveled up them, but there was still no sign of any scars.

"No visible scars," the barbarian responded quietly. "So the kind that lurks in your head, then. They take longer to heal, though, and I don't think there is much magic in the world that can correct them."

"Not that you would know about that."

Skharr stopped and studied her carefully as if he tried to decide if she was joking or not. He didn't seem like the type of person who had nightmares over his past battles. There were likely so many that if he did, they would start to become mixed and confused.

"Is that what you think of me?" he asked.

She shrugged. "I…well, perhaps. I assumed you didn't let such things affect you as much."

He tilted his head and shrugged. "That is…interesting. Either way, you'll need to lead me. I wanted us away from the other group in case they decided they wanted to start another fight, but this godsbedammed temple is a maze and I have no intention to try to navigate it on my own."

She motioned for him to follow her through the hallway that led to the right. "It takes time but I have finally managed to learn the layout without losing myself too often. I did not believe I would be here long enough for that to happen but once I arrived, I could not bring myself to leave."

"That sounds familiar," he answered. "But it isn't a feeling you should entertain. The longer you allow it a foothold, the more difficult it will be to break free. And more importantly, the more influence you will have over the witless sycophants who live in these places."

The paladin looked at him as they came to a halt outside her quarters. "What is that supposed to mean?"

"You working your womanly magic on the temple guards," Skharr asserted with a firm nod. "I noticed that they were particularly ineffective in our fights and I had to assume that something you did had weakened them."

That brought a smile to her lips for the first time in what felt like years as she opened the door and let him enter before she did. "I've not worked any magical wiles on them, and if you mean something else entirely, I have not indulged in that either."

"Why not?" The barbarian regarded her with an expression that was both speculative and challenging. "I've found that a nice rough fuck is one of the finest ways to improve one's mindset."

The worst part was that he wasn't wrong about that. "All the guards here have taken vows of celibacy, and they would think any attempt on my part to have them break those vows would be to entrap them and see them expelled. They fear the paladins more than almost any others in that regard."

"Well." Skharr cleared his throat. "That explains why they were such poor fighters. That much pent-up need in a man will always be a distraction and your womanly powers come into play again."

"How?"

"Well, if they are inclined toward women, they would find themselves distracted by your presence. It would remind them of their pent-up condition and they would thus prove themselves less skilled in combat."

She couldn't understand that. It didn't make much sense even though she tried to wrap her mind around it while she gathered her things.

"That sounds distinctly like a problem they should see to," she pointed out, retrieved her pack, and sifted through the mess of clothes flung about the room. "And it has little or nothing to do with me."

"True enough. You have nothing to do with it but it is a tactical consideration. The idiocy of others always needs to be accounted for."

That sounded a little more accurate, or it made a little more sense at least. She hefted her sword, studied the filigree, and ran her fingers over it.

"Am I on sabbatical, then?" she asked and glanced at him where he attempted to help her to pack everything.

"Aye." He nodded. "We are."

"Paladins have sabbaticals," she reminded him and checked the pack that held her armor. "I'm not sure what you would have. It isn't as though anything you do would change how you would act normally."

Skharr laughed. It was a deep, pleasant sound that she realized she had missed after so much time away from him. How strange that he hadn't come to mind much while she was out and about but she'd thought of him increasingly while she had wallowed in her misery at the temple.

"I am the first Barbarian of Theros," the warrior replied with a cheeky grin. "And I make my own godsbedammed rules as I please."

"No doubt and yet here you are, responding to Theros' call."

"Bullshit. I came because a friend was in pain and there was a possibility that I could help."

CHAPTER TWO

"Where are we going?"

It was a good question. The sun had begun to rise in the east and the city already showed signs of life as the gates opened and wagons with produce from the surrounding countryside streamed in. Everyone around them seemed sure of their purpose and destination, but he had no clear idea of where they would go.

Skharr seemed content to simply get her out of the temple as quickly as possible, mounted on her horse, and out into the cool, fresh air of the world.

One of the advantages had been meeting Horse again. She'd discovered that the barbarian had an effect on her in that she now spoke to any and all four-legged members of any party she was in as if they walked on two legs. It had earned her a few odd glances from the other paladins but as she had more than earned her position as the head of their order, none of them questioned her openly on it.

The stallion nudged her leg gently.

"I know. I've missed you too, you big bastard," she murmured

11

and stretched her hand to scratch at the top of his head. "Less so the big bastard you travel around with."

"I can hear you," Skharr said and glanced over his shoulder at her.

"It's good of you to remind us that your sense of hearing is still functional," she retorted with a grin. "Has he been in this poor a temper all the time you've traveled without me?"

Horse snorted loudly, and she took that to mean a yes as well as a demonstration of how frustrating it had been to travel the lands without anyone to understand his pain.

Further confirmation came when the warrior turned with a deep scowl on his face. "It was one time and that was only because…well, it was a particularly bad day. I'd dealt with a gods-bedammed Kraken that attacked our ship and I snapped at you only once. I gave you apples afterward as an apology."

"I see what you mean," Cassandra whispered and patted the beast's neck until her mount, a gray gelding, snorted and tried to nip the stallion to force him back a few steps.

"So, barbarian?" she asked once her companion had fallen silent again. "Do you have any idea where you want to go this early in the day or did you hope I would direct you like I did at the temple?"

Skharr looked at her and grinned. "I merely wondered which of the inns are the most likely to still serve patrons. Or already serve patrons this early. If you have any suggestions, I would be glad to hear them. I arrived this morning and have tried to find you for most of the day."

"I cannot say I've explored much of the region," the paladin replied and frowned as she looked around. Her night of sleep had been rudely interrupted and she had a feeling that rest would not come for a little while longer.

If she had to go without enough sleep, the barbarian was the right person to travel with, especially if he was similarly deprived of rest.

"I would assume the Goose's Neck is still open," she said with a soft sigh. "I've heard the city guards talk of going there after their work at night is finished when the sun rises."

"The Goose's Neck it is," he agreed. "Lead the way."

"And what do you plan to do after we have drunk and eaten our fill?" Cassandra asked. "That might take a while but my habit is to constantly look to the future when I am out and about."

Skharr dug in one of Horse's saddlebags and rummaged through for a few seconds before he withdrew a ball of thick red yarn and tossed it to her.

She caught it easily and studied it with a frown. It was quality thread and she wasn't sure how he'd found it. In all honesty, she hadn't thought he had an eye for that kind of thing.

"What is this supposed to mean?"

"The way I see it when I consider your circumstances, you have a choice. You can become Ytrea again and live out your days as you might have been meant to. On the other hand, you could return to Theros' service and find a way to fight your ghosts. Sometimes, the first option can lead to the second, but it is perhaps the most natural of them. There is little to be said beyond that."

"You can be an ass," she pointed out and tucked the ball of yarn into one of her saddlebags.

"That has never been in doubt," Skharr answered with a grin. "Or a man-whore, as appropriate."

She shook her head and guided her horse into the courtyard of a small building with a wooden sign that displayed a goose with an especially long neck hanging outside. The neck looped itself a handful of times before it culminated in the goose with its beak open to scare a handful of men on horseback away.

There was a story behind that sign. She knew that much although she couldn't recall it and wasn't sure if she'd even heard it in full. A young lad who looked like he had just woken up approached them and tried to take the reins of both horses.

Her gelding paid him no mind but Horse snorted and jerked the reins away from his hands.

"Oy." Skharr grunted. "Mind your manners or they'll not give you apples."

The stallion appeared to heed the warning, tossed his mane, and let the boy lead him away.

"Be sure to have some apples delivered to his stable if you want him to be cooperative," the barbarian instructed and slipped the youth a handful of coppers before he let him go on his way.

He realized that Cassandra was studying him closely and he shrugged.

"The beast has followed me through some terrible places in the world," he said quietly as they entered the inn. "I would be a horrid friend if I did not reward him for his loyalty."

"I didn't say anything."

"And yet you thought it."

The establishment was somewhat deserted and only a handful of guards sat around two of the tables. They narrowed their eyes when they saw him enter but made no attempt to stop him. Instead, they looked away and returned their attention to their drinks.

They knew her, at least, even if they didn't know him, and knew better than to give a paladin trouble, no matter how tired they were after a long night. Skharr led them to a table on the other side of the room, sat carefully to test his weight on the chair, and shook his head.

"You haven't slept much either, have you?" Cassandra asked as she sat across from him. "Have you been around the whole town looking for me since you arrived?"

He smirked. "I was exploring and got lost. A group of the local guards harassed me a little until they realized who I was and directed me toward the temple."

"Why did you not simply ask for directions at the gate?"

"I did not think I needed them. This is a comparatively small town and I could see the temple from the gate. Once I was inside, however, there was an issue with this whole godsbedammed city being built by a drunk madman."

His description wasn't amiss. There was no real design around the settlement. The construction of walls had only made the area that much more confusing as the buildings were gradually positioned closer together, which made the narrow streets narrower and led to a wide variety of structures closing some roads off entirely.

It was a point of pride for the locals, she'd learned. They decided it would cause any invading army to get lost if they tried to navigate the city. This was the second wall they'd had to build so they could perhaps be excused for thinking like that.

She didn't agree with it and didn't like it. More than anything it offended her tactical sensibilities since it would result in sacrificing the civilians if it ever happened. The fact that the civilians themselves were the ones to say it simply felt wrong. Perhaps they were far enough removed from the wars and the battles at the borders of the empire to remember the appalling state cities were left in once the attackers were done with them.

Still, perhaps it was best that they remained ignorant of it.

The innkeeper had the same bleary look in his eyes as his patrons—like he had partaken of his wares the night before but had to be present for the day.

"Would you like some breakfast?" he suggested. "I have eggs, sausage, and bacon brought from the farms and some freshly baked bread."

Cassandra tilted her head in confusion. She couldn't smell any trace of baking bread from the kitchen, which meant that if it were freshly baked as the man had stated, it came from one of the nearby bakeries that were already plying their trade and delivering orders.

"All," Skharr responded. "And some mead if you have it on hand."

"For the both of yous?"

"Aye," she replied. The idea of food was certainly appealing, especially when the aroma of sausages and bacon cooking started to spread through the room. The table with the guards was served first, but their platters came in rapid succession.

The innkeeper was a fast worker and carried all the platters at once despite looking like he was three steps from his last. She had to give him that. Decades of experience enabled him to be able to care for his patrons no matter how tired or hungover he was.

"I think I'll need to sleep again after this," she commented and took a bite of one of the sausages on her platter after Skharr handed the man two silver coins.

His expression sobered somewhat and he nodded. "Haven't you been sleeping well lately?"

"No. I take it you have some experience with that as well?"

"Nightmare-filled rest is not particularly restful." Skharr added bacon and some of the eggs to his bread slices and made them into a sandwich before he took a large bite. "The longer it lasts, the less rest you find. But if you feel as though you'll get more rest now, I say you should take it. And I would add a large, pleasant meal is a good way to tire your body for that purpose."

It was interesting that he seemed to know what he was talking about.

"What kind of nightmares plague you?" Cassandra asked around a mouthful of bread.

"Past battles. Past mistakes. The kind that ended poorly and left their mark."

"That is somewhat lacking in detail."

He shrugged with a grin. "I was never much of a storyteller. You might want to talk to a bard about that."

"Given that not much is known about Skharr DeathEater before he became the Barbarian of Theros, I doubt any bards would know what you were doing at that time."

The warrior leaned back in his seat and swallowed a gulp of the somewhat sweet mead before he wiped his lips with his forearm. "Bards tend to not sing about the wars. Most of them do not spend enough time on the front lines to be able to do so. If they happened to be caught in one, they would focus all their efforts on leaving rather than looking for muses to inspire their art. No, it is better and easier to sing and tell tales of tasks performed by mercenaries for one god or another, as there are descriptions of what happened far from where they took place."

She realized that he might have a little suppressed annoyance on the subject and if she pressed him about it, her curiosity would likely pull the stopper out. Or perhaps he simply tried to distract her from the topic she had tried to get him to provide details for.

It was obvious enough that he wouldn't tell her what haunted his nightmares and she doubted that any attempt to push him on the matter was a good idea. She had seen the man angry before and nothing in her wanted to see that annoyance directed at her.

Skharr looked at his platter, drank deeply from his mug, and sighed heavily.

"There are more than a few," he admitted finally. "But the one that plagues me most is the moment when I discovered I had buried my blade in the chest of a close friend from times past. I had taken work and fought for the other side and in the chaos of the battlefield when the fight grew intense, we encountered one another. I didn't recognize him in armor and he might have been trying to retreat when I killed him."

"How do you know he couldn't recognize you either?"

The barbarian shook his head. "It's not difficult to make me out, even in full armor. I was consumed by bloodlust by that point and killed anything that appeared in my path, and he appeared at the wrong moment. When I saw and heard him die, it snapped me from the haze. Once the battle was over, I took my pay and settled on a farm outside a dangerous forest where I would not be accosted."

"I assume you were, though," Cassandra whispered in an attempt to turn the conversation to more pleasant matters. She didn't want him to spend too much time in dark thoughts of what had been done in the past. "Otherwise, you might have remained in a life of peace, yes?"

"Aye, and yet not by bandits or deserters."

"I can't imagine that an army would take the time to bother a small farmer when it would end in dozens of their men dead."

"It was not an army."

"Who then? The monsters from the forest?"

"In a manner of speaking. Theros appeared out the woods to send me off. He had a dungeon he wanted me to clear and made me an offer with a contract for the task."

"It seems odd that he would give you a contract instead of simply sending you there."

"He did not appear as himself—or, at least, not in any way that I would have been able to recognize him as a god of any kind. It was the last thing I would have expected from an old man who traveled with a donkey and a walking stick. I suppose an old man who journeyed through those woods on his own without a need for any escort or guards should have warned me, but I did not consider that he might be a god."

Cassandra chuckled and shook her head but was surprised when a wave of exhaustion washed over her. A good meal in good company had worked wonders, and her body begged for more rest. The thought was quickly reinforced when she failed to stifle a massive yawn and barely hid it behind her hand.

"Do you think you might be able to take one of the rooms for the day?" Skharr asked. He had mostly finished his meal already.

"You need your sleep as well. Would you not like to spend the day with me?"

He smirked as they stood from the table and approached the

innkeeper who still seemed to nurse a powerful headache from the way he rubbed his temples.

She placed a couple of silvers on the counter to catch his attention. "We need a room for the day. Perhaps for some of the night too, but I doubt it. Two silvers should cover that, yes?"

He nodded, palmed both coins, and took a key from one of the nearby drawers. "The rooms are clearly marked with a carving in the wood. All mattresses are made of goose down and recently filled. If you need a bath, tell one of my staff and they'll bring it up."

It sounded like he had used that speech enough times that he didn't even need to think before he repeated it. While it called into question whether the mattresses had been filled recently, at this point, she felt she could simply curl on a flat slat of timber and would sleep like a babe.

They ascended the stairs, where each of the four rooms was clearly identifiable by a carving on the door. She pushed on the door marked *3* to match the key and locked the door behind them before she leaned against Skharr and breathed him in slowly.

"It is one thing to fear one's death. I've seen it many times. But the feeling is very different when you see a dragon in the air and know you will die."

He slid his massive arms around her and held her close for a moment.

"Why is a living touch so important?" Cassandra asked after a few seconds of comfortable silence.

"It reminds you that you are still alive and seek to live more," he answered and his voice rumbled from his chest and vibrated pleasantly against her cheek.

Without thinking, she grasped the shirt he wore and dragged him to the bed. She pulled most of her clothes off on the way and discarded them carelessly on the wooden floor.

"Hold me," she whispered and fell onto the mattress, which

did feel like it had recently been filled with soft down. He joined her and grunted quietly as the bed groaned under his weight.

As she shifted to press back against him, a hint of movement touched her backside and elicited a small smile.

"I do believe that your dragon is waking." She looked over her shoulder and noticed a hint of redness in his cheeks.

He snorted softly. "I cannot hold you like this and be a man made of stone. That is too much for even me."

"Good." Cassandra wiggled a little closer to him. "Perhaps that also tells me I am still alive."

"Wonderful," he complained. "I'm left to my affairs with only my dragon for company and no cave to explore."

She smiled when she heard those words but couldn't hear any that might have followed as she drifted into a dreamless sleep.

CHAPTER THREE

Despite the discomfort of need, Skharr was dragged into the realms of dreamless sleep. It had been a long journey to reach the town and once he'd arrived, he'd begun a frustrating search of the city to find Cassandra. This had been followed with a good strenuous battle against the guards to gain entry to the temple.

He was able to endure for a while without the luxury of sleep but when it was available, he wouldn't turn his nose up at it.

With that said, it unsettled him to ache for the woman in his arms and be unable to act on his needs. It was an even more uncomfortable feeling when she woke, moved, and groaned softly. This dragged an immediate reaction from his cock that was practically painful by this point.

She didn't appear to notice or if she did, made no mention as she groaned again and stretched lazily against him before she turned and pressed her lips to his.

That, regrettably, didn't help.

"Thank you," she said, pushed into a seated position, and rolled her neck and shoulders slowly. "There is no other man in my life I feel I could simply...be with."

Skharr nodded and sat as well. "I'll admit there is a case of... pent-up passion within me, but I always consider myself your friend above all."

She smiled, brushed her fingers over his shoulder, and squeezed it lightly before she sidled to the side of the bed. She made no reply to his statement other than that and gathered her clothes that had been discarded haphazardly on the floor, then pulled them on.

"Have you decided yet?" he asked as he dressed.

"Decided on what?"

"Who you will be moving forward."

She tilted her head to regard him with a curious expression. "Do you mean will I be the Ytrea I was during my sabbatical or if I will return to being Paladin Cassandra?"

"You might want to consider the fact that you need to make the decision to be a paladin with your whole heart," he replied with a shrug. "Theros might have made a mistake but in the end, you need to be true to what you want to do."

"Be a paladin or make clothes?"

"Or do something else entirely. I mentioned the two because those are the only two sides I have seen of you. If you want my advice, you will discover who you want to be. Let your inner barbarian loose. Whichever you choose, I believe Theros will accept."

"A paladin's promise is no different than a god's," he continued after a moment and rested his hands on his knees. "He recognizes that he failed you. I believe you have this one chance to make sure—both for yourself and for Theros—and find out what you wish to make of your life."

Cassandra laughed and shook her head as she approached him. "You do realize that you make me want you more merely by speaking to me?"

"It is not by design." He waved her declaration off. "I've paid the price to speak to you as a friend—a man who cares enough to simply hold you and give you what you want. If Ytrea is who you desire to be, Theros will need to go through me to voice his displeasure in your ear."

She nodded slowly. "I understand. I might need to think on it."

"Bullshit." Skharr grunted and shook his head. "You had more than enough time to consider it at the temple. This is not a question that requires reason but rather one of where your heart lies. You either want action and to help others with violence, or you wish to help others with what they look like to themselves and others. Neither one is better when the heart is determined to help."

She sucked a deep breath in, sat on the bed next to him, and clasped her hands together.

"I can always make dresses when I am older," she whispered with a smile. "But I will not be able to swing a sword my whole life."

"That depends entirely on how long your life lasts, but aye." He grinned. "Is that where your heart lies?"

"Perhaps." She turned to look him firmly in the eye. "My heart still wants to wade into the thick of violence when provided with a good enough reason."

The barbarian studied her carefully. "And what reason might be good enough for you?"

"I thought that the need to right wrongs, behead skeletons, and kill the dragons that tried to kill me are all equally valid when it comes to what calls me to action."

"How many dragons have tried to eat you?" he asked and narrowed his eyes as they stood and walked to the door. They collected their packs and exited the room to descend the stairs and hurry out to the stables where their horses waited for them.

"Oh. Only the one. But it is on my list of things to accomplish."

He nodded and they retrieved the horses in silence. The sun was high and bright, which told him that they hadn't slept the entire day away. It was perhaps an hour to midday, which meant that if they wished to conduct business in the city, there was still time for it.

"The dragon did not try to eat you," he corrected her once they'd left the key to their room with one of the stable hands and guided their horses to the doors.

"What?"

"The dragon you fought. It had no intention to eat you."

"It certainly seemed determined to do so. The godsbedammed beast was practically on us before we could react. We panicked and tried to retaliate."

"Dragons are territorial creatures like wolves and tigers. While those might piss or spray to alert others to their territory, dragons tend to use a fluid that usually catches fire when they breathe fire on it to mark their territory. It reeks of something... sweet, almost."

"Are you saying it simply tried to mark its territory?" Cassandra scowled and looked skeptical as she led her horse out first with him close behind her.

The heat settled around him as he stepped out of the stable. It reminded him how close they were to the coast and how far south he had traveled.

"Oh, no. Dragons do not like humans. We compete for the same food sources, for the most part, and usually try to drive them out, destroy their eggs, and kill them. Whenever a dragon sees humans approaching, it flies away and returns later."

"Are you saying they don't eat humans?"

"Not if they have other choices. Those who do will be the injured, weak, or old. The only reason why a dragon would fight like that is if you approached its nest and it cannot move it away. They remember, somehow, that humans used to steal their eggs and they protect the nests now."

"It could have tried to kill us and then eaten us—not that difficult when you think about it."

"You were close enough to feel the heat of the flames, yes? To see how long they lasted?"

Cassandra clenched her jaw and an odd look crossed her face. The barbarian knew immediately that he had touched a nerve attached to a memory that she preferred to keep in the past.

Surprisingly, she steeled herself and nodded instead of changing the subject. "Aye. The others were burned almost immediately. I didn't see it and no one at the temple was willing to tell me what happened to them."

Blunt honesty had always been his approach in situations like these, yet he hesitated when he saw the pain that was still very fresh in her eyes. At any other time, he would have faced the facts without conscious thought about how others might see them but now, he deliberately held back.

It was extremely odd and not like him at all.

"How did you survive?" Skharr asked.

Cassandra cleared her throat and looked away toward the walls. "I held a shield up. I called for them to help me but they were already running away. The flames reached them in a wave before they could turn back and the shield was what saved me."

"How would they help you if you carried a shield?"

"I didn't carry a shield. It was magical—a barrier like those I would generally throw up to block a volley of arrows or something like that. As the flames wrapped around me, so did the shield and I assume…that is how I survived."

She had put considerable thought into it. The warrior nodded, drew a deep breath, and placed his hand on her shoulder. Even Horse appeared to sense her distress and nudged her side gently before he stepped back like he didn't care.

That drew a laugh out of her and Skharr grinned as well and patted the stallion on the neck.

"Your…fellow paladins…"

"They are all dead, I know, and turned to ash. If they had stood their ground with me, they might have survived as well. We might even have won but because they ran away, they were killed."

He nodded. "Aye. And contrary to what most folk think, dragons prefer fresh flesh to ash. They use the flames sometimes in their hunting to drive animals from forests and thickets since they cannot fly through those and try to draw their preferred prey into the open where they use their flight efficiently. Especially the larger ones. Smaller and younger dragons do roost in forests and the like, though, since it keeps them hidden from the larger dragons that might kill them."

The paladin looked at him with a small grin. "And you learned that while fighting many dragons, did you?"

"Amazingly, most of what I learned of the beasts were from books and tomes. I learned long ago to keep my distance from them, allow them to have their piece of land, and find mine. Of all the creatures in the world I would rather not fight, it is them."

"Because they can fly?"

Skharr nodded. "Aye. Something...deep within me regards that as somehow more terrifying than the powers of a lich. I know that might not seem like the most rational response, yet it remains true in my mind."

"I can understand that," she replied.

"But I have learned anything I can about the creatures and I was very surprised to discover that they avoid us when they can. And that is the only suggestion I can think of if you have revenge on your mind. Learn all you can about an enemy you plan to kill —all weapons, friends, and perhaps any way to cheat your way to a victory. It all starts with understanding the fucking shit before you run into it."

"We didn't—"

"I know, I know. None of you expected to face a dragon, but that is where knowledge would have helped. Things might have been very different if you knew where dragons like to nest and how to see where they are nesting. Not that I blame you or your paladins for what happened, but now that you know what you face and intend to avenge your fallen, you'll want to be sure you are prepared."

"You think I want revenge on the dragon?" Cassandra asked.

"You did mention that you had that on your mind. I assumed it was what you planned to carry out as soon as possible."

"And you would simply charge into it with me? Without so much as a question about my sanity?"

"Your sanity?" Skharr asked skeptically. "I always assumed you had no such thing."

"That is fair."

"I know you are intelligent enough to not rush into a battle without proper preparation. And in this case, your first step to prepare for the battle is to have me at your side."

"And such a humble companion beside me should be considerable help indeed."

"Humility is little better than lying when it isn't necessary," he countered with a smirk. "Would you have me say I am not a mighty ally to have when fighting monsters?"

"No, I suppose not."

"And should you find you need to do something that is a little dishonorable to win—perhaps even to cheat—wouldn't you much rather have me around to guide you?"

She laughed. "That is true and not very paladin-like of me."

"Not to be harsh," he added, "but abiding by a paladin's rules of conduct does tend to land you in danger and almost kill you. I would suggest being a barbarian instead."

"Perhaps. And yet not an ordinary barbarian. A barbarian princess."

"You do know the clans do not have any concept of royalty, yes?"

"Then I will be the first barbarian princess." Cassandra winked. "It would make it much more special."

He laughed at that and even she couldn't resist a small grin.

"You would be right about that, of course," the warrior admitted.

CHAPTER FOUR

"Why are we headed to the Guild Hall?"

Skharr looked around as they approached the steps on the approach to the Hall itself. He was surprised she hadn't noticed where they were going. It had been one of the few places he had made a point to fix in his head while he explored at night but perhaps her mind had been elsewhere.

The stairs were made of marble and the Hall looked like a temple in its own right, a perception accentuated by the way the white pillars gleamed in the summer sunlight.

He shrugged. "Something I learned when I was young was that if I made plans, I should not do anything for free. If we intend to hunt that dragon, we might as well see if there is a contract open on it and make coin from the effort. If not, I've found a good way to familiarize myself with the surrounding lands is to find minor work in the region—something small to limber us up again."

"I hadn't thought of that."

"If you want to be a mercenary in your own right, you need to think like one. Another point is that the Guild Halls are the best places to learn more about any of the larger monsters in the area."

She shrugged as they began to climb the steps. "I know a little about the dragon."

"Right."

"Mmhmm."

"Was it a large dragon?"

"Not...perhaps not as big as I assumed it would be. The body was perhaps as large as a horse's, but the wingspan was the greatest surprise. Each wing was as long as it was from snout to tail, and it used these to fan the flames into us."

The barbarian nodded. "It was an older creature then. What was the color of the scales? And was there any difference in coloring on its underside?"

"The scales were a dark-green. I thought it was black, at first, but it gleamed green in the sunlight and in the flames. There was no difference on the underside that I could see."

He tilted his head in thought. That did narrow down the different types of dragons they needed to prepare for, but it was still risky. Most beasts that size had to have their scales softened somewhat before they could be attacked, and he knew they could find acid that would help. Knowing where the creature was most likely to nest, however, required a clearer identification of the species.

And depending on what it was, one nesting on the Seastones would certainly pose problems for the ships that passed through the area. If that were the case, there would likely already be a contract on it.

"You look...you have that look on your face. The kind where you try to wrap your mind around something and it doesn't quite go the way you wanted it to."

"It's nothing like that," Skharr replied shortly. "And yet, here we are. We have vowed to defeat the godsbedammed beast and nothing will stop us from doing precisely that."

"I assume the godsbedammed beast you mentioned might

make an attempt to stop us," Cassandra noted as they passed through the entrance.

The building was surprisingly cool inside despite the heat outside. He had a feeling it was the purpose of all the marble used in the construction of the building. There was also the possibility, of course, of spells put into place by the original architects if that was what they attempted to achieve.

It was pleasantly cool but not quite chilly. If there were spells involved, they had probably included some to ensure that it didn't get too cold either, especially if the outside temperature dropped.

"I cannot help but wonder if they had buildings like this however long ago and if it might even be older than the city itself," he said softly and although he kept his voice low like all the others present, he still heard it echo.

"It might," Cassandra conceded. "Or it might have been built as a temple in a city that was here before. The city disappeared but the temple remained and was used as a Guild Hall when another city was built around it."

"Does that kind of thing happen?"

"More than many people think. History has a way of moving on without us sometimes."

It was an interesting thought and he considered it as they continued through the massive chamber inside the Guild Hall. All those present spoke in hushed whispers and it didn't appear to be out of respect for any kind of rule but was rather an innate respect for where they were.

Or the knowledge that their voices tended to carry.

One of the men in the Hall noticed them and his eyes almost bulged out of his head as he approached them.

"Are you...you are... You must be...Skharr DeathEater, yes? The Barbarian of Theros?"

Skharr narrowed his eyes. The stranger looked a little young to be in the chamber with a group of mercenaries, although the scars across his arms and shoulders did indicate that he had some combat experience.

"How old are you?" Cassandra scolded and her face settled into the look he assumed was natural for a paladin. "This is no place for teenagers, no matter how experienced they may be."

Her companion recognized what the situation was a moment before the annoyance appeared on the stranger's face.

"He's part elf," the barbarian said quietly.

"I'm part...yes. Elf blood makes me look like a child. It's been pointed out before but I'm older than both of you combined. So, if you would move past that..."

Her eyes narrowed and she looked around them before she studied him carefully. "My apologies. I did not mean to insult you."

The elf looked like he was about to snap at her a second time but he sighed and shook his head. "You're not the first to mistake me for a child and you won't be the last."

"How old are you if you don't mind me asking?" Skharr felt he needed to break the silence that had fallen.

"A few hundred. A mere child by elf standards, anyway, but the human side of me kicked in after the fifth decade. And you are Skharr DeathEater, yes?"

"And this is Cassandra, the paladin." He nodded in her direction.

"Former paladin."

"Ah, yes, I remember. I am the Theros Guildmaster. I've heard about both of you and your adventures. I am sorry to hear of your misadventures, Paladin."

"Former paladin." She cleared her throat. "What is your name?"

"Nasan. There is much in the world I would never wish to face. I have been lucky to avoid dragons thus far in my life. Well then, are you here for work?"

"Do you know anything about the dragon that attacked us?" Cassandra asked. "Has it been...were there more?"

"We spread the word quickly that there is a dragon in the Seastones. Many ships pass around them, so we'll wait for any of them to advise us as to whether they've seen the creature. Of course, if they don't reach their destination, that will be all the word we need on the subject. There was a temple in the area that might be where it made its nest. Some...five decades ago, the priests there worshipped the beasts and tried to find a way to call them. It might have worked but we'll never know. Not many have gone there before the paladins tried and...well, as far as I know, they didn't get very close to the actual temple."

The half-elf talked quickly and he motioned for them to follow him.

"That temple..." Skharr said as they approached the map where Nasan pointed to the various locations. "Is it high in the mountains?"

"Aye, past the Seastones and into the mountains. There were rumors of monsters that protected it, so no one approached it before."

The barbarian shook his head and studied their surroundings.

"You don't believe a word of it, do you?" Cassandra asked with a hint of mockery in her tone.

"No, I believe it can happen. I also believe it is in a remote location in the mountains and many would prefer to speak of monsters instead of the truth."

"What truth might that be?" Nasan asked.

"That the climb to it would be an absolute bitch."

The half-elf chuckled softly. "Well, I would imagine if that was enough to stop them before, word of a dragon circling the region drove them even farther away."

Skharr shrugged. "I suppose. But while we could gossip the day away, we have to make coin. Have you any work in the area for us?"

"Nothing simple or easy but if you have a mind for something more lucrative, we have one on the Royal Guild that is well-funded. It does come with a few complications, however."

"What else is new?" the warrior asked. "Have you any idea what these complications might be?"

"You'll have to deal with a recalcitrant royal."

Cassandra narrowed her eyes. "Royal? Does that mean they are somehow related to the emperor?"

"They are directly related." Nasan cleared his throat and retrieved the contract from his desk. "There are many of those spread about the empire these days, given that the last emperor could not keep his cock contained. They've come out of the woodwork like roaches now that the new one has made himself known. Either way, there will be problems with anyone who has to deal with the royals these days."

"We'll take the work," he stated firmly.

"You are a bold man."

The young emperor seemed to make an effort to look as pleasant as he could.

Elric had been around him since he took the throne and the boy had adjusted to his responsibilities rather well. Tryam had a commanding presence about him and the ability to rely on the counsel of those who knew better than him, which made up most of an emperor's responsibilities.

The rest, of course, was to tolerate people who were disrespectful, if only because their disrespect was expertly veiled.

It was one of the few failings of the new emperor and he'd told the young man that. Tryam trusted him to tell the truth at all times, and while he was sure that would change one day, it was a welcome change from before he came to power. Of course, it was only a matter of time before he allowed success and the power of his position to go to his head, and anyone who said anything that displeased him would see their life forfeit.

For the moment, however, a young man of sound mind sat on the throne. The guard captain had studied enough history to know how rare that was. If there was ever an opportunity to change the empire for the best, it was now and he would make sure that no one spoiled that.

Even the two shitheads who were only alive because they had a claim to the throne in their own right as they were the grandchildren of Tryam's father's brother. Certain laws surrounded how those related to the emperor were treated, which was why the young ruler tried to keep his features calm.

"Of course," he said and a smile settled on his lips again. "Please, do carry on."

Elric imagined that he was only able to maintain that expression because he pictured their heads on spikes, although perhaps he projected his wishes on the boy.

"The taxation efforts in the region, while remarkable, simply cut into our abilities to maintain the area," one of them said. "If you would funnel some of what you have taken in tax into our coffers, we would be able to maintain things as we have before."

It was utter and complete bullshit and all those present in the room knew it. Tryam had elevated taxes in the richer sectors of the empire to pay for the end of the various wars his father had started. He had balanced it by reducing the taxes the local nobles and lords could levy at the same time. Most of them realized that this was a temporary measure that would result in elevated profits in the future, yet these two had taken it as an invitation to avoid their responsibilities to pay for their lavish lifestyles.

No guard patrols and no road maintenance meant the presence of bandits in their lands had flourished beyond reason. When the emperor summoned them to explain themselves, they had the gall to pretend that their lower tax revenue meant they could not afford to maintain their lands while they continued to spend lavishly on their personal lives.

It was like they thought no one knew of the month-long parties they had hosted, even though they had invited their ruler to partake.

Unfortunately, he had to pretend that was not the case because of the political connection he shared with them. It was difficult for Elric to stop his features from showing the pure disgust he felt in the pit of his stomach.

"You have to understand that when we don't have the coin to maintain the lands, the tax revenue drops for all involved," the other pointed out to enthusiastic nods from his cohort.

"Are you saying you do not have the coin in your coffers to pay for the maintenance of the lands I have granted you?" Tryam asked.

"Keep in mind that lying to your emperor is forbidden," the guard captain interjected.

"No, but—"

"And yet you declare yourself economically incapable of maintaining these lands despite your coffers being well able to do so." The boy shrugged and looked at the papers in front of him. "Perhaps lands in the south might be better suited to your needs. There are fewer roads to maintain there."

"That is not the issue, Your Grace…"

Their voices trailed off when one of the guards slipped into the room, approached their captain, and whispered something in his ear. He could see that the two royals were desperate for the interruption and probably hadn't expected to be interrogated like they had been.

The emperor motioned for the leader of the guard to approach and Elric circled the desk and leaned close to his ear.

"Word has arrived about Skharr, Your Grace," he whispered.

Tryam shook his head. "Anything you say to me can be said in the presence of my kin. I would entrust them with my life if it were necessary."

He was playing at something but it wasn't at all clear what.

After a brief pause, Elric cleared his throat, straightened his back, and spoke in a firm and clear voice. "Word about Skharr DeathEater has arrived, Your Grace."

"The barbarian?" the emperor asked and regarded him almost impatiently.

"The...the very same, Your Grace." Yes, he was most certainly playing at something since he knew Skharr was a barbarian.

"What about him?" The emperor leaned forward and looked genuinely worried. "Has he died?"

"No." Elric sighed. "Perhaps worse."

Tryam's eyebrows raised. "He fights for Janus now?"

"No. He's been asked to fulfill a contract put forth by the Royal Guild. A recalcitrant noble, Your Grace."

"Oh." He leaned back in his seat. "Will we lose an important royal?"

It began to make sense now. The boy likely knew the contract had been sent out—and had probably signed the order himself—and wanted the two men in front of him to hear the news as well. He seemed to emphasize the fact that a noble was named in the contract and one of royal blood no less.

"If I might respectfully intrude, Your Grace," the man with long golden curls said hastily. "Am I to assume that you have entrusted the life of...one of our kin to the hands of a barbarian?"

"It would seem so, yes. I honestly doubted that any would take the work, yet my dearest cousin persists in his plots against me and my purposes. Were it as trivial as your misunderstandings, I might have summoned him to be dealt with in like manner. Unfortunately, his actions have taken a dark turn. The barbarian is competent enough, however. I wager he will have little difficulty reminding him of the will of his emperor."

"But...and forgive my questioning your will," the other with black hair added tentatively and shook his head. "Why would you commit the fulfillment of your wishes to...one as...a man who...well..."

"One who you might not know or trust," the blond finished and his eyes widened. "If you will forgive my bold tongue, Your Grace."

"Forgiveness is earned, not given freely in this court," Tryam retorted and rose from his seat. "Elric, perhaps you would care to educate my kin on the barbarian."

"Of course, Your Grace." The guard captain bowed before he turned his attention to the two men. "You know the barbarian was instrumental in bringing the emperor to his throne. He even saved his life on more than one occasion when attempts were made on his life."

"Of course. Yes, we know, now that you mention it." Both men nodded. "And what title have you granted to the filthy barbarian?"

It seemed like Tryam had waited for a slip like that since his reaction to the word looked a little more exaggerated than it might like it was a performance.

"The title I granted him is my friend," he snapped, raised his voice, and drew himself tall. "Remove them from my sight. Tell them they can return once they display a modicum of respect for their family."

"No, please, Your Grace!"

"You misunderstand!"

They voiced their protests but it was far too late for that as the guards had already begun to escort them roughly out of the chamber. Elric maintained a stoic expression for as long as he could until the doors closed before he finally allowed himself to smile.

"And here I thought you still had a great deal to learn about the delicate art of politics," the captain of the guard said and chuckled.

"I would say I still have a great deal to learn."

"Yes, but that was masterfully handled." He raised his hand and two servants approached with refreshments. They were new girls, both extremely attractive and likely daughters of one lesser noble or another, and smiled flirtatiously at Tryam as they left the drinks and food and moved away.

The emperor was not a man made of stone, and he stretched his powerful arms as he carefully watched their dresses that swayed enticingly and showed enough of their backsides to call his interest.

Elric took the moment of opportunity while he was distracted to pour himself some of the drink, had a quick sip, and took a bite from one of the pastries that he'd selected at random. His ruler had food tasters but none were present and Tryam wasn't likely to wait for them. He had a bad habit of forgetting how many people out there wanted him dead and were willing to do whatever was necessary to see it happen.

There was no taste of poison and none of the effects either. He knew a few of the magical ones took a little longer to have an effect, but he doubted those would get through the enchantments built into the palace. And if they did, there would be much larger problems than poisonings to worry about.

"Skharr fucking DeathEater," Tryam muttered once the girls were out of sight and he poured some wine for himself. "Even when he isn't in the city, he is always a good way to rid ourselves of pests."

"Do you think we will have a dead royal on our hands?" Elric asked.

The emperor shrugged. "Only if he deserves it. One thing I believe about Skharr is that he is a keen judge of character. He will know what to do and how to carry it out—perhaps a little bluntly, but the job will be accomplished."

CHAPTER FIVE

"I cannot say I've ever heard of the Royal Guild before," Skharr mentioned, his tone curious.

Cassandra wondered if there was any point in trying to convince him to ride Horse, which would allow them to reach the nobleman's villa a little faster. She respected his stamina—more than most—but sometimes, it was best to simply increase the pace.

The glaring heat of the noonday sun was certainly something she was in a rush to escape from. They'd started early in the morning after they accepted the contract and despite this, it did not appear that they would arrive at their destination before the sun had begun to set.

It would also take them a while to accomplish what they had set out to do, which meant they were likely to spend the night out under the stars and face another long journey in the heat before they reached the city again.

Of course, she didn't know if it was wise to assume they would be successful, but it was hard to resist with the indomitable confidence her companion exuded.

"It wasn't used often but the imperial throne reserves the right to issue contracts when they need something undertaken by mercenaries." She shifted in her saddle as she considered her recollection. "Honestly, they haven't used it for as long as I have been alive. The last emperor didn't think mercenaries measured up to the same standard as his armed forces. Either way, it is known as a Royal Guild contract when they do make use of it."

Skharr frowned. "And the new emperor hasn't made use of it before either?"

"Not as far as I know. Not that I have paid much attention to that kind of thing."

"Nor I."

It was interesting that it had been invoked out there and was something close to where he was situated. It was like Tryam made an overt attempt to keep himself apprised of what he was doing. From what Cassandra knew about him, the barbarian did not like the idea of being followed around the empire.

The time was probably coming for him to relocate and find another place in the world away from the emperor's influence to continue his life and his work.

It wasn't like there wouldn't be work for him elsewhere in the world, and perhaps there would be fewer folk who approached him and announced his name to everyone in earshot. And from what she'd heard, numerous people in the empire wished to see him dead as well.

"Do you think the boy is trying to follow me?" Skharr asked as the silence dragged on. "It seems a little odd that the first Royal Guild contract in decades happens to be in my region. It might be a coincidence but I doubt it."

The paladin shrugged. "It could be. If so, how long do you think the emperor has tracked your movements?"

"I always assumed he had better things to occupy his time—like running an empire."

He had a point with that, although all the talk was that the boy had already proved to be an excellent emperor. Perhaps he left the ruling to others while he used the time to check how his favorite barbarian was.

"Is that the location out there?" the warrior asked and raised his hand to shield his eyes so he could see farther despite the glare.

She mirrored the motion and squinted into the distance. A small fortress stood directly ahead of them, with stone walls erected around a hill that overlooked what looked like a fertile valley where almost a dozen farms were established and grew a variety of different crops. She did not like the warm sun but it seemed the plants did.

"I would say so. Do you think the reason why the contract was left vague as to how we are supposed to deal with the royal in question is because the emperor does not want you to kill them?"

"It might be. Or it could be that he wants the ability to deny any involvement if this should go badly for him. Either way, I don't much care as long as the coin comes through."

"So, the point of being a barbarian is that you know what is happening in the world around you and you simply don't care?"

Skharr nodded. "That sounds right, I think. Although a part of it is understanding that not all problems involve me and shouldn't. Most folk assume that barbarians are ignorant morons, and so you find yourself in the situation where they assume you don't care about the problems of the world if you are not paid to solve them."

"It's an interesting view of the world. Have you always seen it this way?"

"Not really. But you'll adapt to it eventually if you truly want to be a barbarian. You might want to find your armor as well. If the man expects trouble, he might have his men ready for a fight."

He was right about that, although she wasn't sure why she'd taken so long to put her armor on. It was blessed and would therefore be cooler to ride in than her clothes and lighter too. Perhaps Theros would not like someone who was not his paladin to use armor he had blessed her with, but if he wanted it back, all he had to do was ask.

As Skharr predicted, men waited on the walls, their crossbows at the ready, and watched them approach the arched entrance.

The only real surprise was that the gates were still open. She had expected the inhabitants to have shut them and told anyone who approached to fuck off, yet they allowed two strangers to enter without being challenged.

Perhaps they anticipated that they represented the emperor and carried his orders, and any attempt to stop them would therefore make any hidden rebellion far more overt. This in turn likely meant that if they resisted, they would beat the two within an inch of their lives and let them go with nothing but the clothes on their backs. If that happened, they ran the risk of being murdered and robbed on the road, which would lead no one to suspect that the royal was involved at all.

That wouldn't be the case in this situation, of course, but they didn't have to know that. If they had any idea that Skharr Death-Eater and a former paladin now moved through their gates, she surmised that they would certainly have locked them and risked whatever the emperor's wrath would entail.

Or they would both be felled by a horde of arrows and nothing else would come of it.

Cassandra brought her horse to a halt and dismounted smoothly as Skharr took his bow from Horse's saddle and began to string it. A handful of the guards started to approach, unsure of what to make of them.

"You may inform Lord Cassian that the emperor's envoys have arrived." The former paladin spoke in a clear and commanding tone. It was enough to make the men look at one another, unsure if they should challenge the visitors or do as they were told.

One of them sprinted into the keep to find their lord while

the rest moved closer and tried to decide why the barbarian was arming himself with a massive war bow.

"That will be all," Cassandra snapped when the group came a little closer than she would like. Had they remained out of striking range, she would have simply continued to ignore them.

"The emperor sent you two?" the captain of the guard asked and narrowed his eyes.

"Excellent, we have established that your hearing is not impaired," she retorted, sighed, and attempted to look as annoyed and bored as she could.

"Why don't you carry his colors?"

"Because we are mercenaries who carry his orders." She brandished the contract, which very clearly displayed the emperor's seal and signature. "I assume that means we do carry his colors— perhaps not as obviously as we should, but still. Do you think we should have had a banner made?"

The question was directed at Skharr, who shrugged and grunted noncommittally. It was as good an answer as he could offer and she nodded.

"Agreed. There is no need."

The doors to the keep were opened again and the lord in question stepped out with a small entourage and a handful of young servants to escort him. One carried a parasol to keep the glare from his eyes and another used a feathered fan to keep him cool as he approached the steps leading into the courtyard where the envoys waited.

"It would appear that the Lord Cassian has finally deemed it necessary to grace us with his presence," Cassandra said waspishly. "Put the bow away, big one. You won't need it. The royal will not give us any trouble now, will he?"

The lord stepped down a few of the steps before he realized precisely how large the barbarian was and decided he would be better off if he maintained his distance from them.

"What is the meaning of this? Why have you interrupted my afternoon rest?"

Skharr grunted derisively and the paladin couldn't help but share in his laughter.

"Indeed. I assume his afternoon rest would have been interrupted by his evening repose eventually."

"What is the meaning of this?" It looked like the vein on Cassian's forehead was about to pop. His bright green eyes revealed anger and the soft brown curls that framed his face bounced with every word. He looked young—perhaps young enough to be the emperor's brother, although a cousin was a little more likely given that he'd been granted lands of his own.

"They came with a guild contract bearing the emperor's seal," one of the guards stated when he realized they were expected to answer the question. "They stated that they needed to speak to you."

"I know that part, you misbegotten halfwit. What is the contract that brought them to my doorstep?"

Cassandra unrolled it and cleared her throat. "For the intention to consort with the enemies of the empire and attempt to undermine the emperor's authority, the verdict against Lord Cassian is that of treason. His punishment shall be remanded to those willing and able to execute it. No punishment shall be handed to those who carry out the orders of the contract for any actions necessary to implement said orders. That is a little vague. Now, I suppose you won't willingly turn yourself over for punishment?"

"To you and your mute barbarian?" Cassian smirked. "I hardly think so. I would imagine he is meant to stay silent and seem intimidating because of his size. Were he asked to fight, he would run. Which begs the question of why you would bring your man-whore with you to fulfill this contract?"

"Man-whore?" She looked at Skharr, who shrugged. "You might as well be, I suppose. You certainly have a way about you, although when he comments on your size, he might imagine the size of your dragon and hope to confirm if you are, in fact, proportionate."

It was a guess on her part but the shocked look on the noble's face when he heard her words was certainly the kind of thing she expected from the likes of him.

The barbarian simply rolled his eyes and moved his hands to his belt buckle.

"No, no. I don't think we have time for any actual measurement. Besides, the contract calls for the man to be punished, not to have his ego utterly crushed. Still, the contract does say you will not be punished for whatever needs to be done to exact punishment so…I suppose that will work as well. Your Lordship, would you like to have your ego crushed by having your dragon compared to that of my man-whore as you called him?"

Cassian looked like he wasn't sure what to do about them before a smile came to his lips. It was a somewhat insane look, the kind that said he'd seized on something he thought he could use to silence the annoying woman in front of him.

"It is regrettable that you never managed to reach my gates," he said smugly. "You might have been able to fulfill your obligations if it had not been for the group of bandits you encountered along the way. Alas, they stopped you and killed you long before you ever caught sight of my glorious walls."

"I assume he doesn't mind that any number of other mercenaries are willing to fulfill the contract," Cassandra said and shook her head. "Then again, a man with a sword that could be better described as a small knife might not be able to think that far ahead. Of course, the longer it takes, the higher the value of the contract will be. Eventually, with the attraction of such substantial coin, he will be mired in fifteen different sieges against those gates he holds so dear—assuming the emperor does not decide to simply send his troops. At that point, an actual army might arrive. Instead, he could have avoided annoying us and submitted to the punishment the emperor had in mind for him all along."

Skharr simply shook his head and Horse whinnied in agreement.

"True. He would not consider such things. I suppose it will be our duty to remind him."

Cassian almost spluttered at her and turned to his servants like he intended to berate them for not doing anything before he realized that he had guards in the vicinity whose job it was to do that for him.

"I've had enough of this!" he shrieked. "Guards, kill them! And ensure that their bodies are found in the locations where there are numerous bandits to blame their demise on."

This was how the situation would end no matter what she said, although Cassandra had to admit that she enjoyed toying with the royal's ego. Still, if they had to engage in some kind of battle, she wanted to make sure they would survive it. The two dozen or so guards wouldn't be more difficult to deal with than a fucking dragon, after all.

The crossbowmen on the wall were the first to react and they leveled their weapons and fired on the visitors before any of the guards could obey their lord's orders. Then again, perhaps those on the ground were less enthusiastic about attacking two fighters who bore the emperor's seal.

Cassandra raised her hand, extended her will from her fingertips, and made the air thicker than water ahead of them to stop the projectiles before they could reach within fifteen feet of where they stood.

"Skharr, if you wouldn't mind?" She turned to him as the bolts fell. "And don't kill them. We aren't here to punish them, after all."

He sighed loudly, moved his hand away from his sword, and turned to face the group of guards that had begun to advance with his bare hands.

"Wait, did she call him Skharr?" one of the men asked as they drew their weapons.

"Shut up and kill him, you idiots!" the captain snapped, drew a sword, and charged their target first.

The man did appear to have some skill with the weapon and carefully maintained his balance as he rushed forward. The blade flicked toward the barbarian's stomach but he simply stepped aside before he twisted and moved closer to one of the guards who attacked with a spear.

The warrior knew they'd heard his name and now tried to determine whether they fought against *the* Skharr—the one they had all heard about. Reputation had a unique quality in combat, especially against those who weren't prepared for it.

"Come on, then, you sludge-brained, yellow-bellied spawn of Janus' poxy whore. This is your moment to test your mettle against the Barbarian of Theros—but perhaps your balls have shrunk with fear and you can no longer think clearly. That would happen if your minds were located in your cock, which I assume they are since you cannot seem to use them at all."

One spear missed his shoulder and another slashed a shallow wound into his chest. He grasped both weapons and twisted to wrench them from the hold of the men who carried them. The jerk and sudden release were sufficient to make them stumble and sprawl, tangled together enough to hamper their recovery.

"That was disappointing. I had hoped you'd last a little longer. But perhaps your friends can find enough of their manhood to at least attempt an attack. I cannot believe that all you bum-sucking toadies have been emasculated simply by my title."

Cassandra drew her sword and advanced toward the captain, whose attention was on Skharr as well. Perhaps he had heard all the tales and now wondered if he was paid enough to fight the barbarian.

"Keep your mind on the battle, captain," she said and tapped his shoulder with her blade. "Unless you have no intention to fight?"

He whipped to face her but she was ready and slid her blade over his shoulder to leave a shallow cut in his arm before she dislodged his sword from his hand.

"You have better things to do with your life than defend some rich prick," she told him as she lifted her sword quickly to rest against his neck, which effectively ended the fight in him. "Like watch Skharr DeathEater, the Barbarian of Theros, battle with your men. It should be interesting, especially since he will try to keep them alive."

Perhaps it would have been better for her to fight the half a dozen or so guards. She wore armor blessed by the gods, while her teammate didn't wear his armor or even a helm.

She raised her hand to block another volley of bolts from the walls. The warrior snapped the haft off one of the spears and flung the other part away as the rest of the guards launched into an attack.

"You're right," the captain admitted. "This is more interesting. And I would rather be here with you than face him."

"Be wary, captain. If I wanted to kill you, there would be scant seconds before you measured the length of your entrails."

"True, but I would still rather you than him."

The former paladin could understand that at least. Skharr rushed at the guards armed with little more than a stick and she still couldn't see how they could stand a chance against him.

"Well, now," he bellowed with a broad grin. "Let's see if your shriveled balls can at least stoke a little fire in your bellies given that they have crushed the life out of your common sense."

He thrust a spear to the side, ducked under a sword swung at his head, and hammered the broken haft into the armored gut of one of the guards.

It knocked the breath out of his opponent in a single blow and as the man bent to try to breathe, the barbarian arced his weapon onto the back of his head. The force of the impact shattered the piece of wood but the guard fell without a sound.

The sword sliced into his side and Cassandra stepped forward to engage, but she heard him laugh, almost as a warning, before he whipped his torso around and his elbow collided with the side of the swordsman's head. The crack was heard throughout the courtyard, and even with his helm on, he fell without even a gasp of protest.

"I can see why you would rather not face him on the battlefield."

The barbarian certainly looked like he was enjoying himself. The other four surged into a combined assault but she could see the fear in their eyes. One had already tried to pull away when Skharr roared something she couldn't understand and attacked. He still held a piece of the broken haft in his hand and swung what was left across the jaw of one of his assailants. As the man staggered back, he knocked the other two off their feet.

It was not a pretty fight, but the warrior certainly had the advantage. He was almost as large as both men combined and was more than strong enough to overpower them. His massive fists battered the two men until neither moved, although it looked like they were still breathing and they groaned when he used them to support himself as he stood. With a broad grin, he rolled his shoulders and patted the men carefully.

"That was perhaps a little better, but if you'd been able to detach your brains from your balls, you might have the wisdom to stand down. It would have deprived me of a little fun, of course, but would certainly have made things easier all round."

The last man appeared to have second thoughts and took a few steps to where Cassian waited for them beside the last three guards.

Of course, this number did not include those on the walls and more were no doubt stationed across the fortress and could likely be called in if needed. Those above no longer released bolts, however, and simply watched in fascination and perhaps a little horror as the battle unfolded below.

Cassandra decided that Skharr had dealt enough damage and had enough fun on his own and she rushed up the steps. The barbarian moved a little slower, having put a fair amount of energy into those he'd left battered and yet breathing below. She moved faster than he did, flicked her sword so she held the pommel forward, and drove it into the face of the one who tripped over himself to escape the warrior.

He fell onto the steps, spitting teeth and blood, and she immediately spun to focus on the three who remained. She had an advantage over her teammate as their weapons bounced off her armor, whereas he needed to move a little faster to avoid them. He'd largely been successful but she had seen a few shallow wounds. They weren't enough to stop him but were certainly more than she sustained through her breastplate.

One dropped when she hammered the pommel of her sword into his gut and lifted it quickly to drive it into his chin hard enough to snap his head up and fell him with a moan.

The other two retreated quickly, although the paladin managed to catch one with a powerful hook. Her gauntlet dug into his jaw and almost lifted him off his feet with enough force that he sprawled on the steps and curled instinctively to escape her.

It brought the kind of exhilaration she hadn't felt when she was a paladin. Buoyed by the feeling, she grasped the last guard by his collar, dragged him back, and flung him almost effortlessly down the steps.

With a deftness that matched his partner perfectly, Skharr was there to stop the guard's descent. All he had to do was extend his arm and it caught the man across the neck, whipped him in midair, and hurled him onto the stone with a breathless whine of pain.

"It's good of you to join the fight," the barbarian taunted, wiped some blood from his lips, and inspected it before he spat more out. "I thought you would chat to the captain all godsbe-dammed day."

"You took your fucking time," Cassandra answered with a grin. "I thought you needed a little help with the rest of them."

Skharr smirked. "Well, if you had jumped in earlier, I wouldn't have begun to have so much fun with those I had my hands on."

Cassian's eyes were wide. He looked around and shoved his servants between him and the two mercenaries before he spun and ran toward what he thought would be the safety of his keep.

The former paladin surged forward, swept his long, flowing silk robe up from where it trailed almost ten feet behind him, and yanked it back. The action was hard enough to pull his feet out from under him and he fell with a heavy thud.

"You...you'll pay for this!" he shouted once he'd recovered his breath. "I'll make you pay in blood for what you—"

Without so much as a thought, she dropped to her haunches and swung her gauntleted hand across his jaw to silence him, and the royal immediately went limp in her grasp.

"Do you think that is enough punishment?" Skharr asked, folded his arms, and watched as some of the servants slunk away, reluctant to be involved in the fight. The guards had begun to recover, but they had no desire to find out what would happen if they pushed the barbarian any farther. Even those who hadn't been involved in the fight now lowered their weapons.

"It might be," Cassandra replied as she inspected the noble's face and head for any injuries. "I see no need to kill him outright, but we'll have to wait until he wakes to see if knocking him senseless was enough to drive the point through his skull. If not, we may need to beat it into him—and kick as well, perhaps. But death, I feel, would miss the point of this lesson entirely."

"You're not wrong," he conceded, stretched, and turned his attention to one of the serving staff, who inched away from him when his gaze fell on her. "I mean none of you any harm, at least as long as none of you mean me any harm. With that said, if any of you have something cool to drink, it would be appreciated."

A young woman who carried the parasol took a step forward. "Apolo...apologies, DeathEater, but if he were to discover that we helped you, we would be punished."

The former paladin looked at him and he shrugged.

"No one will force you to do anything if you are afraid to," he answered and settled his gaze on his partner, who hovered around the unconscious royal and tried to find a way to wake him. "Yet I have a feeling he'll not be in any position to punish anyone, not for a good while."

One of the servants cleared his throat loudly. He carried a silver tray with a handful of chalices and a large silver jug. Beads of condensation had begun to form on the outside, evidence that it was chilled.

"The heat has begun to tell on me," the lad stated loudly and placed the tray on a nearby table. "I must go inside and...and regain my senses."

The rest of them agreed, put their various items of service down hastily, and hurried inside before they closed the doors of the keep behind them.

"I knew they would see the light of Theros eventually," Skharr commented with a grin. "Will you join me in a drink, Cassandra?"

"In a moment," she answered and studied the man she'd knocked unconscious. There must surely be a way to bring him back to consciousness.

CHAPTER SIX

Skharr had no idea what had been prepared for the royal by his servants, but he could say it was godsbedammed tasty.

A little sweet and a little sour, it suggested something fruity he couldn't quite place and a hint of wine. Perhaps, he thought idly, it might be a wine made from orange slices.

It was ice-cold as well, which was certainly a blessing in the heat. He filled his chalice again, took a large sip, and nodded.

"You should have some of this," he suggested to Cassandra, who was still huddled over the fallen royal. "Before it warms and you're left with something so sweet it cloys in your mouth."

"You do remember we have work to do here, yes?" She scowled at him. "There's no chance that we'll reach the city by nightfall, which means we need to finish the job and get moving if we want to avoid another long march tomorrow. Of course, we could avoid it better if you would simply climb onto Horse and ride him."

"Why would I ride Horse?" he asked. "Besides, who could have too much of this warmth and sunshine?"

"I could!" she retorted. "I have and I wasn't walking either. I was riding, which meant my horse didn't have to walk in the heat for longer because I refused to take advantage of his greater speed."

"I won't discuss it," he answered and kept his voice low as he took another sip from the cool drink. "I won't ride my brother. You know that. If you want to wake the bastard, I'll go find a bucket and some water—preferably spoiled—to wake him with."

"There's no need for that," the former paladin said and shook her head. "I think I know exactly what we need to bring him back to us."

"A spell of some kind?" the barbarian asked. "I have a feeling you paladins might have learned a little too much about healing to let something like a pain in the head teach that shit a lesson."

"Aye, there are probably a few spells that could clear his head and make him as clean as a mage's asshole. Of course, he'll also be ready to demand that we release him while he throws in more than a handful of threats for daring to lay hands on him. Given all that, I think he is entitled to my less refined methods."

Skharr tilted his head and watched as she raised her gauntleted hand and drew the back of it across his cheek. That drew a groan from the royal, then another, and he finally opened his eyes again.

"What the...you...you'll all pay. I'll...my..." He blinked a few times before his vision cleared and he realized who was looking at him.

"Go on, then." Cassandra chuckled and patted him on the cheek. "What will we pay and to whom?"

"You...the emperor will take a pound out of your flesh for every drop of blood you've spilled of mine." He hissed and tried to grasp her. "He'll send a squad of killers to deal with you once he knows you've touched his kin."

"He does know who we are, doesn't he?" Skharr asked. "I've never been one to depend on my legend, but it does help some of the time. Self-serving shits like these whose pricks are so far up their own assholes that they spew their seed every time they speak would be far easier to deal with if they knew who they were facing."

"I imagine we'll have to educate him. You like doing a little of that too, yes?"

He shrugged. "Yes, but if we are pressed for time..."

His voice trailed off as he looked at the gate. He could hear the clattering of hooves on the same road they'd used and the loud whinnying of about a dozen horses. Perhaps more, he thought cautiously, but it was difficult to tell from only the sounds once there were more than five.

"Is that the emperor come to gut us for touching one of his kin?" Cassandra asked as she stood and looked at the gate as well.

"I doubt he'd come himself," the barbarian answered and shook his head. "But I doubt he would give us the work and then punish us for it. The contract does say we are absolved for whatever we need to do to fulfill the contract."

"What it says and what the emperor does might not be the same," she countered and pulled some of her hair back. "He might have come to kill us simply to ensure that none know we were here. It wouldn't do for word to spread that he allowed royals to have their asses beaten to a pulp."

She directed the last few words toward Cassian, who wilted quickly as his courage failed.

The clatter of hooves grew louder and a moment later, the first man rode through wearing plate armor with all the emperor's livery. He carried a banner emblazoned with the same and was quickly followed by a dozen men in identical armor. Skharr recognized them as the Emperor's Elites, and on horseback too.

He didn't think he would ever see them too far from the emperor, but when he looked around the group, there was no sign of Tryam. It made sense, of course. The royal wouldn't make an appearance at a scene like this, even if he didn't intend to kill all those present.

One of the riders slid smoothly from his saddle. He wasn't

nearly as tall as Skharr but he had the look of a fighter and a man who commanded respect.

His grimace as he dismounted suggested a pain in his back, a common complaint among tall men who spent too much time in the saddle. Without a word, he stretched to ease his muscles and recover from the ride for a moment before he turned and removed his helm.

The familiar face caught the warrior by surprise. He hadn't expected to see Elric away from the emperor's side and certainly not this far from his ruler. The man didn't appear comfortable with the arrangement either.

His lips settled into a scowl when he saw the guards roll and groan on the ground, in pain from their treatment at Skharr's hands. Although the barbarian couldn't tell if his reaction was disgust at how easy it had been for him to overcome them or if it was merely annoyance over the need to deal with the situation himself.

"Skharr DeathEater," Elric called as he began to climb the steps. "This is an interesting way to find you again, wouldn't you say?"

He regarded the Elite captain warily. "It's not the worst way to reconnect but it's odd to see the captain of the Elites here, and so quickly too. You had better not ask me to go on another dungeon run."

"Captain!" Cassian shouted and tried to push up from where Cassandra had left him. "Captain, thank the heavens you've arrived. You need to help me. These two accosted me, attacked my men, and injured me."

"Well, this is interesting," Elric declared as he approached the warrior. "If I had placed any coin on it, I would have said you would have left none of them breathing. I've seen your work in the past and I assumed you were the type who rarely left anyone alive."

"I know how to control myself. Fighting is a good way to

release pent-up energy and if I were to kill all those I fought… Well, the world would be an emptier place for it."

The guard captain chuckled. "The emperor mentioned that we would have a dead royal on our hands. Is this the pile of troll dung?"

"Captain…you know this man?" Cassian propped himself on his arms. "You must help me. I am cousin to the emperor. The blood that runs through my veins is the same that runs through his, and you will protect me as you would the man himself."

Elric scowled at him and turned to Cassandra. "I don't suppose there is anything you could do to silence the turd?"

She turned to the man, who covered his head hastily although it did him little good. The former paladin hammered her fist into his gut and forced him to curl in his tangled robes.

"Much appreciated." Elric bowed his head to her. "And here I thought you would be the more pleasant of the two given that your party includes a fucking barbarian."

"I would have gagged him." Skharr folded his arms. "She is by far the more brutal of the two of us."

"Did you forget that you trounced a group of guards with a broken spear haft?" She shook her head.

"It was a friendly brawl between— Well, they weren't friendly but I was. It was an enjoyable battle between us, although I do think they could have provided a little more in the way of real resistance. I am sure they will think the same once they are conscious and able to walk again."

"Please. I've seen you be brutal, barbarian."

Elric nodded. "As have I. She has a long way to go to reach what you are capable of."

"Captain!" Cassian had recovered his breath and now dragged himself across the ground. "You must help… You must…punish them. Assault on me is assault on…on the emperor himself. You must arrest this barbarian and his…his female warrior."

"I thought I was her man-whore," Skharr said affably.

"That is what he said," Cassandra agreed.

"You cannot believe that I will intercede on your behalf," Elric told him.

The former paladin took that as a nudge and drove her boot into his gut to double the man over again.

"You were saying?" the warrior asked. "Kicking a defenseless man on the ground is what most would call brutal, wouldn't you say?"

The Elite captain shrugged. "I would have done the same thing. That man is one singularly annoying arrogant shit."

"It is the princess attitude," Skharr said and shook his head. "She has had to learn the skill of ass-kissery."

"I've what?" She scoffed. "I've kissed no ass."

The rest of the Elites approached, unsure of what was expected of them. They looked at their captain as if to determine what they should do, and his calm demeanor was enough to put them at ease and make sure that all hands remained away from their weapons.

Those of Cassian's guards still on the ground showed no sign that they wanted to be in the middle of a fight again. A few others drew water from the well and cleaned themselves with it, although Cassandra needed to kick the royal again to quiet him.

"She does not look like any princess I've met before," Elric admitted.

"That is true but it is because she is a barbarian princess," Skharr explained.

"There is no— Barbarians have no royalty, right?"

"Correct. Which is why you have likely never seen any like her before, given that she is the first of her kind."

"I...I think I understand."

"I like that." Cassandra nodded. "Princess Cassandra, first of her name. Although it begs the question of when I'll be queen. I suppose I would need to command groups and perhaps find a whole barbarian tribe to lead."

"Clan."

"What?"

"Barbarians have clans," the warrior explained. "Tribes are closer to what orcs call their groups."

"What is the godsbedammed difference?"

Elric cleared his throat. "Tribes are more individualistic. You'll find they act almost like city-states, which means each orc tribe has almost everything they need to survive within their ranks. Clans are more loosely organized and dependent on each other to maintain themselves. They are independent to some extent but still rely on those clans that are better at one thing than the others."

Skharr tilted his head as he considered it. "I've never thought of it that way but I suppose he is correct."

"I've fought a handful of battles with the barbarian clans, and those more experienced with it explained it to me. It made sense, although I have no idea if it is true. The DeathEaters especially are more than capable of dealing with their own business and are quite isolated from the rest."

"And yet we..." The barbarian narrowed his eyes and shook his head. "We rely on the dwarf cities in the region, which in turn rely on the other barbarian clans. It is a cycle that is required for survival in the world's most inhospitable areas."

"Captain...please!"

Cassandra leveled her boot into the royal and he fell again and whimpered pathetically.

"I'm afraid I must ask you to stop beating the insufferable shit-stain," Elric said finally. "It would be unfortunate if he were to suffer damage to his head."

"More damage than he has already, I suppose you mean." Skharr frowned. "Perhaps one of your men might want to see to him? Ensure that he has no lasting damage?"

The Elite captain motioned to one of his men, who jogged forward and took a small vial of health potion from his belt. It appeared as though the emperor sent his Elites out well-equipped—or better-equipped than most of his soldiers, at least.

"Keep note of how much he takes, corporal," Elric snarled. "He'll pay for every drop."

The barbarian nodded. "Now, why are you here? I would have thought you would be at the Imperial City, fighting off the hordes who want to kiss the boy's feet or something."

"It is what takes up most of my day, yet the emperor wished to ensure that whatever happened here, it did not end in the death of the godsbedammed royal because he...uh, said something stupid in your presence."

"He should have been more worried about him dying because he said something stupid to the barbarian princess here." The warrior nodded at Cassandra. "He called me a man-whore when we first approached and said she only brought me because I was cheap."

"What did you answer?" Elric asked her.

"I was a good sport, I think," she replied with a grin. "I asked him if he would like to compare his prick to the barbarian's dagger. That enraged him enough that he set his guards onto us."

"And fun was had by all—although I still think it could have been a little more entertaining. I suppose they didn't do too badly for a group of brain-dead, fear-castrated ass-suckers." The barbarian completed the story with a grin but no one seemed to have heard.

The Elite captain studied Cassandra with a small frown. "I have to say this is not how I imagined a barbarian princess would appear."

"You should have seen me when Skharr and I first met," she responded and looked at the royal who was dragged roughly to his feet.

"When you were a clothing merchant?" her teammate asked.

"No, when...you remember, when I wore the scale mail undergarments?"

"That...does not seem appropriate for a battle, if I might say so," Elric muttered. "Although that is closer to what I imagined for barbarian royalty, I suppose."

"I carried an amulet that empowered the undergarments to act much like full plate armor, although without the weight and restrictions." She rolled her shoulders in the armor she currently wore. "Which is not to say that this isn't the kind of thing most kings would kill to wear into battle."

"It's blessed by the gods, is it not?" Skharr asked. "I suppose we could say that the barbarian princess title is a religious one and you would be able to wear whatever armor you wished. You merely need to state that it is as the gods demand or something. Of course, barbarians do not give themselves to magic or worship of the gods."

"That is true enough," the Elite captain answered. "Although for a princess, I am sure they could make an exception. You wouldn't...happen to still have the amulet and scale mail undergarments?"

"I do. I thought about wearing it but I doubted that these men would respond with the respect and awe I am owed if I were to appear in naught but my knickers."

"I would beg to differ," Skharr grumbled. "Given that the sight of you in naught but your knickers is something that most would be in awe of—ow!"

Cassandra scowled as she punched his shoulder. "You'd best see to it that the royal has learned his lesson so we can claim on our contract."

"Aye. We'll handle him from here." Elric chuckled and shook his head. "A good amount of coin has been offered on this one."

"He sent it out for me specifically, didn't he?" Skharr scowled at the thought.

"Not necessarily, but he knew where you were and he knew that if anyone was brave enough to confront a royal, it would be you. And he was right too."

"You have folk following me, then?"

The man looked up and realized that he had revealed more than he intended. "There is a reason why I'm a captain of the Elite and not his master of spies. I have never had much skill at court politics or intrigue. I fear you might have more skill at it than I do."

"We haven't set that particular bar high, have we?" The barbarian smirked as Cassandra took hold of the royal's chin and forced him to look her in the eye. "How is the boy?"

"He'll be amused that you still call him the boy for one thing." Elric chuckled. "Tryam has taken to the responsibility of being emperor rather well, I would say. Better than I might have thought."

"He went through the trials that made him fit to be emperor," Skharr recalled. "He might have much to learn yet, but he'll have the core skills he needs. And there are many who can do what he can't, as long as he knows who to trust."

"You are one of those he trusts. I suppose I am another, and I try to keep the opinions I express to him as honest as I can although I do also make an attempt at respect."

"It won't be long until he sees your honesty as disrespect in and of itself. Never trust a king's loyalty to last, and that counts doubly for emperors."

Elric laughed. "I have thought the same thing myself. I wondered how long it would be until he thought one comment or another was too glib and had me whipped or hung. But for the moment, he has a good head on his shoulders and is the right amount of paranoid. He is trying to bring about an end to the incessant expansion wars his father was involved in, and while that is a popular decision, there are more than a few who would see him dead for it. They assume that any successor will be easier to control."

The barbarian shrugged. "They might be but as easily might not. Are all emperors sent on the same quest as Tryam?"

"Only the illegitimate presumptive heirs, which at this point is all of them since the boy hasn't found any wives or concubines yet. I think he is saving himself for when a marriage of alliance is necessary. But…well, rules can be changed. Seers can be bribed to say that all is well and it will end with someone on the throne, no matter what."

"Well then, it's best to ride home and make sure no one tries to kill the boy before he does some real good."

Skharr offered his hand to the captain, who grasped it at the wrist in a firm warrior's handshake.

"It is always a pleasure to see you, DeathEater."

"Likewise. Tell the boy I send my best. And remind him that he need not be married to a woman to fuck her. He should get it out of him with someone of his choice instead of with whoever is around when he is at the peak of need."

"That will merely make him turn out like his father. But I'll deliver the message anyway."

Elric marched down to where his men still held Cassian. Cassandra turned away and climbed the steps.

"What did you two talk about?" she asked and wiped some blood from her gauntlets.

"Old times. Past glories. Exchanging gossip. It seems the emperor desperately needs to find a cave to hide his dragon in."

"You wouldn't want him to hide it in simply any cave. Unlike you, any child he has will inevitably shout about the throne he or she is owed at some point. For you…well, I imagine there will merely be a horde of tall, red-headed bastards wandering the empire over the next few decades. Hell, if the emperor has any wits about him, he'll find those bastards and raise them to be his personal guard. They'll only be half you but it will still be more than twice most men out there."

Skharr shook his head as they descended the steps again to where their horses waited for them. "There…wouldn't be that many."

"Please. That royal shit-stain might have spoken out of turn but you described yourself to me in those same words not long ago. Or are you saying that the fire your dragon produces does not travel far?"

If he were honest, he hadn't thought about it much. He acknowledged the possibility that he'd left bastards around the empire, especially in the early days when he had recently left the clan and the novelty of women who were not barbarians was enough to have him raging at any opportunity.

The idea grew steadily more real as he continued to think about it.

"I can see your mind churning over the concept and I'll allow you to consider it for a moment." Cassandra laughed, mounted her gelding, and patted him on the neck as he pranced away from where the Elites' horses stood.

"It is not a pleasant thought." Skharr growled his annoyance.

"Most men do not like to think of the subject," she conceded as they moved toward the gates again. "And yet it is the women who are left to care for the results once you've found yourself another dungeon to attack. I would imagine that more than a few of them would have paid a visit to the local mage or herb dame and asked for a charm or a bitter tea that would prevent the possibility of a child. Mostly because there are still those who think that raising a bastard is somehow less honorable than raising a legitimate son."

She was right. He didn't like to think about it and it left him feeling like a bastard for not wanting to consider the possible pain he might have left behind when he didn't mean it.

"I'm sorry," she said once they were clear of the gates. "I did not mean to bring your mood down."

"No apologies are necessary," he replied and shook his head. "I do feel a right fucker for not allowing the thought into my mind before."

"Well, if my experience is any indicator, you certainly made it a worthwhile moment," she stated.

"True." He smirked. "But I was not always the lover I am today. Experience honed my skills as it does for us all, and when I was younger, I did not lack enthusiasm, and yet..."

Cassandra laughed when he left the sentence unfinished. "Well, younger men tend to not lack enthusiasm. But at least you admit that you have come a long way from a simple fucker."

"I suppose some might say I am still a simple fucker." The barbarian shrugged. "But in the end, what matters is that I know I am simple and strive to improve myself with every passing day."

She nodded. "One can't ask for more than that, I think."

He patted Horse's neck. "I don't suppose you left any bastards behind who will need tending?"

The stallion snorted and tossed his mane.

"You're right," Cassandra noted. "Horses judge a great deal less for foals born out of wedlock."

That drew a laugh from the barbarian and even Horse nickered softly.

CHAPTER SEVEN

"It doesn't seem possible."

Nasan didn't look like a half-elf who was surprised by much in the world, given that he had been in it for so long, yet there was an unsettled look on his face.

"You didn't think we would be allowed to lay hands on a royal?" Cassandra asked and nudged the contract a little closer to him. "I'll be honest, I didn't believe it myself, but there you are."

"Sure, there is the surprise in that too, I suppose. But it's not the most surprising thing I've heard today. You say the Emperor's Elites arrived to ensure that the work was done properly?"

"I don't think they knew what the job being done properly meant," Skharr answered, folded his arms, and scowled at one of the nearby windows.

"Is there a problem?" the guildmaster asked.

"I think he is annoyed by how the emperor appears to be tracking his every step," she explained. "You do know he helped to put the man in power, yes?"

"Everyone knows the story. I merely assumed it was false since it included a part where the two of them killed a dragon."

Skharr growled in frustration. "We did not kill a dragon. We successfully…avoided a dragon on our way into the dungeon."

"Ah. That is a little more believable. I still have my doubts but I won't bother you with those." He shook his head and the barbarian was suddenly annoyed at him for no reason.

Perhaps it was the fact that he looked like he was barely old enough to apply a razor to his jaw but filled a position of some power in the Theros guild.

As long as the work was done and the coin was paid, however, he wouldn't complain much.

"Well, the contract has been marked closed and I have been authorized to pay you." Nasan retrieved a hefty purse about the size of Skharr's fist and it clunked heavily on his desk when he put it down. This left Cassandra with nothing else to do but hand the contract to him.

The warrior collected the coin purse and nodded to the former paladin to join him in leaving the Guild Hall, although he had a feeling the half-elf somehow expected more from them. It was almost as if he thought they were more than mere mercenaries.

The problem with legends, Skharr knew, was that they often clashed with reality, no matter how much folk wanted them to be true.

"You'll let us know if there is more work to be done in the region, yes?" Cassandra asked when her partner's back was turned.

"Aye," Nasan replied. "I suppose there will be many folk in the area who would want to pass work on to the fucking Barbarian of Theros, but I'll be sure to sift the idiots out and those less likely to pay."

She patted the man on his shoulder and broke into a trot to catch up with Skharr, who was already halfway to the door.

"It wasn't bad for a few days' work," he commented and tossed the purse up for her to catch.

It was not a difficult catch and she performed it deftly before she shook the purse a few times to determine how many gold coins were inside. "No, but I think folk pay you more for your reputation, as much as you bitch and whine about it. It'll be what made you a rich barbarian in the long run."

"It'll also be what kills me," he pointed out. "So it will be a race as to whether I can spend all my coin before someone knifes me in the gut or poisons me. I would prefer a knife over poison, honestly."

"Do you speak from experience?"

"Yes. The last time someone poisoned me, it took the intervention of a friend to save me and even then, it was a narrow call."

"Interesting. And here I thought barbarians were immune to most poisons."

"Where did you hear that?"

"I never heard it so much as assumed it. The talk is that barbarians are half-troll and they are notoriously resistant to poisons and venoms and the like."

He regarded her speculatively. "It's untrue, and yet… It would be interesting to spread a rumor like that. If nothing else, it will perhaps stop folk from trying to poison me."

"There you are, then. I am helpful already. Does that mean I am owed half the purse?"

"That was the case already." Skharr smirked and patted Horse on the neck as they stepped out into the sunlight.

Cassandra grinned and tucked the purse into her belt. "Well then, what do you have in mind next?"

"I need to speak to someone in the underworld in the city."

Her eyebrows raised as they reached the bottom of the steps and the city began to press in around them again. "Anyone in particular?"

"Yes, and no. Someone who runs the underworld will likely attempt to contact me, especially if I visit the right places in the city. It's another benefit to having your name known and being tall enough that folk can see you from half a mile away."

She laughed. "I think I know where you need to go then, if only by reputation."

That seemed to be enough to encourage him to follow her and Skharr did so without argument. They hurried through the narrow streets and wound upward into the area where the richer citizens appeared to spend their time, although it was still a fair distance from where they lived.

The clearest indication was that it was where the finer craftsmen in the city displayed their wares. It left no doubt that they were in a cleaner, richer section. Cassandra motioned him toward one of the inns ahead of them, where a group of patrons enjoyed their meals and drinks outside in the sun.

"There?"

The former paladin nodded. "The guards who visited the temple often spoke of it as somewhere they always wanted to go but were never allowed since most of the patrons were criminals who paid a great deal to make sure none of the guards interrupted their business there."

"That sounds suspiciously like hearsay. Are you sure you don't merely want to eat somewhere with finer fare than our last meal?"

She snorted. "You don't know what you speak about, barbarian. I've been on too many campaigns to be fussy about food or drink. But if you want to find the upper echelons of the city's criminals, it would be a place to start."

He could agree with that, at least. And even if she were wrong, there was the possibility that they would enjoy a decent meal there. Skharr approached and noticed that more than a few of the patrons watched him closely as he stepped inside. One of the stable hands rushed down the street as they delivered their horses into the care of the others, and while it was possible that he was going to fetch something for a customer, the barbarian had a distinct feeling that he had gone to inform someone of the new arrivals.

Cassandra placed her hand on the shoulder of one of the serving women. "Apologies, but is there a place where a woman might change her clothes and freshen up before a meal?"

Her accent had changed into something a little more formal and likely the kind of voice folk expected from women in these places. She could have made the change consciously, although Skharr wondered if it was perhaps a reflex from her time as a paladin.

Either way, the young woman pointed at a room away from where most of the tables were. It was nice and private and a woman would be able to freshen herself before a meal without drawing attention.

"Freshen up?" the warrior asked in a whisper as they moved to one of the tables as far from most of the patrons as they could.

"I am dressed in my traveling clothes. Nothing would appeal less to the people here and the last thing we want is to have the owner ask us politely to leave."

"How would he make us leave if there are no guards?"

"I suppose he has roughs of his own to call on."

"Good. I've needed a good fight for a few days now."

"You… We were in a fight a few days ago."

"Precisely."

Skharr grinned as he sat, then drew a deep breath and leaned back, and showed no sign of leaving to freshen himself. Cassandra merely sighed and placed the coin purse on the table before she hurried to the room pointed out to her.

One of the serving girls approached his table once the former paladin was out of sight. She wore a broad smile that he assumed was how most of the patrons enjoyed being greeted.

"I hope this afternoon finds you well, good sir," she said. "Might I interest you in something to drink or eat? I might recommend our white wine stores, kept cool in snowbanks in our cellars to make a refreshing drink in this heat."

"Might you?" He grunted. Perhaps this wasn't the kind of place for him after all. "Two chalices and a chilled wine bottle, I think."

"Of course."

She bowed and paused to look at a handful of other serving girls who watched her closely before she retreated.

It only took her a few moments to return with what he had ordered, the wine chilled enough that there were droplets on the outside of the bottle. She was followed by the other girls who had watched him before.

He straightened in his seat and tried to determine what was happening. After a moment, he realized that all of them tried to offer him smiles. It seemed he made them nervous but that they were also intrigued by the novelty of having a barbarian in the area.

"Will you have anything to drink, good sir?" one of the others asked before the girl who had spoken to him before had placed the bottle and chalices down.

"Oy, it's her table. Don't push in!"

"She don't mind the extra help." She flicked some of her black curls behind her ear and smiled again. "What about something to eat then?"

The woman with the drinks scowled to show that she did mind the extra help, although she was a little too professional to physically shove her aside.

This suddenly posed another possibility for why they acted so oddly. Skharr wasn't sure he liked it. It was flattering but it was the kind of thing that would not be taken well once a certain barbarian princess rejoined him.

"How long have you been in Bora-Cera, sir?" a third asked and made no attempt to help offer him refreshments.

"Don't pry!" the first one snapped and elbowed the third girl hard in the ribs. "Don't forget that our patrons wouldn't like excessive curiosity about their lives. But if he were to stay in our establishment, I might suggest the Emperor's Room, where the beds have recently been—"

"Oy! You lot!"

The barbarian grinned as Cassandra stepped out to deal with the group. She wore different clothes, although he had no idea where she had kept them on her person. It seemed pointless to ask, however. They were made mostly of leather with a deep purple tinge that reflected the light, but he wondered how comfortable they were and how hot they would get.

One of the waitresses stiffened and he realized that she had a dagger pressed against her hip.

"Find your own mound of flesh to fawn over." The former paladin hissed a warning. "That there is my man-whore."

All the others backed away immediately, and Cassandra flipped her long curls, now released from the bun in which she had bound them before. The one with the dagger against her hip acted as though it wasn't the first time she had been threatened thus and immediately retreated with an apologetic smile.

"You scared them off before we could order food," he told her and tried not to reveal how arousing the sight was. She probably hadn't intended it that way but he couldn't help the feeling.

Besides, as a paladin, she knew how to take the fight out of someone simply by being intimidating. That was likely her intention, whatever effect it had on him.

"They'll be back once their employer reminds them that they are supposed to be working for a living, not batting their eyelashes at any handsome man-whore who might cross their path."

She had a point, although the warrior needed a moment to process her words. He was essentially still lost in studying the figure who looked quite ready for a fight in her leathers.

"I won't fight that knife," one of the waitresses said, still in earshot.

"Forget the knife. I won't fight that ass."

Skharr smirked and shook his head.

"What?" Cassandra asked and poured herself some of the chilled wine.

"You made quite the impression on the staff," he said casually and waited for her to finish filling her glass before he filled his. "But I imagine they'll have a story to tell the others later, so it should not be too much of a problem. I doubt it was the first time they've dealt with a dagger in their backs."

She shrugged and sipped the wine. "It's refreshing. Did you order this?"

"They recommended it."

Although she looked disgusted, she did not retract the compliment and took another sip.

"Would you care to explain the outfit?" he asked after a moment of silence had passed between them.

"It is…something I threw together," she admitted.

Skharr tilted his head to examine it a little closer. "It is…effective."

That drew a laugh out of her, and she shifted in her seat to allow him a better view. "Oh? In what manner?"

"I would assume the charm you wear around your neck is the same one you wore to make your scale undergarments as effective as full plate armor. Might I assume that you are wearing them now?"

"Yes," she answered. "You can assume but I suppose you'll have to wait until I undress to find out."

"I do hope that is soon."

"So do I." She winked.

Before she could say anything else, she paused, looked around, and settled her gaze on a small man who wore a black cloak that covered most of his face and appeared to be watching them.

"And who the fuck are you?" Cassandra asked. It seemed she did not want Skharr to be interrupted while he told her how good she looked in her new outfit.

"Skharr DeathEater, Barbarian of Theros." The little man spoke in a gravelly voice and ignored her entirely. "It is a wonder of wonders to see a legend walk among us so freely."

"Speak your piece and fuck off, stranger," Skharr answered and leaned forward to catch a wisp of beard on the man's chin before he lowered his hood even more. "Before I throw you out myself. There is no point in involving the city guard in this, I suppose."

The man laughed. It was an ugly, grating sound on the ear.

"That is an interesting proposition coming from the likes of you," he said and shook his head. "I come bearing a question from a variety of interested individuals who have a mind to find out what you are doing in the city of Bora-Cera and how long you plan to remain. There were many suggestions as to how to discover the answers to these questions, yet I held to the point that to simply ask you would be the safest and wisest course of action."

He froze in place and Skharr smirked when the stranger realized that Cassandra was already a little too close to him with her dagger pressed between his thighs.

"You might want to reconsider," she whispered harshly and he tried to back away from the blade that dug into his genitals. It continued to follow him across the chair until he'd run out of space to retreat to, stopped by the back of the chair. "Would you call this situation you find yourself in a safe one?"

"No...no. No, I would not. And I promise that I mean...I mean no harm in...in coming here."

Skharr smirked but his eyes narrowed as he watched her lean closer, a dangerous look in her eyes. It could have been an act to scare the man to the point of voiding his bowels, yet there was a sick feeling in the pit of his stomach that told him there was much more to it.

Something in her fully intended to kill the man by castration with a sharp knife.

"Your timing is poor and rude on top of that," she whispered. "Do you not realize that you should respect royalty when it sets foot in your city?"

"Ro...royalty?"

"The barbarian princess comes into your city and you waste all your attention on a mere barbarian?" She shook her hand and with the way the man jerked and whimpered, Skharr assumed the blade had drawn blood.

"Ah...apologies...uh, Your Grace."

He relaxed as the blade pulled away slowly and she moved to her seat again and sheathed her blade. The man's cloak had fallen back in the engagement and the thin, almost gaunt features that had been hidden were now visible. Even the thin, graying beard didn't do much to make him seem a little closer to human.

The warrior consciously relaxed as well when he realized that his whole body had been tense and ready to lunge into action if her actions proved to be more than simply an act.

"Bar...barbarian princess?" the man asked and pulled his cloak up to cover his face again.

"It is a religious title among my people," Skharr lied smoothly. "They generally do not deign to wander outside of the clans."

"I...I see."

"We would appreciate it if this knowledge were not spread," he continued. "There is a reason why our royalty remains a secret from the outside world after all."

The stranger's eyes narrowed to show that he didn't quite understand, despite his next words. "I understand. None of this shall pass my lips."

That wasn't how the barbarian assumed it would be, but that

wasn't important. He knew that many among the DeathEaters would have a riotous laugh over him spreading rumors about the existence of royalty among the barbarian clans, although a few others would not be so forgiving.

But the more the story spread, even denials among the clans would be seen as the barbarians' attempt to keep their royalty hidden from the world.

"I beg your forgiveness, Princess..."

"Ytrea," she answered and looked a little calmer as she continued to support what Skharr was saying for the moment.

"Princess Ytrea, of course." He cleared his throat and looked a little closer to his original and more confident state.

"You have us at a disadvantage, stranger," Skharr pointed out and sipped his wine. "You know both our names but you have yet to introduce yourself."

"My name is not important." His eyes widened when he caught a look from Cassandra. "And yet...in the interests of respect, you may call me Seiben. It should be known that the Undercouncil knows you have no business with them in Bora-Cera and that you have no intention to interfere with our business in the city either. Yet, there is an interest in sharing the knowledge that would guide you to those who are best-informed on the subject of older dungeons in our vicinity, particularly the Saren Dungeon—the one founded by the dragon priests."

The barbarian leaned forward. "Speak plainly. I have no plans to involve myself in politics or dishonest dealings in this city, one way or the other. If that is all you need to pass on to your employers, be on your way."

"I am sure they will be most pleased to know that you have no intention to interfere with their business interests. Your honor comes with the knowledge of your reputation among their contemporaries in Verenvan, so your word is beyond question. But if you were to find the Mage Salernus' shop in the Mage Quarter three blocks from here, I do not think you would waste your time. In the interests of keeping an open mind, you should not be surprised by what you find."

That was about as helpful as the weasel would be, Skharr realized, although it begged the question as to why the local Under-council was suddenly so helpful.

Seiben stood and turned away but paused and looked over his shoulder. "If you need to speak to me, eat at the Northman's Flagon. I'll be sure to not allow any slights to occur."

He began to walk toward the door and the barbarian smirked when he adjusted his crotch once he was far enough away from them and mumbled something about the godsbedammed barbarians before he was out of earshot.

It would be some time before the girls returned to find out what they would have to eat, but for the moment, he was more than content to enjoy the wine and good company. He was relieved to see Cassandra—or Ytrea if that was what she wanted to be called now—had calmed visibly now that the human embodiment of slime was gone.

"Now," she said and took another sip from her glass, "continue the talk."

"What ta—" His words were cut off immediately when she kicked his shin hard.

"Did that remind you?" she asked and winked. "A woman always wants to hear what her barbarian man-whore thinks of her outfit."

"You didn't need to kick me for that." He growled and resisted the urge to rub his leg. "But yes, I remember now."

CHAPTER EIGHT

"I don't understand why we are visiting this...Salernus person based on the word of a sewer rat who works for the criminals of the city," Cassandra protested.

"There is no point in not at least speaking to a mage about it," Skharr countered. "If there were dragon priests, it stands to reason that they had magical powers. If they did, there might be some knowledge about what we will face. If not, we can find charms that will be useful and fuck off."

"How do you know that a mage the criminals of the city rely on is someone we can trust?"

He shrugged. "Given that the criminals of the city rely on him, I assume he would not be able to afford it if talk spread about him selling faulty items. I doubt he would survive it either."

She nodded.

"Even so, you will be able to see if the items are of any worth, yes?" he asked

"Of course." She smiled. "I've had my experience with charms and the like and I should be able to identify those we could use."

That was all he needed to hear. He had no magical talent of his own, which meant he mostly had to trust the word of the mages he bought from. They had been more or less reliable, although he was always left with the feeling that they would attempt to push an unnecessary purchase in with those he needed since it wasn't likely that he would be able to tell the difference.

"Salernus," Cassandra said quietly. She pointed at a sign held up by a beam that spanned the street and was supported by both buildings. The windows were open and a gentle breeze ruffled through the plants on display. There must be a spell in place to make the wind move continually like it did. Skharr was the first one through the door.

Compared to the oppressive heat outside, the interior was cool and pleasant although there were many more plants around them than he was generally used to seeing in mage shops. They tended to have a horde of trinkets out and on display. This one looked a little closer to a herb shop.

Movement came from the back and a young woman appeared, smiling at them. Her bright green eyes complemented her tanned skin and black curls, all of which matched the long, flowing, colorful dress she wore.

"Welcome to Salernus," she said with a thick accent. "How may I serve you today?"

"You're Salernus?" Cassandra asked and narrowed her eyes.

"Aye, although I've heard many question my name."

"Not really." Skharr shook his head. "Your accent…it's from the southern coast, yes?"

"You've traveled there?"

"No, but many of your compatriots have caravans that trade with the barbarian clans. I've heard the accent before."

"I am impressed." She laughed. "Even this far south, not many in the empire know much about my kin on the coast."

"It was one of the few countries the late emperor was afraid to attack. I doubt he would want his people to discuss the matter."

"Well, not many would want to cross the deserts to reach there. Armies are certainly not interested in marching that far."

"Are you a druid then?" Cassandra asked and folded her arms.

"You are well-traveled, I see. But I have learned many of the charms that are required in these parts."

"And dealt with the Undercouncil a great deal as well?" Skharr asked.

Her pleasant demeanor shifted into something a little more nervous, and he noticed her hands slide into the long sleeves of her dress, most likely to grasp a pair of daggers.

"Do not fear," Cassandra said and glanced at the windows to make sure they had a way out if they needed one. "We are not with the city guard. Your services were recommended and we were told you might have some knowledge about the Saren Dungeon."

Salernus removed her hands from her sleeves, which meant the daggers didn't pose a danger to them yet, but she looked as though her guard was still up as she studied them carefully.

"You don't appear to be the type who would consort with the Undercouncil."

"We aren't," the former paladin snapped.

"But we have found ourselves at both crossed purposes and united purposes with criminals in the past," he added. "When it was confirmed that there was no intention on my part to inter-fere with their business, they decided to send me to the dungeon. It could be because they are desperate for a way to rid themselves of me."

The druid nodded and rubbed her hands together. "It is possi-ble, although they have a vested interest in clearing the Seastones as well. They have used them to smuggle anything they might need from the outside."

"That isn't surprising given that most of the trade in this region goes around the Seastones," he commented.

"Not around the Seastones," Salernus corrected him quickly.

"Through them. I mapped the waterways under them and taught the Undercouncil how to use them in exchange for protection that would not have been afforded me by the city guard."

Cassandra took a step closer. "You would have mapped them because you spent a great deal of time around them, yes?"

The woman nodded and smirked. "Indeed. I spent time in the area some five or six decades ago when I was apprenticed to Maskos, one of the dragon priests. I never honestly believed and when the temple fell into disrepair, I left."

"And yet you needed protection. From the priests?"

Salernus scowled like the former paladin had begun to annoy her.

"Either way, the dragon has been driving the smugglers who use the Seastones away, so the Undercouncil would prefer it if the beast were done away with."

"Is there any way for us to approach the dungeon without going over the Seastones?" Cassandra asked. "Under, perhaps?"

"Yes. But that won't stop the dragon from attacking and you would have to climb up through the tunnels to reach the temple itself."

"A map would serve us well," Skharr interjected.

"I do not work for free."

"I assume you have one already created for those who might need it." He took a gold coin from his purse and tossed it to her. "And we would appreciate advice on where you would be the most likely to enter if you wanted to do so."

She laughed, stretched into a nearby desk, and took a small scroll from within, which she handed to his partner. When Cassandra opened it, they only needed a brief glimpse to confirm that it was a detailed map to navigate the narrow reaches beneath the Seastones.

"Does it look accurate?" the barbarian asked.

The former paladin nodded. "Most of these cracks are spanned by small bridges that allow folk to travel over them."

"I generally advise the smugglers to steer as close to the coast as they can given that the deeper you go in, the more you'll find that the stones shift and move to alter their paths and make a maze. But there are many ways for you to enter if you choose to. Once you reach the inner circle, the sea pulls back. The tide comes in and floods the area but no deeper than your knees. The priests did not want their temple to be flooded from below."

Cassandra sighed and tucked the map into her pocket. "Right, then. I think we could find our way through there."

"But the dragon will still be able to attack you from above," the druid warned. "I would move silently and if you smell bile in the water or on the sand, I recommend you direct your path around it."

"A dungeon full of dangers?" Skharr asked and his voice dripped with sarcasm. "And here I was worried that it would be a boring journey."

"The dragon is not all you have to fear, of course. Numerous monsters have made their home there, although they fear the dragon as well. The smell of the bile might drive them back if you have no other choice."

"A choice between monsters and dragons," Cassandra whispered. "This is most certainly not a boring journey. I think we'll need some charms for the duration."

"Most of the smugglers ask for charms that will dampen any noise they make. The one I sell works on smells as well, so it will make it more difficult for the dragon and other monsters to find you but that is about as far as it goes."

"Do you have any that act against venom?" the barbarian asked as she placed two charms on her table.

The druid nodded and looked around before she slid her hand into a small glass box where a few dozen wooden chips were intertwined with a handful of vines. She carefully plucked two chips free and bound them with some rope.

"I've never seen that spell before," Cassandra whispered and rolled one of them between her fingers. "It's effective, though. Some spell dampers would not go awry either—the kind that would not interfere with any magical items I carry on my person."

"Of course." More charms were produced and the former paladin inspected them all as closely as possible. She leaned forward and ran her fingers over them. Skharr half-expected her to start sniffing and tasting them, but she didn't go that far.

"Do you have some magical talent as well?" Salernus asked and looked curious.

"Barbarian royalty are the few barbarians who possess magical abilities," the warrior interjected before his partner could do something as boring as tell the truth. "It is not well-known and many would deny that they even exist, but there are a few in the world with mage and barbarian blood."

Cassandra tilted her head and smiled as if she had hoped to keep it a secret and yet would not deny its existence.

The druid looked confused and almost disbelieving, but she certainly wouldn't call two paying clients liars to their faces. Skharr hadn't been sure that she would believe him and as a test, it had likely failed.

"All these charms come to…twelve gold pieces and three silvers. Would you like to make it out to a bank paper, or—"

The barbarian shook his head, retrieved his purse, and produced the required coinage.

"Don't you think it a little dangerous to travel with that much coin on your person?" the woman asked.

"I'd like to meet anyone stupid enough to try to take it from us," Cassandra replied with a smirk.

"I doubt they would want to meet us, however. Will there be anything else?"

"Only the most fervent wish of good luck from me to you on your journey," Salernus answered. "I fear you will need all the help the gods may provide."

"It couldn't hurt," the paladin answered as they collected their purchases and exited the building. "I don't know why but something about the woman…unsettles me," she whispered as they left.

"Druids tend to have that effect on people. They are closer to nature than most other humans. I think they possibly have a trace of dark elf blood but I don't know enough about that to comment on it."

"Why do you spread the legend of the barbarian princess?" Cassandra asked as they moved closer to the town market.

"It is…amusing," Skharr admitted. "I picture the reactions of my fellow barbarians at the concept of having royalty who are magic wielders like a paladin is, and it would go from instant violence to unending laughter. It's the kind of reaction I always try to stir in my fellow barbarians."

"You aren't fond of them, are you?"

He shook his head. "Most of the clans already dislike each other to some degree. Over the years, I've found that even the DeathEaters are flawed."

"Is that when you learned about the southern coast?"

"No, that was when I was involved in a handful of wars for the empire. There were always questions about why the emperor never attacked the Talim Kingdoms and talk about when the empire would push down there. When I spoke to a few of the generals, they told me the kingdoms are allied with the orc tribes that make their home in the deserts. Any invasion would have to pass through the tribes' territories, and that is the kind of nightmare no general would ever want to put his armies through."

She nodded. "You would think mages would be able to clear the way, though."

"Orcs have their shamans too, you know," he answered. "And they have practiced battle magic for decades. Although…"

The former paladin looked at him and tilted her head as she waited for him to continue. "What?"

"Well, I've never seen an orcish shaman, which begs the question of whether they even exist or if they are merely rumors and legends the orcs themselves have spread to make sure folk fear to attack them."

"That is an interesting point. Whatever it is, I doubt there will be any who would put it to the test if the rumor was effective enough. Which I suppose it was if it prevented the emperor from invading."

Skharr couldn't disagree with that. They continued through the market and he made a note of where the children around them were at all times. The fact that they appeared to draw away from the two of them was a sign that they were experienced pickpockets and stayed away from anyone with a weapon who looked like they would cut hands off on a whim.

Children didn't live for long on the street if they couldn't identify who was the most likely to kill them for attempted robbery. Even turning them over to the guards was sometimes a better fate, which was what most of the parents and farmers tended to do, although it could not be guaranteed.

The guards would not hold a pickpocket for long, and for most of the children, a few days spent in a cell with regular meals was considered better than the alternative of freezing and starving on the streets.

"Do you miss it?"

Skharr looked at Cassandra and slid his hand to his purse to ensure that none of the thieves around them could lift it while he looked away.

"Miss what?"

"When you traveled across the land with armies, were paid well, and had steady work without the need to look for it. I can concede that I will eventually miss the sense of duty that came with my responsibilities as a paladin, no matter how miserable I felt while bound by my role. So do you miss being a soldier or that kind of mercenary?"

It was a good question and he considered it as they bought the food they would need for the journey.

"There are elements I sometimes pine for," he admitted finally once their purchases were paid for. "The camaraderie is always something I miss most of all. And yes, the combined sense of duty and a cause to fight for until eventually, you realize you have fought for so many causes that are all the same. The ugly truth emerges over time—that so many die young while those who make the mighty speeches remain safe in their well-guarded seclusion at the top with a pile of money. Many of those who survive are left penniless with the wounds of mind and body that will last their lifetimes, and this knowledge makes you finally acknowledge that the causes are all bullshit."

Cassandra studied him for a moment and nodded. "I think you've carried those feelings inside for a good long while."

"True. And yet not long enough."

Even thinking about it was enough to sour his mood and Skharr fell silent as they continued through the stalls in search of other supplies they needed before they returned to their inn.

When they arrived, he remained in the stables, conscious of the need to spend time in silence with Horse but was surprised to feel a hand on his shoulder. He shifted his attention to where Cassandra stood behind him.

Perhaps she had decided to spend time with her horse as well, although he couldn't recall if she'd told him his name already.

"I'm sorry that you carry such nightmares with you everywhere you go," she whispered and leaned closer to press a light kiss on his cheek. "But I hope you know that you need not carry them alone if you do not want to."

The barbarian lowered his head instinctively and refused to meet her eyes for a moment, but when he felt her grasp on his shoulder weaken, he covered her hand with his.

An unsettling horde of feelings rose within him. They had roiled under the surface for longer than he was willing to admit but it felt good that he did not have to face the demons on his own.

"Thank you," he said softly before he released her hand.

"You need not thank me," she answered and ran her fingers through his bright red hair for a moment. "I know you would do the same for me—and have done the same for me when I needed it."

He nodded. "I'll thank you all the same if you don't mind."

"As if I could stop you." She laughed and walked to her horse's stable. "Fucking barbarians. We'll collect the contract from the guildmaster in the morning and head out early, yes?"

"How do you know there is already a contract available on the dungeon?" he asked.

"Please. If the criminals are losing money, there will be a contract."

CHAPTER NINE

"I 've never been to the Seastones before."

Cassandra brought her horse to a halt and looked into the distance at the view Skharr studied quietly beside her.

They truly were a marvel, and although she had once thought they were a natural design, more information had come to light that made it seem as though there was magical influence in their creation. They could have been a natural formation once but they had most certainly been meddled with.

"I'm not sure I enjoy seeing them, not anymore," the former paladin admitted and shook her head.

The rugged landscape stretched for hundreds of miles but looked like it had once been a single rock that had shattered into thousands of pieces to allow water and weather to seep in and erode it. Chunks were missing that had fallen into the water below but from afar, it was easy to see what it had looked like once. Perhaps thousands of years before or even longer.

"We should get closer to see if the view is a little more comfortable from there."

He was probably right about that, although the former

paladin studied them cautiously again to make sure she couldn't see the dragon flapping its wings while it scanned the area for them. There was no sign of the beast, but she knew better than to think it wasn't nearby.

At least she knew what she was looking for now and could avoid it—or Skharr did. She had no idea what a dragon's bile smelled or looked like. Given that she couldn't remember having come across it the first time she had approached, she doubted that she would be able to see or smell it this time.

Finally, somewhat satisfied that the beast wasn't aloft and watching them, she spurred her horse forward to rejoin her companion. She hadn't insisted that he ride again, partly because she knew it would be a fruitless effort but mostly because she dreaded approaching those fucking stones again.

Of course, the slow approach somehow felt worse but the wait was over for the most part. Instead of taking the pathway directly into the Seastones, which would force them to cross over the top, they followed the road that led to the beach and from there, traveled under them.

Hopefully, the druid's map would be reliable and they would be able to navigate through without mishap.

From below, the rocks were somehow more impressive than they were from above and seeing them from the beach three or four miles away was an unsettling sight. Many hung precariously in the air, somehow thicker at the top than they were at the bottom, while some stood taller than most buildings.

There were pathways, that much was clear, and they searched for one that led them deeper into the Seastones until they reached the base of the mountains in the distance. This would hopefully bring them to the temple where their contract waited. Cassandra had been right and there was a contract. She assumed it was issued the moment those with the coin to pay for it knew Skharr was in their area.

The waves crashed on the beach and the surf pounded on the rocks ahead of them, the only sound aside from a handful of seagulls that hovered lazily in the breeze. A few decided to dive into the clear, cool water on occasion to come up with fish and sometimes with nothing at all before they soared and returned to hovering.

How were they not terrified of the dragon?

Cassandra pulled her horse to a halt once they reached the track that headed toward the rocks. It vanished into the water after less than a mile.

"We could wait for the tide to go down again," Skharr suggested when he caught up to her. "Or push on through the water. Which do you think is the best course to take?"

She shook her head. "We don't have time to wait for the tide. If the dragon sees us, it will be a truly short journey. I'll feel more comfortable once there is something between us and it above our heads."

"The stones won't be much protection if the dragon does see us."

"I know, but the protection is essentially to prevent it from seeing us. And I'll feel a little better. Come."

She nudged her horse forward again and the beast trudged slowly into the water. It wasn't deep and barely reached its knees as it began to wade through.

The real problem, she deduced, came from the waves that still moved with the tide and drove into the rocks. It wasn't hard enough to splash much but it was certainly enough to make her mount's footing unstable.

Even so, the road was more secure than she gave it credit for and still intact despite the water. It seemed to shed any sand that was pushed onto it so it was clearly visible to any who traveled along it.

The fact that the horses were calm was probably the best indicator that they were still safe from any monsters, winged or not, that might attack them on the ground.

Still, there was no point in taking risks. Cassandra grasped the reins a little tighter as the stones loomed directly over her head. They truly were impressive this close, although she had no intention to spend any more time around them than was absolutely necessary.

"Oh, this is much better," Skharr quipped as they followed the road under the stones. "Instead of a dragon looking down at us, we'll worry about the odd waves knocking rocks loose that crush us to death. Much better."

"It's preferable to dying by fire, I think," she replied, although she also felt a hint of foreboding as they followed the path under the rocks.

On the bright side, between the shade cast by the stones and the spray from the sea, it was as cool as they could ever feel without using magic. The former paladin drew a deep breath and enjoyed the smell of the water.

"You're smiling."

She startled and looked at Skharr. "What?"

"You're smiling. Out here in the middle of the Seastones, you look about as relaxed as I've seen you since…well, ever."

The man had a point and she knew there was likely some kind of explanation that confirmed her to be utterly mad. She had no real problem with that. After all, a barbarian princess needed to be a little mad.

She held the reins a little tighter, shook her head, and decided not to give him an answer that would allow him to make a mockery of her good mood. Perhaps he wouldn't but she did not want to jeopardize it.

It was interesting to see small outcroppings on the rocks that had begun to grow a few trees. Vines climbed everywhere and made it seem like the stones grew out of the earth somehow. As they began to move in deeper, a handful of those that had already fallen collapsed into the water below. Others leaned on their neighbors and made it almost impossible to determine the safest path between them.

Behind her, Skharr maintained a constant vigil of the area above them.

Cassandra snapped her gaze up as well at the crackle of rocks falling from the heights to splash loudly into the water below. Her heart jumped into her throat and she moved her hand reflexively to her sword, but all she could see were the seagulls as they launched from their perches and flapped away.

Their loud caws were a source of alarm because the two adventurers had attempted to make as little noise as possible to avoid attracting the attention of anything hovering above them. After a long pause during which they scanned every inch of their surroundings, no more movement came from above.

"The dragon might be taking time to rest," Skharr told her. "Most lizards are particularly active when it is warm, but I am not sure if the same applies to dragons given that they create their own fire. And there were a few that lived in icy mountains."

The question remained as to whether dragons were lizards at all, but she did not know enough about the beasts to make any real comment. They looked like lizards, although massive, and there were huge reptiles out there that were certainly not dragons.

"Of course, if it is resting, it means the monsters will be more active," she reminded him and nodded at the plants and vines that grew higher among the stones, where she could see more movement. Unfortunately, it was difficult to tell precisely what it was.

It could have merely been the wind moving through the plants, trees, and vines that grew all the way up and created a web across and between the stones to make it practically impossible for anything to fall from above without being caught in the middle.

Still, she couldn't shake the feeling that something was there, watching them and waiting for them.

Perhaps not the dragon, but certainly something. The former paladin had long since learned to trust the instincts that nagged at her and she let her hand rest on her sheathed sword before she nudged her horse forward again.

"What is his name?"

She looked at her companion, who walked beside her.

"What?"

"Your horse. What is his name?"

"I…haven't had him long enough to name him. The temple gave him to me without telling me his name. Do you have any idea what it is?"

Skharr shook his head. "He won't talk to me. I assume he is not used to having folk talk to him. We'll warm up to each other but it might take some time."

Cassandra grinned and leaned forward to pat her horse's neck. "Is that true? Or do you simply not want to talk to the big barbarian man-whore?"

"You won't ever let me forget about that comment, will you?"

"Why would I? It's not as though he was the only one to name you thus. It seems those related to the emperor think you are one and who am I to disagree with them?"

"Barbarian royalty, apparently."

"There is no such thing."

"And yet that did not stop you from referring to yourself as such."

He made a good point there, but she wouldn't admit it. Instead, she turned her attention to her mount. "Do you see what I mean? He can be a grumpy old fuck, but if we can learn from Horse, he is tolerable even at the worst of times. I cannot speak to that but I think he is worth talking to at least."

She did feel a little silly about speaking to a horse like that, but the beast did appear to listen. Perhaps he didn't understand or didn't want to, but she'd learned a long time before that horses relaxed when they were spoken to.

"I don't think he believes you," Skharr told her.

"What did he say?"

"He does not like barbarians in general," he answered. "But he prefers you because he knows you are not a barbarian, no matter how much you proclaim it."

"Did he tell you his name?"

"Well? Do you have a name?"

Horse nickered softly and tossed his mane as he trotted forward to nudge the warrior on the shoulder.

"Don't you worry, there will be no replacing you," he said reassuringly and scratched the beast's nose. "She'll need a horse of her own if she travels like we do. Even if she does ride."

"Don't you talk about me like I'm not here," Cassandra protested and shook her head. "See, he can be a grumpy bastard when he puts his mind to it."

That appeared to get a chuckle out of the gelding, although she couldn't be sure what the soft whinny meant as he shifted from one foot to the other.

"He shouldn't be the one to name you," she whispered. "He calls all his horses Horse and thinks that it is a royal enough name that he does not need to strain his creativity."

Skharr shook his head. "Now you are talking to your horse about me as though I am not present. Although, interestingly, he does agree with you."

"Of course he does." She leaned forward to pat the gelding's neck again. "And it proves that he is a smart horse. I think I'll...I'll name him..."

She paused when the barbarian's amused expression changed to one of alarm. He unhooked his bow from where it was secured on the saddle and strung it smoothly before she could consider what to name her mount.

His eyes were focused upward and she followed his gaze to

where something moved across the rock. A handful of some-things, she amended quickly. Perhaps dozens of them, although she couldn't tell exactly what they were until a few of them thrust their heads out of the cover of the trees and vines on the stones.

The creatures looked like birds, but small, needle-like teeth extended from their beaks. They hissed and screeched at the humans below them.

One of them finally released its hold on one of the stones, extended wings like a bat's as it glided to a neighboring stone, and looked down again from its new perch. It appeared to be about as long as an alligator she had seen in the swamps not too far away, including the tail that extended to almost the same length as its body.

She studied it closely and scowled. The wings were not large enough to allow the creatures to fly easily, but they could glide from stone to stone. Dozens more of them began to do so and shifted from one rock to the other. Both the limbs from which the wings extended and their hind legs had claws.

They looked almost like bats except for their sickly gray skin, a complete lack of fur, and the elongated beaks with the teeth.

"What in the hells are those?" Cassandra whispered and drew her sword slowly.

"I have no fucking idea," Skharr answered, finished stringing his bow, and took a handful of arrows from his quiver. "Yet I do not like the way the flying ass-ugly goblin turds are looking at us."

The former paladin shared his dislike and scowled at them. She swished her sword as the creatures gathered on the crests of the stones to their left and continued to stare at them from their elevation of about twenty yards.

The barbarian had already nocked one of his arrows when the first one jumped clear of its secure vantage point and curled its wings to dive swiftly to where the two humans stood. A moment later, three more joined it and it wasn't long before the other creatures started their attack as well.

The barbarian steadied his raised bow. The string sang loudly and the arrow streaked upward at an impressive speed. As usual, his aim was impeccable and Cassandra decided that it seemed like the kind of skill a barbarian princess would need to acquire.

She smiled as the projectile cut directly through the chest of the first creature to dive. It went limp immediately and the wings opened to slow its descent as the others shifted trajectory to avoid a collision with their dead comrade.

The arrow continued upward and into the chest of another that was close behind, and it too sagged in midair.

"So you aren't so hard to kill. You merely look like fuck-ugly hell-spawned nightmares. Beneath all that ugly, you're simply hard-headed limp dicks with wings."

He smirked at the effects of the first arrow, nocked another immediately, and loosed it to eliminate another of the beasts. This time, the target was pinned to one of the nearby stones. Skharr loosed a third but it missed entirely when the creature rolled away and the projectile continued its flight until it thunked into one of the nearby stone outcroppings.

That was all he was willing to fire at this point and he flung himself to the right with a massive splash as three of the creatures plummeted to strike at him. They barely managed to reverse their trajectory to avoid the water.

Cassandra assumed they did not enjoy being in the water and perhaps were unable to swim and needed help to climb out of it.

Before she could think of any way to make use of that knowledge, she swung her sword to catch one of the beasts as it swept down to attack her.

The blade sliced through the flying creature's neck and it splashed into the water a quarter of a second before something hammered into her chest. She looked down and realized that she'd been lifted out of her saddle. Her horse galloped away, neighed loudly, and kicked at one of the creatures that attempted to attack him as well.

Oddly enough, she couldn't feel the individual claws digging into her flesh. Her captor's hold was painful and thoroughly uncomfortable, but she wasn't dead and both her arms were free.

The former paladin knew she would not be able to attack with her sword from that angle, so she drew a dagger from her belt and screamed as she drove the blade deep into the beast's leg. The injured limb released her and the monster screeched, but it twisted and tried to reach one of the stones while it struggled to fly with her in grasp. She pushed higher and buried the blade in its chest.

The attack drew no shrieked response but the claws went limp. Cassandra fell and landed in the water with enough force to knock all the breath from her lungs. Her leathers immediately began to grow heavy and she struggled to her feet with a slight feeling of panic. Finally, she managed to stand and realized that the water was fairly shallow.

It was odd how the impact with it had disoriented her. She stabilized herself and drew a deep breath as she took stock of her situation. Her sword remained in her tight grasp but her dagger was buried in the monster's chest. It had fallen hard onto one of the stones and tumbled into the water a short distance away from her.

She would need to reclaim her dagger eventually, but she had her sword to defend herself with for now. Skharr crouched low in the stream as well, his bow in hand, and aimed up as the creatures flew to the stones. They could not reach their previous perch using their wings but they could climb and skittered up quickly.

Those still in the air screeched at the humans but avoided the horses as it seemed they were too large to drag up after they were killed. She doubted that would continue, however.

For now, though, none of them had resumed their airborne

assault. They reached the outcroppings and screeched at the two adventurers but showed no intention to attack again.

The water had soaked thoroughly into her leathers, which made them feel a little heavier and more cumbersome than she liked. Not only that but the claws of the flying monster had left a handful of gouges deep in the armor.

"Are they not coming down?" Cassandra asked and eased to where Skharr had pulled the horses together and tried to calm them.

"Aye, but our troubles are not over." He snatched a few arrows from his saddlebags and shifted his gaze to movement across the ground and through the water.

These beasts looked surprisingly like those that watched them from above, but were considerably larger—twice as large, in some cases, although their length was more or less the same. They glided through the water with only the slightest ripple and she frowned as she studied them closely. Something like bones in their heads and the front of their legs cut through the water and made it look like they were swimming.

It seemed as though they were perhaps the males or females of the first group and possibly explained why those above had avoided the water. A few of the larger ones feasted on the corpses of those that had fallen while the others turned their attention to the humans.

Skharr was ready for them and loosed an arrow with a faint splatter of water from the wet string.

It sang on its steady path and one of the monsters rolled to thrust large splashes at it in a possible defensive reaction, but it suddenly lost control of its limbs when it punched directly through the heavy bone plate at the front of its head.

Another arrow followed moments later and the second creature fell, but the others surged forward when they realized they were under attack by the massive barbarian.

"Have you not learned the lesson?" he bellowed. "I must

assume you are as stupid as you are ugly but then again, a stupid bag of flying troll turd dies the same as one with a brain."

He seemed unconcerned that he wore only a gambeson with nothing else between his body and the razor-sharp claws that would surely tear through his flesh.

Cassandra couldn't allow that. Her armor was likely strong enough to prevent any attack from getting through. She could feel that a few bruises had formed around her ribs but nothing that would make her unable to continue to fight.

That was something that could not be said of Skharr if they reached him. A third monster floundered in the water but while his aim was unerring, he didn't fire fast enough.

Her arming sword felt light in her hand, but her attempt to move through the water was nightmarishly slow, no matter how shallow it was. She gritted her teeth and thrust forward between her partner and the monsters as he retrieved more arrows.

They were less than ten yards away from him when she reached the closest of the creatures. It turned barely in time to see her and its powerful jaws snapped and flung a splash of water into her face. Dark-green blood rose from the wound she inflicted but it raked its claws across her shoulder.

Something hot filled her as she drove past the creature toward two that tried to flank Skharr and stay clear of the possibility of another arrow loosed toward them to eliminate another of their number. She hacked into the monsters almost before they realized she was there. The first one's body jerked in its death throes. Its body separated from its head and the other one lunged to defend its dead partner.

The power of the creature immediately thrust her into the water again, but the former paladin buried her sword into the soft underbelly of her adversary. She thrust it deep enough to punch out the other side with a spray of its blood.

The force of impact almost hurled her off her feet but she managed to catch herself before she fell on her back in the water.

Immediately, she steadied herself and turned her attention to the other beasts. Skharr used his bow to fell one, and the creatures appeared to foam at the mouth in their frenzied desire to attack him but seemed to avoid her. Wherever she moved to through the water, they drew away.

One more was killed before the larger creatures began a retreat. Those that were close enough tugged at the corpses of the fallen, likely to drag them far enough away to be consumed safely.

"Are you all right?" Cassandra called to Skharr.

"Yes." He growled, closer than she'd thought he was. She jumped and turned, surprised to see him so close to her already. "The question is are you all right?"

She raised an eyebrow. "I'm the one with armor."

"It is in shreds."

She looked down and narrowed her eyes when she realized that he was right. The hardened leather armor she had worn had been torn to shreds. The godsbedammed bastards had struck her more often than she thought they had in the heat of the moment. Their assaults left her with pieces of leather hanging from her body to reveal her bruised skin beneath as well as the scale mail undergarments.

"Fuck," she snapped in irritation and yanked the damaged pieces off. Perhaps she should have realized what had happened when she was no longer encumbered by the soggy leather.

"In all honesty, though, you look better now."

Cassandra glared at him. "I liked the way the leathers looked too. They were darker and more menacing."

"Yet now, you'll be far more of a distraction should we have to fight any humans."

He was right about that, even though the likelihood of facing people rather than monsters seemed somewhat remote.

"We need to keep moving," she insisted. "There is no way to

tell if those in the rocks would like to try to attack us again now that the larger ones are gone."

The barbarian nodded. "I'll need to recover my arrows first."

"Do it quickly."

"As you say, Princess."

"Fuck off."

CHAPTER TEN

To pull the rest of the leathers off required that she move away from the water. Skharr guided them to one of the stones that was tucked back a little and wouldn't provide an easy trajectory for any of the flying monsters that still watched them. There, the sand banks sloped out of the water and made it a little easier to begin to remove the pieces.

Cassandra liked the way the leathers had looked on her but it was somewhat liberating to remove it all and assume the appearance she had considered for herself at the outset. The scale mail was mostly something folk expected. She wouldn't have minded wandering around naked, although the hint of modesty in her protested that it probably was not a good idea. Even so, she wouldn't put too much thought into that. Folk expected a barbarian to look like they did in paintings and as they were described in ballads.

If the truth be told, she had half-expected Skharr to tear his clothes off and rush into battle with his cock out when they first fought together. While she was relieved that he was more sensible than that, it was a little disappointing as well. At least in her case, she was able to find something that matched what she thought a barbarian was meant to look like while she remained fully protected.

All that aside, the fact that the warrior had watched her undress, tilted his head a couple of times, and even cleared his throat while he acted like he hadn't watched her intently when she looked at him was even more gratifying. Her reaction wasn't ordinarily the kind of feeling she would have had toward many men who ogled her, yet she had ogled him on more than one occasion.

Turnabout was fair play.

"Do you see something you like?" Cassandra asked once she had removed the ruined outer layer of her armor.

Skharr nodded, approached her, and smirked. "You could say that. I am glad to see you still wear that medallion. Those godsbe-dammed sharp-toothed bags of goblin shit would have ripped you apart if you hadn't worn it."

"It is why I committed the way I did. I knew I wore real armor and you did not."

He took the medallion in his hand and nodded. "A sound tactical move on your part, I must agree."

The former paladin took a step back and regarded him with a raised brow. "Are you seriously discussing tactics and the magical doo-dad I wear around my neck when you have this body to admire?"

She grasped her breasts in both hands, which made them even more difficult to ignore than they already were. He smirked in response. "I am capable of performing multiple tasks at the same time."

"No, you should not be when you have cleavage like this to consider." She pulled her hair out of the way to give him a better and unobstructed view. "And do you want to see something?"

The look in his eyes already answered the question, and the

way he cleared his throat and licked his lips before he looked away only drove the point home perfectly.

When he saw the smirk on her lips, the barbarian knew he was caught with nothing to say one way or the other and he leaned into it. He was not a bashful man and she didn't expect to see him blush, but it did appear that he thought their minds needed to be on something other than sex.

Finally, he gave in, smiled, and nodded. "Yes."

His voice was considerably rougher than it had been before, and if he hadn't worn a thick gambeson, she had no doubt that she would have been able to see his dragon— as he liked to call it —had grown large and ready.

Cassandra approached him slowly and something like fire burned in the pit of her stomach as she jumped up lightly, wound her legs around his waist, and pressed herself close enough to him that she could feel the reaction she teased from him. She pressed her lips firmly to his as her arms slid around his neck and dragged him closer.

He settled his hands on her hips and held her in place and she couldn't help but grind her body against his in a slow, rolling motion. It made him suck in a deep breath when she pulled away from the kiss and bit her bottom lip.

"If we didn't have the stench of blood hanging over us, I would take all the fire your dragon had to give me right here and right now."

Rather than wait for his reply, she pushed up as far as she could and placed her next kiss on his forehead.

"What was that for?" Skharr asked as she slid down again.

"My thanks for saving me."

"As I recall, you were the one who jumped in to scare the beasts off. I think they did not attack only because they had no intention to face you outright, whereas they were more than willing to tear into me."

"That may be true," she admitted with a smirk and walked to

where the horses still waited for them. "But you know that was not what I referred to. And I know that you are looking at my ass as I walk away. You should make it a little less obvious if I can feel your gaze on it."

"Good, I thought I was too subtle with my staring," he retorted, and Cassandra tossed him a flirtatious glance over her shoulder to reward him for it. "It is the kind of ass that inspires a dragon to wake and plunder while causing me troubles."

"You know, I did come up with a good name for my horse now that I've had time to think on it."

"Did you?" Skharr asked and scowled at where the monsters continued to tear into the corpses of their fallen. She doubted he would be able to recover the arrows he used given how the beasts attacked their feast. The only chance he had at that was after the monsters passed what they'd eaten and they did not have that kind of time.

"Aye. Did you have any ideas? That are not Horse."

"What is the problem with Horse?" he asked and patted the stallion's neck before he checked his quiver and counted the number of arrows that remained. "It is a noble name and since I cannot speak as he does, it would make sense to name him something that describes him instead of assigning a name that is somehow an insult."

Cassandra nodded. "Yes, but there is a problem with that."

"What?"

"We can't name both our horses Horse. The confusion would be disastrous. As such, I have settled on the name Strider—it's simple, descriptive, and to the point."

The barbarian tilted his head in thought and finally nodded. "It is a kingly name. Do you think Strider is a name for you?"

Her mount showed no sign that it was listening to him, and she laughed.

"True, he does not care what a barbarian thinks. What say you, then, Strider? Is that a name you could live with?"

Strider snorted softly in response.

"He says it will do for the moment," Skharr translated as he patted Horse again.

She did want to know if there was a name her mount would prefer, but her companion stared at the outcroppings above them where the monsters continued their vigil. There was nothing they could do to shoo them away but the hope was that if they moved out of sight, the creatures would decide not to follow.

They seemed intelligent, at least. The way they had avoided her when she had inflicted lethal wounds suggested that they were capable of thought, despite her partner's insults to the contrary. They were not mindless beasts that threw themselves into the battle, willing to die if it meant they would defeat the humans.

It wouldn't always be what they encountered but it was interesting to see. Most of the creatures that threw themselves at certain death were generally under the control of other monsters —those that were more likely to pull away if they knew what kind of danger they were in.

The fact that they watched as closely as they could meant that those that flew were likely the females. They lived higher in the stones where their nests and young were, while the males were too large and too heavy to climb. Perhaps they were willing to eat the eggs as well if they were given the opportunity.

Some academics would want to study them, likely with the help of a handful of mages who would be able to prevent the creatures from attacking and a group of warriors that would be at the ready in case they did.

If she had to guess, there was likely no magic in these beasts at all. They were merely the local predators that had survived in the Stones, even after the arrival of a dragon.

All this notwithstanding, the assumption remained that the closer that they got to the temple, the more influence its magic would have over the creatures in the area, which was likely what had drawn the dragon to it in the first place. There was nothing in the world she wanted to do more than avoid the dragon, but she had a feeling that even those monsters influenced by the temple would stay away from it.

Those that didn't were likely no longer around.

The idea that they could move when the dragon wasn't active was not the feeling she enjoyed hanging over her. It was an unsettling kind of compromise and she constantly studied the skies between the Seastones and waited for it to appear in the cracks.

"There is no sign of it yet," the former paladin whispered as she brought Strider to a halt. The tide had begun to ebb, which made the water much shallower. In an hour or so, they would walk on dry land again.

"The dragon will have a difficult enough time seeing us," Skharr pointed out. "And it might not be in a position to attack."

"What do you mean?"

"All these animals are here," he explained and pointed at the stones. "Dragons tend to not allow anything to live near their nests, yet this one has."

"Do you think it simply hasn't dealt with them yet?"

The barbarian shook his head firmly. "I read that dragons cleanse any region they nest in with fire and kill any and all creatures larger than a spider to ensure the safety of their nests. They then mark their territory to make it clear that anything that comes close will meet the same fate. This one, it seems, has not done so."

"Perhaps it hasn't nested here properly," Cassandra suggested and shifted in her saddle as she cast another fearful look upward. Even talking about the creature felt like it might summon it, at least in her mind. "Perhaps it was brought here by the temple but has no intention to remain?"

He shrugged. "Perhaps. To be honest, nothing about this makes sense to me."

There were too many coincidences, she conceded. Someone who had been at the temple unaccountably waited in the city to help them. The coin and the contract were ready for them almost immediately. If she wracked her brain, she could probably identify a few others. While she didn't quite share his suspicions, she could understand where they came from. For her, all she cared about was staying as far away from the dragon as possible until they were in a position to kill it.

Emerging from beneath the Seastones was still somehow more impressive than seeing them from above. They entered an elaborate labyrinth mostly created by the slow beating of the sea against the rocks over countless years. It was complex and difficult to navigate, but with the map, Cassandra could state with some certainty that they moved deeper into the maze.

This was, interestingly enough, the right way to go and they began to wind along the path through the stones. The deeper they went, the less effect the water and wind had on the rock. While this narrowed the passages, the cracks ran from top to bottom so the adventurers were never quite closed into what would feel like tunnels. Still, the constricted space and the darkened area around them made her wonder if they were now protected from the possibility that the dragon would attack them.

Of course, that was not much of a comfort. The dragon's breath was not how they sent their fire. Rather, it came from a liquid in their body and that would fall through any crack that was visible from above and would burn hot enough to cook anything caught in the flames.

But perhaps it would not see them moving below.

"Eyes ahead," Skharr said softly and took his bow from the saddle. He'd left it strung after he'd dried it, prepared for anything that might attack them from above or below.

The tide was out fully by this point—if it even reached that far, although the dampness suggested that it might—and the horses' hooves clopped loudly on the rocky floor of one of the narrower passages. Their route led them ahead into one of the brighter areas they'd seen during what felt like hours of navigating the maze.

Whether it meant that they were close to the temple or if they worked through to the other side of the Seastones, they wanted to be ready for anything.

Cassandra had her arming sword drawn and she nudged Strider to move forward, ready to meet any attacks. Her armor would protect her, while Skharr would be far more effective with his bow against their enemies from a distance.

He would be more than useful up-close as well, but she couldn't draw his bow. Perhaps she should make time for her to learn to use it. She knew about DeathEaters and their bows, which were more than legendary among the merchant caravans that traveled through those mountains. As a paladin, she had always assumed that she would have to face one of those attacks herself if she was called on to escort a caravan through the region.

Now, she considered whether or not she wanted to be one of those archers herself. It truly was odd how life worked itself out.

Strider was immediately nervous when they stepped into the open and a hint of wind brought a foul smell to her. The scent of rotting flesh was quickly and immediately confirmed when her gaze located a variety of bones scattered across what looked like a courtyard in front of an opening on the hard stone of the mountain.

They had reached the temple, it seemed, but something waited for them there.

Cassandra dismounted quickly, scrutinized the area, and tried to determine what the bones were from. Some of them appeared to be smaller creatures, perhaps even the seagulls that inhabited the foliage that filled the Seastones, but others were considerably larger. Most seemed to be the beaked creatures they had fought earlier.

"A snake," she whispered. "Not many other fucking monsters would leave the bones out like this."

Skharr nodded in agreement, a couple of arrows already in his hand. He nocked one quickly and aimed at the entrance as the stench suddenly grew worse and a low hiss greeted them from inside.

"I guess we'll see why we haven't seen many creatures this close to the entrance," he muttered, drew the bow, and watched the aperture intently.

Movement immediately caught Cassandra's attention. Dark-green scales launched her heart into her chest and she wondered for a moment if she was looking at the dragon again.

When more of it moved into view, however, it was immediately apparent that it was not a dragon. With no legs and no wings, it slithered across the ground and coiled in front of the entrance to glare balefully at them.

"You made a good guess," the barbarian whispered as the serpent's mouth opened and a tongue about as thick as his arm flicked out before it bared its massive fangs.

Less than half of the creature was coiled outside and as it pushed forward, more emerged. The body was about as thick as Cassandra was tall and the fangs were easily the length of longswords. A clear, milky liquid dripped from them.

If being impaled by the fangs didn't kill her, the venom almost certainly would.

"It wasn't a guess," she retorted and tried to hide the fact that her mouth was dry simply from looking at the creature. "Well...it wasn't only a guess."

Skharr nodded and it was somewhat comforting to see his brows furrowed and that he dried his drawing hand on his gambeson before he dragged in a deep breath. These signs of his nervousness somehow reassured her that he would press in and work harder than he would have otherwise.

"Do you feel a little envious?" Cassandra asked in an attempt to lift their spirits.

"Of the size?" He grinned. "A little. I don't suppose we woke it?"

"We might have," she answered with a small smirk and shook her head. "Fucking barbarians."

"Are you ready?" he asked as the snake began to move toward them parallel to the walls of the courtyard so it could attack from the side. The structure was in ruins but they could still see what had once been an impressive piece of stonework, clearly a part of the temple that awaited them above.

"About as ready as I'll ever be."

"That's good enough."

With that said, Skharr drew his bow smoothly and loosed without so much as a breath between the two actions. The arrow streaked across the distance and buried itself in the serpent's head.

His aim was still unerring, which she had expected, but the fact that the powerful bow's strike was not able to punch into its skull came as something of a shock. A part of her had foolishly hoped the battle would be over that easily, even though the other part had somehow known that it would not be.

Cassandra ran forward when the serpent hissed again and pushed hard toward them. The horses backed into the tunnel they had approached through, and a moment of what felt like sheer insanity touched her.

What was she thinking? It was utterly foolish to rush directly at a serpent almost twenty times larger than Strider was. When one considered that Skharr did something like this on a regular basis, it certainly explained why folk were so desperate for his services.

He already had another arrow fitted to the string and drew it back as the creature moved in to attack her.

She timed the beast's strike and dove to the right so its face impacted the stonework beneath her feet. The power of it was enough to make the ground shake and she rolled over her shoulder and regained her feet an instant later. As the massive body slithered in front of her, she slashed her blade upward.

The thick skin almost stopped her blade entirely but it inflicted a shallow cut from which bright red blood seeped.

It wasn't quite the strike she had hoped it would be.

Still, she had the beast's attention and it shifted away from Skharr, who fired another arrow that hammered into its jaw. The snake hissed and turned to face her as the rest of the body serpentined from inside the cavern and flicked across the entire courtyard.

Cassandra saw the attack with seconds to spare, raised her hands, and pushed as much power as she could into her shield to stop the beast's lunge.

"Over here, you overgrown flabby snot-brained troll dick!" the barbarian roared, dropped his bow, and drew his sword. He rushed forward as her shield collapsed beneath their adversary's assault and she sprawled awkwardly and twisted to protect herself. She barely managed to deflect the strike away from her and the ground shuddered as she rolled clear of the monster and tried to regain her feet.

The warrior pressed his attack and bellowed again as he thrust his sword deep into the beast's belly. His longsword with the silver hilt went directly through the monster's skin and deep into its body, although Cassandra was not sure if it was a fatal blow.

The entire creature writhed in pain and she gasped when the tail whipped viciously to catch him in the chest. It hit with enough power to knock him into the wall and left the blade buried in the beast.

"Skharr!" she called as he found his feet. He attempted to stay upright but staggered, fell to his hands and knees, and heaved up the contents of his stomach.

Of all the bad signs, that was close to the worst.

"Fucking godsbedammed stinking whore's ass." She grasped her sword tighter and narrowed her eyes when the snake turned its attention to the barbarian.

CHAPTER ELEVEN

S kharr was down and certainly did not appear to be in any condition to fight the serpent. He had struck the deepest blow and their adversary appeared to still be pained by the injury, but she wouldn't assume it was even close to dead.

Her sword was a fine weapon but the one buried in the snake would provide her finest chance to kill it.

"Shit," Cassandra whispered. She knew she would not be able to defend the barbarian in time.

He would have to save himself while she retrieved the sword he'd left. Every instinct in her said to rush to his aid but she would have to trust that, even injured, he would know how to stay alive for the precious seconds she needed.

She surged toward it and her boots thumped on the stone and launched her forward as she sprinted as fast as she could.

The snake seemed to ignore her for the most part. Its body slid around to block any escape and it leaned closer to strike at the warrior while he still struggled to regain his feet. He seemed unable to regain his balance but managed to push himself out of the way of the attack and moved forward and under its body as it hammered at him. The strike dug its fangs into the stone and tore a chunk of it out when it raised its head.

Skharr was alive but looked the worse for wear as he stumbled away from the monster that now moved in for the kill. The former paladin knew her time was running out and every thump of her heart told her she needed to somehow move faster.

This close to utter disaster, there was no time to think about what she attempted. Those fangs would be able to punch through whatever armor she wore, magical or no, and even if she hadn't cared about her partner coming out from the battle alive, she would not be able to fight the beast on her own.

The serpent writhed. Its whole body jerked in pain but it still moved to attack the barbarian as she vaulted smoothly over its body to where the sword was buried. The skin was soft and pliable to the touch with a cold, wet feel to it that left her with a slightly sick sensation simply from that slight touch, but there was no time for personal disgust. She would climb inside the fucker and drag its heart out with her bare hands if she had to.

Although she did sincerely hope that such a feat would not be necessary.

Cassandra stopped her slide by catching hold of the hilt of the blade, the only part that still protruded. She twisted her body with agile strength and her boots connected with the stone. Once they had found purchase, she was able to drag the blade to cut a deep gash across its midsection that made it jerk away from Skharr. Its sinuous body writhed in agony.

"I didn't think you'd like that, you filthy gap-toothed sonofabitch!" she shouted, unsure if the creature could even hear her. Whether it could or not was irrelevant. When she twisted the sword in its gut it would certainly feel her.

This was possibly the most pain the monster had ever felt and the deepest wound it had received. That aside, the laceration was far from what could be turned into something lethal. She had caught its attention, however, and drawn it away from Skharr. It turned slowly toward her and for the first time, she realized that its slitted, green eyes had an almost hypnotic quality to them. A hum from one of her charms warned her that magic was in effect and tried to take hold of her.

"Did you think it would be so simple?" Cassandra shouted, dragged the sword clear of the gaping wound she'd left in it, and ignored the blood that gushed from it now that she had the monster's attention. "You'll have to try harder than that, bitch!"

The serpent bared its fangs again and launched a streak of venom toward her.

All she had to do was duck and use its body as cover as she sliced the blade deep into its skin again. She had meant it to be a shallow wound but the sword was lighter than she expected and spellwork had surely been involved in its creation as well. It slid through the thick, tough skin as if it wasn't even there. Another hiss issued from the creature and it attempted to roll its entire body over her. She knew that if she gave it the chance to wind the endless coils around her, it would mean the end and she swung the weapon to force it back as she inched closer to the head.

"What are you waiting for?" the former paladin yelled when it tried to curl into a ball to protect the injured parts while it continued its attempts to attack her. "Do you think you'll be allowed to survive this? You might as well try to take one of us with you!"

She doubted that it could understand her, but her taunt drew the reaction she had hoped for. The head jerked forward with impossible speed and suddenly, the fangs were all she could see before she jumped away.

Her leap gained no distance, however, as her back collided with the wall. Startled, she realized that her adversary had worked slowly to corner her until she had nowhere to retreat to. Hell, something that big would be able to crush her against the wall without any need to use its fangs and she would not be able to do much to stop it.

Suddenly, the bowstring sang again and a moment later, another arrow jutted from the side of the snake's head. It failed to penetrate very far but was enough to divide the serpent's attention for a moment. Thankfully, a moment was all she needed.

Without taking the time to find out how Skharr had managed to reach his bow or fire it, she surged forward with his sword in hand and arced it powerfully into the beast's neck immediately below the head.

Once again, the blade cut like the snake's skin and bone were nothing, but the strike wasn't enough to kill it immediately. The sinuous body began to writhe, jerk, and roll, and Cassandra pushed forward, knowing she would have only one more attempt before she was crushed against the wall.

She needed to get herself a magical blade if she survived this, she decided. The weapon sliced smoothly through the rest of the neck and she jumped and rolled away from where the body still tried to crush her. The head thudded on the stone and foul-smelling blood and goo leaked from the wound. The former paladin scowled and inched away. Its eyes were still open and she had the oddest feeling that it would suddenly snap to life and try to kill her again.

The fear was undoubtedly foolish but it felt very real. Almost as if to fight it, she advanced on the monster's head and before it could attack her, drove the sword through it. She would have to find her own weapon in the tangle of snake that filled the courtyard but that would come later.

Skharr was seated on the ground and still looked like he was about to collapse. He held a small vial of healing potion in his hand, recently emptied, and his bow was on the ground next to him.

"I thought I'd missed my shot there for a moment," he said and shook his head. Blood smeared the back of it, although the wound it had come from was already healing.

"You took a nasty knock to the skull there, barbarian,"

Cassandra commented, approached him carefully, and inspected the injury caused by the impact. "How do you feel?"

"Not…not wonderful," he admitted and still looked pale like he was about to throw up again. The healing potions worked by pushing what the body already did to heal itself to act faster. In this instance, though, it did not seem to go fast enough.

"Are you all right?" Skharr asked once he'd taken a few deep breaths.

"Aye. You?"

"I have a…a slight headache."

"So does that." She nodded her head to the beheaded snake and his sword planted in its skull beside two arrows. "How did you manage to fire an arrow while practically falling over?"

"I…am not sure. I suppose we'll have to answer that later when you eventually knock me on the head and I try to fire an arrow, simply to find out. How did you manage to cut the head off?"

Cassandra shrugged. "Your sword did most of the work, but I feel I could have hacked it off eventually, given the time and no resistance."

The barbarian shook his head and struggled to his feet. She was there to catch him if he fell, although it was more likely that he would drag her down with him. Still, although he staggered at first, he managed to remain on his feet and after a moment, walked to the head of the dead beast.

"Women," he muttered. "They are always quick to ask a man to do the hard work, even when she is perfectly capable of doing it herself."

"I heard that," she snapped.

"I said it out loud," Skharr responded and yanked the sword out. The blood seemed to be repelled by the blade and within seconds, it was as clean as it had been in the moment when he'd drawn it from its sheath.

With a little more effort, he plucked his arrows from the head and turned to where she rubbed her chin idly.

"What?" he asked. "Are you wondering where your sword is in that mess?"

"No. Well, yes, that too, but I was also thinking about what kind of artist I would commission to paint the scene."

"Scene?"

"You know, the part where I prevented you from being swallowed whole. I think I'll call it...*The Barbarian Princess Saves the Life of the Barbarian of Theros.*"

"With my sword."

"Pure semantics. The point is, if it weren't for me, you would be dead. Therefore I did save your life."

Skharr shook his head. "If that is what you need to tell yourself."

Cassandra grinned and moved to where her sword was not, in fact, wrapped inside the still-twitching corpse but had conveniently been shoved across the rocks.

"We should move inside," the warrior told her brusquely. "Before something decides it is hungry enough to eat the snake."

"True, but you do not appear to be in any shape to attempt a dungeon of any kind yet." She placed a hand on his shoulder. "I cannot think of a more gruesome place to rest for a moment, but you do need it."

She would admit that she needed a moment of rest herself, but he made no argument. Once the horses were retrieved, they advanced toward the entrance—which still reeked faintly of death and decay—and sat out of the sun on the steps leading to it.

"You should eat," the former paladin suggested once they were situated. "It might seem crazy to you but it will settle your stomach. Some of the way bread especially."

He scowled at her but offered no argument and instead, heaved one of the packs from Horse's saddle and took some of the food from it.

It would have to be a short stop. He was right, after all. Scavengers would find the sight of something so large and dead inviting, yet they were far from ready to continue their journey.

The barbarian did eat but with no real enthusiasm and he seemed to fight the nausea from the knock he took to his head. The healing potion was working already but he still had a way to go before he made a full recovery. In solidarity and because she was hungry as well, Cassandra ate some of the way bread and washed it down with water from their skins.

"I think I understand why folk have never heard of you before you became the Barbarian of Theros," Cassandra commented as she pushed her hair from her face. She hoped the banal conversation would keep her companion distracted from his misery.

"Because I did nothing of note before I was the Barbarian of Theros," he asserted with enough confidence that she was half-tempted to believe him.

"No. It's because you were known by other names that you chose to leave behind when you had a mind to become a farmer. The kind of names that one might wish to run from."

Skharr regarded her for a long moment before he chuckled softly. "Yes, I suppose that is correct."

She leaned forward, her eyes narrowed. "Were you known by any names I might have heard of?"

He scratched his chin, took another bite of way bread, and sipped his water. "I've had various names over the years but not many that would have been known to the outside world. One of them was Scourge of the Waters, as I recall. I was reminded of that one when I was on a ship with a dwarf friend of mine. Although it had been many years since I left that life, the captain of the ship remembered me as the particular barbarian known as the Scourge."

"So you spent time as a pirate?"

"There was a time…well, yes. It was a little more complex but ultimately, yes. Piracy was how we sustained ourselves."

"We?"

The barbarian nodded. "I will admit it wasn't my finest hour—a time when I was in the mood to fight for anything I wanted, no matter who was in possession of it. If word came out that the Barbarian of Theros and the Scourge are one and the same, I would be met with fewer rich contracts and more executioners' axes."

"Is there anything you might have done in particular?"

He snorted. "I pretended to be one of the emperor's inspectors and boarded a small merchant vessel that carried silk across the water. On the first night, we slit the throats of the crew, threw the bodies overboard, and took the profit from the silk for ourselves. Another time, I pretended to be a priest of Carran. I was drunk and somehow landed in one of his temples. It was manned entirely by women. They had a vineyard and...I do not recall much of the two months I spent there. I left once word came that a proper priest was on his way."

"I think you would make a fine priest to the god of wine and revelry."

"Oddly enough, I did. But there is more to it than drinking and fucking all day long."

"What of the emperor? I know you helped to bring him to power, but he seems more...well, attached to you than one might think."

"I worked on his behalf to clear yet another dungeon, although I gave my word to Janus that I would not speak on the matter."

"The High Lord God Janus?"

Skharr nodded. "He is an ass, but I doubt he would take any man breaking his word to him lightly."

Cassandra nodded. "Fair enough. Are there any other gods you might have run into since we fought together?"

"I met Theros a few more times, including the instance when he sent me to find you. I also met Ahverna face to face—the goddess of thieves, as I recall. She isn't as powerful as the other gods but quite impressive in her own right."

"Her own right?" She raised an eyebrow. "I suppose she found you equally impressive?"

He shrugged. "I helped the dwarf who served her."

"Of course." She paused, frowned slightly, and drew a deep breath. "So…Theros did send you to find me then?"

"Aye." The barbarian looked at her. "He…well, it was obvious you were in pain and that was not something he wanted for his paladin."

"That is oddly comforting—and oddly annoying at the same time. I think I know how you feel about the emperor following you."

Skharr nodded. "He…well, he admitted there was a side to you that would be affected by what you experienced. Theros has an idea of his paladins and thinks they are purely extensions of his will. He sometimes forgets that they are humans in their own right."

"I see." That made sense. A god would be oblivious to his followers' humanity, although not many of them would be willing to admit they were wrong. "Wait, did he trouble you because his paladin had screwed you blind?"

"I was never blind," he argued. "There were no torches and we were underground. Did I struggle a little to walk afterward? Perhaps, but I wasn't blind."

"Oh, of course, use that excuse."

"And yes. Yes, he did reprimand me on the topic." He pushed up from his seat and seemed to feel better already. "Are you ready for the dungeon?"

"What?" Cassandra bolted her feet. "A god is upset with you for defiling his paladin?"

"It wasn't as though I'd deflowered you or anything like that."

"I did not say deflower and of course not. But I was sore for a week!"

"From our fucking?"

"Partly," she admitted. "The fight did play a part as well."

"But you can heal yourself."

"Interestingly enough…" She sniffed as if reluctant to continue. "My ability to heal myself didn't fix my groin. I assumed it was Theros allowing me to learn from my transgressions."

"What did you learn if you don't mind my asking?" Skharr patted Horse's neck.

Cassandra mounted Strider, drew a deep breath, and shifted in her saddle. "I learned that I could attack my fear and go back for more."

She couldn't see his expression as she had taken the lead and now headed into the ruins of the temple.

His silence spoke volumes and a broad grin crossed her face. "You're looking at my ass again!"

"Do you have eyes on the back of your head, witch?" he retorted.

"You will address me properly by my title of Barbarian Princess Witch!"

It was a mouthful but utterly accurate.

CHAPTER TWELVE

There was certainly enough to remind them that the ruin was once a temple dedicated to dragons. Skharr kept his bow strung in anticipation that something might be waiting for them.

Despite that, he doubted that they would encounter monsters close to the entrance. The serpent guardian appeared to eat anything that lived and breathed so would have made it difficult for other creatures to make a home nearby.

That theory was not something to wager their lives on, however. Instinctively, he moved his hand closer to where Horse carried the bow on his saddle.

Cassandra continued in the lead and from the way she held her right hand on her sword, he knew she shared his feeling of unease.

"It makes you wonder why they left," she whispered. "Or why they were forced out. Do you think the snake might have been responsible?"

The barbarian shook his head. "Something we could kill would not have posed too much difficulty for a group of priests—assuming they were magically capable, of course."

There was nothing to guarantee that, though. They did not even know if the druid in the city had told them the truth.

The former paladin came to a halt, narrowed her eyes, and pulled Strider around to face the walls they were moving past.

"What is it?"

"A mosaic—or perhaps a mural. I am not sure. It's been falling to pieces for a while."

"No surprise there," Skharr commented and settled on his haunches. "I would wager that this is where that snake spent most of its time."

"Why do you say that?"

"Lack of dust, for the most part. If an area like this were left abandoned and without movement, everything would be covered in dust."

She looked around for a moment and shook her head. "I think I can still make some of it out. Here…here—see the coloring? That looks like a group of people, right?"

He approached the mural and narrowed his eyes as he stretched his hand to run his fingers over the place she had pointed out. "Perhaps."

Cassandra took that as encouragement to continue her investigation and nudged Strider to allow her to continue her inspection of the mural. "There are more of them here. They look like they are carrying…cows, sheep, goats. The kind of things they might sacrifice."

The farther along the mural they went, the clearer the images became and seemed to confirm that the figures depicted brought the creatures up the mountain as some kind of sacrifice.

"And there is the dragon," Skharr pointed out.

It was well above most of the other images and breathed fire on the group, although it appeared to only target the sacrifices.

"The figures are…worshipping it," he whispered but shook his head a moment later. "No, they are on their knees but facing away from it. Do you think they were able to control it somehow?"

Even as he spoke, it sounded impossible. Besides, the natural assumption was that the mural was created by them and would describe the events from their point of view. This did beg the question, however, of why they did not worship at the feet of the dragon.

"I assumed the druids had something to do with their demise, but what if whatever dealt a blow to the temple wasn't human at all?" Cassandra suggested. "What if the dragon or some entity that had a dragon in its thrall was what struck them?"

It was an interesting idea and he would prefer to know if they would have to battle something that could control a dragon before they stumbled onto it.

"We need more information," Skharr noted. "Or we could wander in to play sacrifice to whatever the fucking priests lured here."

The former paladin nodded in agreement. "We might have to consult with Theros and ask for some guidance. I would not want to be lost here."

She made a good point. He turned as she dismounted.

"Do you think Theros would respond to your call?" he asked.

"If not mine, then certainly yours," she answered and dropped to her knees in a practiced motion. "You are still the Barbarian of Theros, after all."

"I won't kneel for him."

"I doubt he would expect that of you. Now, be quiet. I need to focus."

Skharr did as he was told and watched her close her eyes and fold her hands on her lap. It was an odd sight, given the clothes she wore. He knew her eyes were firmly closed but she would know that he was staring at her tits if he remained still for too long.

Instead, he turned and moved to where Horse stood beside

Strider.

"You still don't like me, do you?" he asked and the gelding did not answer. It wasn't uncommon for horses to avoid speaking to certain humans, although that was generally not an issue for him. He treated his beast well and fairly, which meant most tended to be conversational enough.

Perhaps this one simply did not like barbarians as he'd said before.

"I don't suppose you could intercede on my behalf?" Skharr asked the stallion.

Horse snorted in response.

"I do not need to be liked by all horses, but being on good terms with one we are traveling with is a sound idea."

"Shut up!" Cassandra shouted from where she was still kneeling.

The barbarian nodded and with a sigh, adjusted the packs Horse carried to make the load a little more comfortable.

In response, the beast nudged him gently on the shoulder. When he failed to move, the heavy lips nibbled at his shoulder and tugged him insistently. He knew teeth would be used next, and with another sigh, he turned to look at Cassandra, who pushed slowly to her feet.

"Did you hear anything?" Skharr asked. "Or do you need me to call on the fucker myself?"

She didn't answer and when he approached her, he realized that her eyes were still closed. The woman appeared to be in some kind of trance and he had only a moment to consider what was happening before she walked past him.

"Shit," he snapped. "Horses, follow me. And Strider, I need none of your nonsense. Don't talk to me if you don't wish to but follow anyway."

The beast practically rolled his eyes before he complied.

Surprisingly, the former paladin moved at a brisk pace and Skharr had to break into a trot to keep up. Her eyes were still closed, yet she navigated the ruins and caverns as though she could see perfectly.

Skharr paused when she reached a wall with a massive crack in it and without hesitation, climbed through it into the darkness of the mountain above them. As large as this new space was, there was no way ahead.

As if to contradict his thoughts, Cassandra drew her sword and pointed it directly at the wall that blocked their path before her eyes flickered open.

She looked surprised to have moved at all.

"What happened?" she asked, looked around, and frowned at the sword in her hand.

"You hurried away like you knew something," the warrior answered and gestured for the horses to stop. "Or like you had a nest of hornets up your ass. Either way, whatever happened drew you here."

"Why?"

It was a good question and he approached the wall warily.

"Do you think there's something on the other side?" she asked. "We'll have to find some kind of handle or a knob to pull it open."

"How simple," Skharr said snidely. "We could spend weeks here and never find the way through. I have another slightly less elegant solution."

"Oh?"

He drew his sword from where it rested in its scabbard on Horse's back, approached the crack in the wall, and stared at it for a long moment.

"If your idea is to hack into the wall until we reach the other side, I admire your effort but I will not assist," Cassandra told him sharply.

"My plan is slightly more elegant than that," he retorted and after he'd studied the crack a little longer, he pressed the tip of the blade into it.

He expected it to stop after a few inches but to his surprise, the sword continued through until it was buried to the hilt.

"You know, I read a story once about a sword stuck in stone." The former paladin approached and narrowed her eyes. "It was said that only one with royal blood could draw it out again."

"It's not stuck." Skharr drew the blade halfway out again. "See?"

"All that means is that you have royal blood."

"Fuck off." He shook his head, pushed the blade in again, and after a moment, twisted it carefully. It was not likely to be a key but an odd feeling drove him to make the attempt.

To his surprise, the sound of stone grinding on stone filled the room and the crack began to widen. It moved slowly but after a minute, it had opened enough to allow them to slip through.

"How did you know to do that?" Cassandra asked.

"I had a feeling."

"Or Theros guided you as well. You didn't ask for his help so he had to be a little more subtle about it."

The barbarian rolled his eyes and allowed her to go through first. She could move mostly unhindered by the rock, but he needed to turn sideways to avoid being scratched.

Unfortunately, the horses would have to wait for them outside.

By the time he wiggled through and stood beside her, the former paladin had lit a torch to illuminate the room they had stepped into.

"What is this?" he asked.

"I would have thought you would know a library when you saw one," Cassandra replied shortly. "Then again, perhaps you don't spend much time around books."

The room was absurdly clean, although Skharr was not sure how that was even possible. He paused next to one of the pillars, where a set of bones were piled on the ground and covered by bright regalia that was still in good condition if he ignored the charring on the bottom of the robes.

The former paladin barely glanced at the remains as she moved to the books, pulled a couple from the closest stacks, and opened them.

"There is no sign of dust," he stated. "It's like someone has been cleaning here—religiously too."

She didn't appear to have heard him and put the torch on a nearby sconce and leaned close to the paper.

"It's in elvish," she declared with a small frown.

"Which means we are fucked, yes?"

"No. Anyone studying the higher magics needs to know at least some elvish since that is the language the spells were written in. You need to understand and mean what you're saying. With that said…this is a problem."

"What?"

"We will need an elf to read this. Or at least, a very powerful mage of some sort."

Skharr looked around the room and shrugged. "Not many powerful wizards will talk to a barbarian,"

"Because your people kill them?"

"Your people?"

She rolled her eyes. "Our people, then."

"Our people politely encourage them to leave, not kill them." He scratched his beard. "I did kill the last one I knew a while back when I helped Tryam ascend to the throne, but that was his own godsbedammed fault. He was a murderous, self-serving slug, although he did have a keen brain in all that slime."

"You need to stop killing all the good contacts."

"Perhaps, but he was an irredeemable asshole to whom I owed a blood debt. He was responsible for many soldiers dying by taking coin."

"Oh." Cassandra turned her attention to the books. "Well, he earned it then. You would not happen to know any elves, do you?"

He nodded. "The one who gave me my dagger."

She looked at him. "The one you used to stab yourself to save me."

"Indeed."

"Very romantic."

"It still hurt like a son of a bitch."

She laughed and her voice echoed through the room. "All right, I might have a way to help us but I need to get this out of here safely. There is no telling what mayhem it could cause."

She indicated the entire room, and Skharr folded his arms.

"We could burn it."

"Unfortunately, that is a choice."

"The world has spun along fine without this knowledge. I assume it will continue to do so if we were to burn it all."

"There could be some good to be found in the pages, however."

"The sad truth is that there will always be good in the hearts of those who start down any road. The paths to various hells are paved with the best of intentions since gone astray. Each story is the same in the end."

"It bites them in the ass," the former paladin agreed. "But I can't bring myself to do it. There…there is too much value in these pages."

"Do you have any other options? Are you able to open a portal to the temple for us to drop all the books through?"

She scowled at him. "You're mocking me."

"Not unless you can open a portal. Can you?"

"No. Unfortunately not. But…give me a few hours to look through it. It might pay to know exactly what we are burning."

He wouldn't understand. Of course he wouldn't. It wasn't that he was as ignorant as he pretended to be, but he would always revert to the barbarian who preferred there to be no magic for fear of it being used for ill-purposes.

She understood that and ignored the fact that he watched her as she went through the variety of books that had been left on the tables, skimmed through them, and moved on to the next one.

It would take a while and Skharr doubted that his remaining with her would do much good.

"I'll check on the horses," he called. "Perhaps set up camp for when you're finished here."

"Yes, yes," she answered, although he doubted that she'd heard him.

It was for the best to simply leave her to her exploration. She wouldn't understand the aversion barbarians had to magic in general, which explained why she didn't realize how funny it was that she posed as a barbarian princess.

One day, perhaps.

The warrior shuffled through the narrow crack again and resisted the fear that it might close while he was inside. Still, he heaved a small sigh of relief when he emerged where the horses waited patiently for them.

"Settle in, you two," he told them. "We might be here for a while yet."

The healing potion had done its magic and he only felt slightly sickened by motion. It would pass once he'd had some sleep but for now, the best way he could help was to prepare food for when Cassandra eventually decided she'd spent enough time with the books.

"I don't suppose you know anything about cooking?" he asked Strider. "Or perhaps you like apples like Horse does?"

No answer was forthcoming and the barbarian settled himself on a nearby rock. There was no wood to make a campfire but there were ways to prepare food without fire.

"I'll get you to like me eventually," he vowed and the gelding pretended to ignore him.

Horse merely nickered softly in amusement.

CHAPTER THIRTEEN

Talking to the dead man wasn't quite as effective as she'd thought it would be. Cassandra scowled as she dropped into her seat and stared at the remains. Without proper equipment, she would not be able to determine how long it had been there although if she had to guess, she would estimate between forty and fifty years.

The bones had been picked clean, which left her with nothing except the clothes to tell her that he or she had been someone important. They had most likely cared for all these books and performed the spell that maintained them in such perfect condition.

A spell she would break so she could destroy everything inside, simply to make sure the wrong hands did not acquire them. She could see how that would end poorly for many people.

But a part of her refused to see all this knowledge turned into ash when it could be used to help instead. Too many would benefit from it for the decision to be a simple one.

"I guess you have nothing to say one way or the other," the former paladin said to the corpse and shook her head. "You would rather see all this gone since it was likely the reason why you died."

There was no answer and while she didn't expect one, there was always the possibility when magic was involved. She'd heard numerous stories of mages who managed to isolate sectioned portions of their minds and place them into containers that would allow them to speak to those in the future. Of course, they couldn't hold long conversations and were restricted to only the topic that consciousness was focused on.

Still, it did not appear to be the case here. Nothing was left of whoever had gathered the books.

"I know I don't have much right to call," she whispered and closed her eyes. "But if you had any advice on what to do in this situation, I would appreciate it."

Theros probably had better things to do than to arrive to help her deal with some books.

"I wouldn't say that I have better things to do," a deep voice said behind her. "You would be surprised how little I have to do. In truth, very little of what I do is necessary, which does give me time to do whatever I want."

Cassandra turned, her hand already on her sword before she noticed an old man leaning on a walking stick. She immediately assumed some kind of magical attack would follow but if so, something was very odd about it.

The sight of an old, cranky donkey beside him was enough to make her wonder if she had misconstrued what was happening.

"Theros?" she asked, took a step forward, and kept her hand on her sword in case she was wrong and she did indeed face an imminent fight.

"Yes. I am glad that I do not need to explain my appearance. I assume Skharr informed you of my preferred travel attire?"

She nodded. "He might have mentioned that you prefer to travel as an old man with a donkey at his side. Although the reason why does not occur to me."

"There are many reasons but mostly because folk either underestimate an old man or attempt to help him. Either one benefits me."

She looked around and her eyes narrowed when she realized she was no longer in the library but out in a forest with a lit fire and the chirping of birds and various other animal noises around them. It seemed as though she was in some kind of dream and Theros spoke to her through it—an odd feeling but not unpleasant.

What was interesting was that she wore her purple robes instead of her barbarian attire, which was something to consider given what they were doing. She brushed her hands over the cloth and tried to imagine what Theros was trying to say about what she wore.

Not that she would change. She was not under his employ, as it were, and he therefore no longer had any say in her actions. Even so, she couldn't help a slight tremor of awe that came with facing an actual god, no matter what form he chose to take.

He did not appear to show any sign that he was displeased and merely sat on one of the logs next to the fire where a pot bubbled with a fragrant liquid.

He motioned for her to sit as well. "Might I interest you in some koffe?"

The former paladin complied and studied the pot curiously as he poured the thick black liquid into two ceramic mugs. He handed one to her.

"This is a dream, is it not?"

"Yes. But the koffe will still have its intended effects. It's one of the perks of being a god."

She shrugged and raised her mug. "To Abirat."

Theros raised his as well and they tapped the mugs together gently. "Poor bastard."

"You know of him?"

"I was...chastised by Skharr, for lack of a better word, because

I did not know his story," the god admitted and looked a little chagrined. "I took the time to learn more about those you have traveled with. And so...to Abirat."

"The barbarian does have that effect on people. I did not think it would apply to you, however."

He shrugged and for a moment, they enjoyed the warm brew without too much said between them. Cassandra wondered if he had called her because he had something to say for himself or if he wanted her to say something. If it was the latter, she had no clue what he wanted from her.

"I'm sorry."

She startled, fought back the need to cough up her last sip of koffe, and cleared her throat instead before she drew a deep breath. There was no point in questioning him since she assumed that if he apologized, he was bound to explain what for.

He watched her for a few seconds like he was trying to gauge her reaction before he took another sip of his beverage. "You are my best and I failed you."

That was not the kind of admission she had expected, least of all from a god.

"I...well. I don't know what to say."

"You need not say anything if you don't want to. I needed to apologize and offer you koffe as a token of my appreciation for you."

The forest faded and Cassandra looked around the library in surprise. Even more startling was that while the fire was gone, the mug was still in her hand with the steaming koffe inside.

"Is this what you needed my help with?" Theros asked and approached the stacks of books on the table. He hummed softly. "Oh, now that is interesting."

She raised an eyebrow and took another sip. It was still warm.

"Simply incredible," the old man whispered and ran his fingers through his beard.

"The issue is that Skharr does not believe this knowledge

needs to be shared. It would be too great a risk if it were to fall into the wrong hands. "

"He does have a point," the god admitted and flipped through the pages of the book he held. "And yet, so do you."

"What do you mean?"

"There are a great many dangers when it comes to knowledge. Skharr's instinctive response that magic will always pose a greater threat than good has a great deal to do with how barbarians are taught. And they have reasons for teaching their young that since they remember better than most the danger that the world was in when the Ancients battled each other. But that does ignore the good that magic has done the world and how it has improved his life."

"I assume you have some kind of solution."

Theros nodded and closed the book. "I have a dungeon defended by a dragon. If I send the library there, it would be considered safe and the knowledge would be kept from the hands of those who might misuse it."

"Janus' followers."

He chuckled and shook his head. "Some, but not all. I must admit that a few of my followers should not learn what is contained in these passages, so there will be no preferential treatment in that regard. But I think you should keep at least something for your trouble. What do you say…hmm this one, I think? It caught your eye before."

"I remember it but I could not read it."

"Find yourself someone who can read elvish. She will have the answers you seek from this history book."

"Is it a history book?"

"Well, perhaps more of a diary penned by that layabout there." Theros nodded to the stack of bones in the corner.

"She?"

"Did I say she?"

"You did." Cassandra narrowed her eyes. "Why do you assume a she?"

He smirked and ran his fingers through his pointed beard. "Are you taking Skharr with you?"

"Of course. We are doing this together, after all."

"Then you should always assume that the person he seeks out will be a she. Do you think it was a random encounter that the paladin he needed would be a female?"

"I...never thought of that."

"Perhaps you should." Theros tilted his head and regarded her with a raised eyebrow. "That is interesting armor."

Cassandra looked down and realized that she was in her barbarian garb again. "Well...first of all..."

Her voice trailed off when she looked up and discovered that he was gone and had taken his donkey with him.

"So leave, then," she muttered. "Anything to keep me from explaining that I am the one who chooses my godsbedammed clothes now."

Saying it aloud did make her feel better. If Theros was still around and had only dropped out of her view, he would hear what she had to say. If not, it was his loss.

She was distracted from this mini-rebellion when she noticed that all the books had disappeared from the shelves and tables around her to leave the room remarkably and hauntingly empty. Cassandra hoped she would have the chance to look through what had been taken for herself when she was able to read them.

Then again, Theros had left her with one of the books, and she picked it up from the table and examined the leather binding and the condition of the pages. It was amazing that it was in such good condition after such a long time.

The former paladin shook her head, tucked the book under her arm, and strode to the crack in the wall that remained open for them. It occurred to her that there was no longer much point to hiding in an empty room.

Skharr waited outside. The hulking mass of barbarian was huddled over some food he was preparing while the horses stood patiently, at rest until it was time to move again. Their packs had been removed from their backs and the saddles set aside for the moment.

How he'd managed to accomplish that with Strider was the kind of question that was perhaps best left unanswered. It could be that he had managed to appeal to the beast's need to rest to get the saddle off him, or he had earned a few bite marks when the beast attempted to force him back.

He looked up from the food and gestured for her to sit. "Did you decide what you want to do with the books?"

"Yes. Or…rather, it was decided for me."

The barbarian narrowed his eyes as she sat. "Will smoke come out of that crack in the wall any minute now?"

Cassandra grinned. "No. But I had a short chat to Theros while I was in there and he offered a solution I think was the best chance we had to keep what was in there out of the wrong hands."

"I see." Skharr pushed one of the platters to her. The meal was cold but smoked sausage, bread, and dried fruit with water would have to do for a meal in an area where they were far from any kind of support. And, of course, they did not want to attract any attention to themselves given the horde of monsters that might lurk in the area now that they had moved beyond the snake's lair.

"He took the books to his dungeon, which he assured me was guarded by a dragon and therefore would be well-protected against those who had a mind to take them. He did leave me one of them, however, and stated that you might know an elf who would be able to translate it."

The barbarian nodded, took a bite of his bread, and scowled. "I suppose he isn't wrong about that."

"I know you might not think that giving those to a god would be the safest choice, but…well, I made the decision anyway."

His expression didn't change. "There isn't much we can do but trust him at this point. Although I am not sure how we might find someone who speaks elvish to translate what it says, which is the point of the search, is it not?"

She set her food aside and leaned forward. "Theros mentioned that you knew of someone who might be able to help."

The look of confusion on his face appeared to be genuine. "Perhaps he means the half-elf who gave us the contract? I would assume his experience with that side of his family would have been minimal, but you never know."

It was a logical thought process for him, but Cassandra fixed her gaze on him. "He might have implied that the elf you know is a woman."

That drew his eyebrows over his eyes in a deep frown until he leaned back on a handful of fallen pillars and nodded. "Ah, I think I know who he was speaking of, although the elf who gave me my dagger was a child by their standards and I would not say I know her. She's probably older than you and I combined in years, though. Still, it's an odd thing for a god to say, don't you think?"

"Not particularly."

Skharr narrowed his eyes. "He did not happen to notice you wearing your barbarian princess garb, did he?"

"He might have."

"And you don't believe he might have been teasing you about it?" he suggested.

She raised an eyebrow. While it was possible that he was right, she wouldn't admit it outright.

The barbarian seemed content with that lack of an answer and ran his fingers through his beard like he was deep in thought about something.

"Are you sure he saw your armor?"

"Yes," Cassandra answered smoothly and a small smile touched her lips. "Yes, he did."

"Well...fuck." He sighed and shook his head.

"All right, then."

It was his turn to raise his eyebrows. "Pardon?"

"You asked me to fuck you and the answer is yes. I want you and I want you right now." She stood, walked to where he was seated, and studied him closely. "I've been in the presence of a god I have followed for years. He saw me as this..." She paused to gesture to herself. "He knows me, he appreciates me, and he even apologized for not doing so in the past."

"He did?"

"Aye. And as I am on sabbatical until I decide not to be, I intend to..." She stepped closer and waited for him to put his food aside before she grasped his shoulder and pushed him forcefully onto his back. Thankfully, his seat had enough space to allow him to lie on it without his head coming close to the edge on the other side, and he grunted as he was pushed down.

She assumed he could have remained seated if he wanted to. The fact that he did not was sufficient invitation and she wasted no time before she acted on it. She reached back to undo the catch on her back that held the top half of her undergarment armor in place and let it fall to the side before she climbed smoothly atop the man and settled on his hips.

It was easy to forget the sheer size of him until she was close. At that point, it was impossible to ignore that he was easily twice her size. She wanted to climb every last inch of him.

"I'll use my attitude to take what I'm offered," she continued, ground her hips gently over him, and smiled when she could already feel a reaction. "I assume that what I feel rising to attention is available for my use?"

Skharr growled softly and she smiled when he raised one hand immediately to her hips and the other even higher. He brushed his calloused digits lightly over her exposed nipples and triggered a shiver down her spine that made her press a little harder against his growing cock.

"You're…you're not merely sitting," he pointed. "You…happen to be moving back and forth."

"It's getting bigger," Cassandra responded and ran her hands up the hard planes of his chest. "I'll take that as an encouraging sign. Answer me. Are you available or should I go and find a dark corner in which to attend to my desires?"

His icy gaze locked onto hers while his fingers squeezed and tugged lightly at her nipple, enough to drag a soft gasp of need from her.

"A barbarian princess takes what she wants of me," he rumbled and a small smile touched his lips.

The former paladin leaned forward to place a light, tender kiss on his lips before she shifted to whisper in his ear. "You're godsbedammed right I will."

CHAPTER FOURTEEN

The night passed in something of a blur, although certainly the pleasant kind. Skharr's skin felt a little raw where her nails had raked across his bare chest, shoulders, back, and what felt like at least a dozen other places.

When night had fallen, there was nothing else to do but remain where they were until the sun rose again. He had therefore waited with Cassandra still in his arms, wrapped in the warm blankets they had brought for the journey.

In the early dawn, he was the first one awake and he could still feel her breathing softly into his chest.

Light provided better visibility in the area and he could see the entrance to the ruins, where they'd left the body of the serpent that had been killed. He was not surprised that the body was gone, but he had expected to at least hear the scavengers doing away with it.

Perhaps it had happened while his mind had been otherwise occupied.

The barbarian looked at the woman in his arms, brushed some of her hair from her cheek lightly and tenderly, and tucked it behind her ear. He hadn't meant to disturb her but she reacted to the touch with a soft growl and grasped him a little tighter than he'd expected.

"You can't have him," she murmured softly. "Elf slut."

He smirked and stroked her cheek again. "What was that?"

"Hmm?" Cassandra grunted and half-opened her eyes to look around, still a little disoriented and unwilling to move away from him. She shrugged and rested her head again like he was her pillow. "What?"

"You said something in your sleep," Skharr said and spoke softly as he stroked her hair. "Something about an elf slut?"

"Oh." She looked up and perched her chin on his chest, her eyes still bleary. "It was a bad dream, is all."

"An odd dream, that," he answered with a small smile as he eased her carefully off him and made sure she was wrapped in the blankets before he stood with a soft groan.

She smiled as she studied him and seemed to admire her handiwork in the form of the angry red scratch marks he was sure were spread entirely across his back. He put no effort into hiding any part of himself from her as he approached their packs and made sure nothing was missing and there was no sign of insects attacking their food stores. That would have annoyed him beyond measure, but it seemed even insects avoided the ruins. They had been everywhere on the road to the Seastones but all signs of them had vanished once they approached.

Intelligent insects, he mused. He would never have thought to see that kind of thing in the world.

"That was the nicest and warmest bed I've enjoyed on a task for Theros in a long while," Cassandra said once he returned to the fallen pillar they'd slept on with food and water to start the day with.

"I imagine there is not much in the way of competition there," Skharr answered and handed her the water skin first as he took a bite of a piece of way bread.

She first leaned closer to inspect the place where he had been injured and grunted softly with satisfaction before she settled again. "True. But I believe you will put all future beds to shame from this point forward."

The barbarian grinned and leaned closer to kiss her lips gently. "You flatter me."

"Perhaps a little. But it is still the truth."

She scooted to the edge, stood, and walked to where their clothes had been discarded. He saw her wince and shift her step a little before she collected his shirt and trousers and tossed them to him.

"It is a shame that we will probably die by dragon fire before the end of this," he commented and took a sip of water before he pulled his shirt on.

"It might not be a probability," Cassandra answered. "I might have already died by dragon fire by this point."

Skharr chuckled deeply. "I'll claim a great deal of credit for my fucking abilities but I doubt I will ever be able to fuck a woman to death. Nor do I wish to make the attempt."

"Either way, I think I know where we might find a few elves who might be able to translate the journal for us." She tapped on the leather-bound book as she pulled her clothes on.

"How?" Skharr asked.

"They arrived as the first high-elf ambassadors to the empire in decades," she reminded him. "They passed through Verenvan not that long ago, and folk have spread word of where they are. It's the kind of gossip that a paladin would be informed of if they happened to require some help. The last I heard, they were situated in Calaser, a small town not far from here. Or she will be there in a week, which gives us time to arrive before her retinue does."

"She?" he asked.

The former paladin rolled her eyes. "You are hilarious. Give it a rest."

"What do you mean?" He assumed there was some vital

context involved in her answer, although he seemed to have missed most of it. Perhaps it was something Theros said to her and it could have had something to do with what she discussed with him inside the library.

"Nothing. Never mind. We need to get moving."

Skharr nodded and pulled his trousers on as well, although he caught her sneaking one last look before he was clothed again.

Perhaps that conversation had something to do with why she had mounted him so aggressively the night before. If that were the case, he owed the god thanks of his own, although it would almost certainly never be properly expressed.

There were towns in the world that people did not even bother to name, and Skharr could tell what they looked like from the moment he laid eyes on them. There would never be any defenses established on the outside. The quality of the buildings would not be an indicator one way or the other, but the way to tell was to see how new they were. If they looked like they had not seen more than three winters, the chances were that it had all been established to take advantage of the trade that traveled through the area.

It was almost inevitable that the settlement would be raided and burned by bandits of some kind before it was five years old. If not, it would be around long enough that folk would feel attached to it. A name would be given and, if they were sensible, defenses would be erected.

Thus far, the trading outpost did not appear to have any real emotional connection to those who lived in the region, but there was enough traffic through the area to show that the situation might very well change sometime soon.

The fact that he could see more than a few imperial patrols throughout the area was a good indication that a bandit raid would not be enough to tear them from their location. A dragon might be enough to do so, of course, if the godsbedammed winged spawn of Janus' sweaty scrotum decided it was no longer happy to only occupy the Seastones.

"This is your first time in a real stable in almost a week," Skharr said cheerfully as he brushed Horse down. "You'll grow into a horse who prefers to spend his time in the open before too long, mark my words."

The stallion's answer was laden with derision, and he shrugged.

"You never know what you might want in your old age, so mock my words at your own risk. You'll find a nice little apple tree that blooms and provides fruit all day for you to grow old under. Perhaps Sera will have somewhere like that for you when we return to Verenvan."

The beast turned to look at him as he finished brushing the day's grime from his coat.

"No, I don't know if there is a real tree like that. I assume there is some kind of spell that allows a tree to flower, bloom, and produce fruit all year round but I've never seen it. But it is good to know that you would be interested in such a thing should it exist."

He patted Horse on the neck and stowed the brush he'd borrowed from a stable hand in a place where the boy could collect it, then stepped out. Cassandra had said that she would find them rooms and food in the inn, as well as ask about whether there was a merchant in the town where they could replenish their supplies before they continued their journey.

As he approached the entrance to the inn, the uproar from inside gave him the impression that she might have been side-tracked.

He was still a few paces from the door when it was thrust open and a scrawny fellow was tossed out. He looked like he'd taken a chair to the face and protected his mouth carefully with his hands as he landed on the cobbles.

"Fucking bith," he lisped through broken teeth, pushed to his feet, and staggered to the main road.

"Oh yes, most certainly sidetracked," Skharr muttered and approached the door carefully lest another individual be flung at him.

He stepped safely and warily into the inn, where the odor of stale ale greeted him immediately. It was a familiar enough smell that it was almost comforting. Perhaps it would be after a few more years traveling like this.

Still, he was immediately distracted by the source of the uproar. The common room of the inn was fairly well-occupied, although most of the space in the center had been cleared and he could hear the familiar sound of fists beating flesh.

"Say it again!" Cassandra yelled clearly over the din. "Tell a princess what she should fucking wear, you piece of pig shit!"

The barbarian was almost afraid to see what was happening, but he had to know. She was still in the scanty armor she generally wore, and he should have guessed that it would attract attention. Still, he hadn't expected that a fight would ensue.

A part of him, he realized, had even hoped there would be none, although it was a very small part. He was always happy for a good brawl but it looked like the former paladin was more than able to take care of herself. This sadly meant that the fight was already finished by the time he arrived.

Three men already lay senseless, bleeding, and battered on the floor while two were still on their feet. One appeared to have taken a few blows to the face already while the other looked relatively fresh.

He could tell what the story was from what little could be seen. The men involved considered her scant attire to be some kind of invitation and never imagined that the woman they approached was a former paladin. They were being taught a lesson in making assumptions based on clothing.

And a few others, judging by what Cassandra yelled at them.

As assured as he was that she required no help with the two idiots, Skharr shuffled to where it appeared most of the drinks were being poured and raised his hand to the barmaid to provide him with a mug of something cool to go with the entertainment.

"Come on," one of the other patrons challenged and laughed. "Of course you want a piece of that. Provided you don't find your face rearranged it is worth the risk, aye?"

It took him longer than he cared to admit to realize that he was being spoken to and he turned. One of the other men drinking near the bar nudged him but with his attention fixed on the combatants, he had not looked to see who he was talking to.

When the group around him noticed, their laughter fell silent and they took a step back so they could look at him without craning their necks.

"My apologies, barbarian," one of the men mumbled before he beat a hasty retreat. Skharr assumed it was because they had seen what one barbarian was capable of and did not intend to anger two.

"Say it to her," he grunted as the barmaid brought his drink.

They understood that the apologies should go to the one who had been offended, and he could see them immediately rethink what they would spend the evening doing.

"You…you two know each other, then?"

He shrugged. "Travel together."

His attention was drawn to the fight when one of the men stepped in and was felled immediately by a fist to his face. Cassandra spun as the other attempted to catch her from behind. She stamped her boot on the man's instep before she grasped his neck and groin, lifted him off his feet, and flipped him to pound him onto the floor.

"I'm surprised you had the balls to think you could slip

anything between my thighs," she snapped at the man. "Because from what I felt, you certainly don't have the cock for it. Anything less than a dragon and you'll simply disappoint me. Unless you're looking for a little snip?"

The men looked at Skharr again and he realized the barmaid now stared at him as well, although her eyes peered well below where the others were focused.

"Perhaps more," he muttered and sipped his drink. There was little to add to that, at least not without the kind of bragging he had never quite been partial to. Some women liked size but not all, and it seemed like it was more a matter of ego than anything else.

The former paladin appeared to be finished with the fight and she looked at him and waved with a brilliant smile, a gesture that suggested far more barbarian to her than even he knew.

"I found us an empty table," she stated with a wink and nudged one of the groaning men out of the way as Skharr approached.

A handful of the patrons stood to give her a standing ovation over the fight, and she grinned and bowed like she was an actress who had performed at a local amphitheater.

"A little food and drink, I think," Cassandra said as he sat across from her and the other patrons turned to their own business. "You know, I think I like a good brawl for the evening. It does wonders to release the tension stored in the muscles. It's as good as a hard fucking. Almost."

He nodded. "Now you understand why I enjoy a good fight whenever I can find one."

"I would have thought your preference would lean toward fucking."

"Oddly enough, folk feel less strongly about a barbarian battering their face than they do about him fucking one of their women. It generally means I have a fuck and a fight for the evening."

She nodded. "I assume they have a less strong reaction if a woman does the fucking."

"I did not think a woman would be as interested in fucking strange men. Or women, for that matter."

"True enough. It would be different if there were as much of a guarantee that the sex will be fun every time for the woman as there is for the man."

The barbarian shrugged in agreement. "I can understand that."

"I know you do, which is why I am generally interested in fucking you. I assume most women who see you have a similar interest."

"Less than you might assume," Skharr admitted. "The novelty plays a role in it, I suppose."

"And would explain why they want to fight you as well. I would have thought that folk wouldn't like you fighting around them."

"They are usually annoyed at the necessity to clean up the results," he told her. "But it would be considered entertainment for their guests so they do not complain too profusely about it. I'm always sure to pay them a little more to compensate for the extra work."

As if on cue, one of the barmaids approached them with a tentative smile.

"Drink and food for both of us," Cassandra requested, took a few extra silvers from her pouch, and handed them to the young woman. "For the trouble."

"No trouble at all, miss. I was glad to watch you beat the bastards."

Skharr raised an eyebrow as she left and he focused on his companion. "I can then safely assume that you did not crush skulls because they were making lewd comments."

"People have made lewd comments at me since I was a teenager," she retorted, "and even when I was a paladin. If I crushed the skull of every man who did so, there would not be many skulls left in the world. It's when the words turn to touch that I start the fight. Do you generally wait or are you the one to throw the first punch?"

"It is better to wait to have witnesses to stupidity before acting," he suggested. "Folk see a barbarian and immediately consider them to be the initiator of the violence and you soon find you are unwelcome in certain towns for it. It's best for folk to see that you did not start the brawl before it starts."

Cassandra nodded. "I suppose we can assume from what the girl said—"

"That the slime-brained gutter-crawling bastards had a tendency to touch when it was not welcome. You were merely the first to fight back."

"Do you think they'll have learned their lesson?"

"Honestly? I doubt it."

She spat on the head of the one closest to their table when the barmaid returned with two platters of food and drinks.

"I suppose we should not become accustomed to fights that are this easy," the former paladin said as she took a bite of the smoked pork belly provided. "I still have no idea what that mage's journal will reveal about killing a dragon."

"If there is anything I learned, it is to take any advantage into battle that you can," Skharr answered. "Especially against dragons. Perhaps killing it will not be necessary and the writings will advise us into how to release it from the Seastones."

Cassandra regarded him with a questioning look. "You don't want to kill it, do you?"

He shook his head. "You might say I can relate to it. What most folk view as a vicious beast is merely a predator that is feared for its size and ability to inflict pain. There is no thought about why the pain is being inflicted or what could be done to avoid it."

"Are barbarians generally this...pacific?"

"Not toward humans, who are known to be violent, unpredictable beasts. Those humans one might consider beasts, on the other hand, might be seen in a better light."

The former paladin smiled and shook her head. Before she could respond, however, they were interrupted by a tall, lean woman who approached the table and sat without being invited to join them.

She was human enough with a few streaks of white threaded through the long black hair she restrained in a severe braid. Skharr noticed the arming sword she carried at her hip and knew immediately it wasn't worn for decoration. It had the look of a weapon that had been drawn often and he was sure the stranger carried a goodly number of scars to prove it.

He raised his hand to stop Cassandra from snapping at the woman before she'd said her piece, and the interloper scrutinized them both before she spoke.

"I was told there were two barbarians in town," she stated finally, her voice gravelly and kept low so none of the other patrons could hear. "Assuming the two of you are not here to cause trouble, I wondered if you were interested in some work in the area."

"Trouble?" the warrior asked.

Their visitor raised an eyebrow at the men that were being dragged out.

"They started it," Cassandra stated and partially emulated Skharr's grunted speech pattern.

"I'm sure. I am the guildmaster in this hole of a town. The only one here, which means I need to identify those willing to take contracts where I can find them. Are you interested or are you not?"

"It depends," Skharr answered. "What is the work?"

"We have a group of deserters who have taken up residence nearby."

"Plenty imperial patrols around," Cassandra said bluntly. "Might be interested."

"The same thought occurred to a handful of skin traders up north. A few weeks later, we discovered that the deserters pay the patrols to turn a blind eye to their business when we found the skin traders' camp burned to ash and the bodies hung on the trees while the men were still alive."

"A mercenary company would be better suited to that kind of work," he pointed out.

The woman appeared a little surprised that he'd dropped his dumb speech but she moved past it quickly. "The fact of the matter is that we can't afford it. The larger caravans are offered the option to pay the bandit scum a fee for safe passages. The smaller caravans are looted if they cannot afford it. They are paying for the contract."

He turned to Cassandra and waited for any sign of what she wanted to do. He could understand if her mind remained fully focused on what they were currently doing, but he felt inclined to pause their journey so they could deal with a group of renegade deserters.

And, if they had any luck, they wouldn't have to explain to Tryam why they had massacred one of his patrols as well.

Cassandra nodded and he turned to the woman.

"Do you have the contract on you?"

The guildmaster nodded, took it from her pouch, and transferred it officially to them before she took her leave.

"Fucking cow," Cassandra muttered. "Did you see how surprised she was when she realized you were capable of forming full sentences? We should have turned the work down on principle."

"If that were the case, we would turn down work from almost everyone, given that most folk are bound by their narrow minds and biases. Of course, there is sometimes no point in trying to change their minds. In that case, it's best to use their mindsets for our benefit."

"I suppose most humans have that kind of attitude."

"Most sentient creatures, to be honest. Even some of the brighter trolls located out west. The kind of thinking that anything that doesn't look like you must be terrible seems to infect even the most intelligent minds."

"Then what is your bias?" she asked and leaned forward. "Assuming your mind is the thinking kind, of course. You seem to accept what life has to offer as it comes to you, not what you expect to come to you."

"That is because I've lived long enough to have had my bias fed to me like a man shoving it down my throat with the heel of his boot. It's worse when you're young. I suppose I have some reflexive dislike of most magical items, but I think I've done well to contain that. As we interact with more of society, you find that not everything matches your expectations like—"

He froze when he felt a small hand creep toward his purse. Almost before he could consider who would be stupid enough to try to steal from him, Skharr had already caught hold of the hand, grasped it tightly, and yanked the owner forward.

The small stature gave the first impression of a child, but he realized that the figure was a little stouter and a little too heavy to be a human youngster.

It was not the kind of build he encountered often. Most halflings tended to avoid the larger folk of the world and hid in forest and thickets as far away from most other species, although they did have trade relations. He assumed that was where this particular one came from.

The three-and-a-half-foot tall female with bright brown curly hair, sun-touched skin, and dark eyes tried to pull away from his hold with little success.

She struggled fruitlessly for a moment until she realized there was not much chance that she would be able to pull away given her limited strength.

When she reached for the dagger at her hip, he yanked her closer to the table.

"Try that and I'll swing you around and use you as a club until your godsbedammed teeth shake loose and relocate to bite you on your fucking ass." He growled to emphasize the warning.

She ceased her resistance, slid her dagger carefully into its sheath, and turned her attention to the two travelers.

"What can I say, barbarian?" Cassandra laughed softly and shook her head.

"Well then, will you kill me or what?" the halfling asked and tried again to yank her arm free. "You're too large for me to manage in other ways."

"Why do women always think I want to bed them?" Skharr wondered and shook his head.

"Biases," Cassandra replied, took a bite of the roasted pork belly, and added a little of the rice that had been brought with the meat. "But what will we do with her?"

The barbarian was aware that the rest of the inn watched them covertly and although this had probably begun before when he encountered the halfling, there would certainly be talk about it. A massive barbarian who crushed a half-pint was not the kind of victory he wanted to be known for.

Instead, he stretched his hand to the dagger, removed it, and placed the weapon on the table. He found a few more knives, some with no handle and a star shape that he assumed were generally thrown. A small flute with poisoned darts hung on her belt as well. Not quite satisfied, he pulled at the top of her shirt.

"Oy!"

The protests were ignored and he tugged two charms on necklaces from the halfling's neck. Once he was sure there were no more weapons on her, he removed the other pouches from her belt and spread it all out on the table.

She looked annoyed, especially since the top of her shirt was ripped to expose a few of the curves she would probably have liked to keep hidden.

With that in mind, Skharr wondered if there were perhaps a

few more weapons hidden in those curves, but without any real cause to search, it was best to leave things as they were.

"You can give me those charms," the halfling demanded, her gaze fixed on a small locket as she stretched her hand toward the item. "It won't cause you no harm."

Cassandra took it immediately and her eyes narrowed. "That will have to wait until you apologize."

He released his captive and felt a twinge of regret when she rubbed the place he'd grasped. His hold had been a little too tight, he realized.

"I'm sorry about that," the barbarian said and shook his head as she slid onto the seat the guildmaster had vacated not long before. "What is your name?"

"Give me my locket."

"Your name first," Cassandra answered firmly. "Or I'll have to see if I can find a more creative location to move those teeth to."

"Barbarian whore," the woman hissed.

"He's the whore," the former paladin snapped.

The answer appeared to confuse their guest, who turned to look at Skharr with an odd expression.

"Not literally." Cassandra cleared her throat. "Besides, his cock is about the size of your arm so you wouldn't want to try."

"It doesn't hurt to think about it." The small being smiled and seemed to think she had found something that unsettled her taller opponent, but she inched away when she saw the barbarian princess' expression change from annoyed to halfway murderous. "Leahlu. My name is Leahlu. And yours?"

"Cassandra," the woman answered after a moment of thought during which she realized that she might have acted a little too aggressively. "And this is Skharr DeathEater."

Leahlu narrowed her eyes and turned to Skharr with a hint of fear in her eyes. "Oh. Shit."

He raised an eyebrow at the reaction and took a bite of his food. "Is there a problem?"

"I would not have snatched your pouch had I known who you were."

"You didn't," he reminded her. "You tried."

"Semantics. Give me time and I would have had your purse and weapons too."

"You can be assured of a wrung neck if you attempt to steal his pouch again," Cassandra warned.

"There is no need for all this hostility," the halfling assured her and raised her hands before she crossed them to hide her cleavage a little better. "Fucking barbarians."

"Fucking barbarian princess," the former paladin corrected her. "I am a little different."

"I'm not sure how. A female human who parades her body like it's for sale and threatens to hurt me does not set you apart from most of the other human females I've dealt with."

"Promises," Cassandra retorted sharply. "Only a—"

She looked at Skharr and he realized she was searching for a metaphor.

"SandStrider."

"Only a SandStrider threatens. I promise." She relaxed a little in her seat and sipped her beer. "And your appreciation of my body is noted. I rather like it myself, especially since the heat makes proper armor impossible to wear."

"You have armor?"

"Of course. I'm not stupid."

"You might not be stupid but no woman in her right mind would wear something like that."

The barbarian raised an eyebrow, and he heard a handful of the other patrons begin to place bets on which of the two women would remain standing.

To his surprise and their disappointment, Cassandra laughed and shook her head.

"I never said I was right in the mind. Only that I wasn't stupid."

"I suppose that's fair enough."

"So," Skharr interrupted, "do we kill her, princess?"

Leahlu turned to him, her eyes wide. "Kill?"

"You tried to steal from me. Most towns would see you separated from your hand for that type of crime. Since none have come to help you while we waited, I can only assume you have no one to support your criminal endeavors, so what we do with you will not matter. If I leave you alive, you might do something stupid like try to take back the possessions you owe me as a penalty for your actions."

The halfling gulped and looked at Cassandra. "You'd let him kill me?"

The barbarian could see that his partner had as little intention to hurt Leahlu as he did, but an idea had begun to brew in his mind. A halfling's help was never something to scoff at. Their size led too many to underestimate them—which was how they liked it—but they were some of the finest trackers and hunters in the world.

From the gleam in her eye, he could tell that the former paladin had come to the same conclusion.

"Of course." The barbarian princess shrugged carelessly. "We are barbarians, after all."

"Are you?" Leahlu studied both of them. "Him, I understand, but you... No, something is missing in both of you. I've heard enough tales about enough creatures to know when to doubt their veracity."

She had a point there, and Cassandra faltered as if recalling their conversation about inherent biases that needed to be struck down.

"A deal, then," he interjected. "Your possessions will be returned to you once you agree to a geas to help us on our next two contracts. If we are impressed with your work, you might even share in the profit we make when the contracts are fulfilled."

He could see the suspicion slide into her eyes that this was what they had wanted the whole time. It wasn't, of course, but he would allow her to continue to think that and not inform her that the idea had come to him on the spur of the moment.

"My locket?"

"The geas first."

"What are the contracts?"

"Does it matter if the alternative is death or the loss of a hand?"

She sniffed and shook her head, knowing there was not much of a choice involved. "Barbarians."

"DeathEater," he corrected her.

CHAPTER FIFTEEN

They located the Guild Hall and it was what Skharr expected it to be in a smaller settlement. The modest building in the middle of the town had been put together quickly and efficiently by those who wanted something simple to last against the elements, at least for a few years, before it needed repairs.

A large fireplace occupied the center of the room with a few desks spread around it. Some simple hay beds were arranged in the rafters. He assumed there were a handful of mercenaries who could not afford to spend a night at an inn and instead, stayed at the Guild Hall while they worked in the area.

The guildmaster saw them almost immediately and narrowed her eyes as they approached her.

"Is there a problem with the contract?" she asked.

"No," Cassandra answered. "We have an addition to our party who we need a geas scroll made out for."

The woman peered at the halfling they had brought with them and Leahlu folded her arms to hide the places where Skharr had torn her shirt. He hadn't ripped her clothing to the point where anything essential was revealed but the end result was still a little more revealing than she might have preferred.

"Do you have issues with her?"

"Aye," he answered. "But she owes us and we'll see to it that the debt is paid once she's helped us with two of our contracts."

The guildmaster had questions, but he could tell that she wasn't curious enough to dig any deeper. She shrugged, rummaged through the scrolls spread across her desk, and pulled a silver geas scroll out.

"Are all parties in agreement with the geas terms, where the signee will be released from their commitment only upon the fulfillment of the agreed-upon conditions?"

All three nodded.

"All right, I'll need your thumbprints on the paper before it can be sealed."

Skharr was the first to prick his thumb and press it into the silver skin on the outside of the paper. The blood disappeared almost instantly, and it was the halfling's turn next.

"Fucking barbarians," she retorted before she mirrored what he had done.

Cassandra then took her turn, although when she pressed her finger to the paper, a soft puff of green smoke rose before her print vanished from the silver paper.

"What in the hell?" Leahlu whispered.

The guildmaster chuckled. "The color of Theros flared on the signing. I suppose it means the work you've signed up for will be incredibly interesting, halfling."

"What does that mean?" She looked up at her new and unwelcome teammates and narrowed her eyes.

"That might have to do with the second contract," the former paladin admitted as she began to return the halfling's possessions to her.

"What...what is the second contract?" Leahlu looked like she wasn't sure she wanted to know, but there was no avoiding it now.

Skharr shrugged. "Taking care of a dragon."

She coughed and her eyes bulged. "I'm sorry, did you say a dragon?"

"He did," Cassandra confirmed.

"A...a small one, yes? One that has recently hatched and is giving farmers troubles with their livestock?"

"No." The former paladin shook her head. "No, it was rather a large fucking one."

"What in the everloving fuck possessed him to take work of that nature?" Leahlu shook her head.

"A god," Skharr answered before he pocketed the scroll.

"A god possessed you?"

"No," Cassandra replied quickly.

"Which god possessed you?"

"Theros, obviously." She shook her head. "And there was no possession. You are not thinking very clearly."

"Or you need to explain yourself better."

"Perhaps I should smack your head into the wall to sharpen your mind."

"How would that sharpen my mind? Beating it will only addle me more."

"Skharr?"

He turned to the two bickering women, although he wasn't sure what it was about. There was no chance that he would come out the winner if he interjected himself into the conversation, so all he could summon was a shrug.

"I was all for using her as a club and relocating her teeth before," he said and shook his head. "I have no idea how you expect me to be the voice of reason in this."

"She was too," Leahlu shouted. "You are not very nice barbarians."

"A reputation you should have considered when you attempted to steal my coin pouch."

The halfling rolled her eyes. "When will you let that go? I barely touched your pouch."

"Lucky for you," Cassandra whispered.

"We'll let it go...two contracts from now," Skharr asserted with a smirk.

The former paladin shook her head. She had a jealous streak in her but even she must understand that there was no future in which he and a halfling measured his dragon—for the halfling's health more than anything else.

Then again, perhaps she released the kind of energy that could be contained after a while before they stood in the presence of the elf they sought.

"Enough!" the barbarian snapped when the two continued to argue. "We have a contract to fulfill and as entertaining as this might be, we certainly will not do so while you two bicker like this. Gather your possessions and we'll go. Now."

He shouldn't even have to remind them that they wouldn't solve issues while they did nothing but work their jaws. It seemed Cassandra had a hearty dislike for the halfling, but he had a feeling that would change if they worked on a contract together. At least that would include the knowledge that halflings were useful when dealing with the dangers that came with traveling through wooded areas.

"Do you have a horse?" the former paladin asked as they approached their beasts.

"There aren't many horses out there I would be comfortable riding, except for the odd pony." Leahlu shook her head. "I'll be more comfortable on my own two feet, thank you."

"With our luck, you'll be as slow as Skharr is on his own two feet," she commented in return.

"Are both horses yours, then?" the halfling asked.

"No. The stallion is Skharr's. We call him Horse. The one we call Strider—the gelding—is mine."

Leahlu shook her head and frowned for a few moments before she spoke again. "I have…oh, so many questions. First and foremost, if both of you have horses, why does the DeathEater walk?"

"Believe me, I've asked myself the same question." Cassandra snorted humorlessly as she mounted.

"Horse is my brother," Skharr answered. "I would not ride my brother."

"Your actual brother?"

"Of course not. That would be ridiculous."

"No, it wouldn't. There might be spells that turn a man into a horse."

"Not in this case."

"So…uh, you won't ride a horse who is…not your brother and yet is?"

"Now you reach the heart of the matter."

Cassandra laughed. "I fear you will have to explain your oddities to every person you meet on the road."

"It is not my fault that so-called civilized folk do not understand the simplicity of how to treat their horses."

"No indeed."

"I have another question," Leahlu interrupted as they began to walk to the edge of the town. "Did I hear you correctly? Do you call your horse…Horse?"

"Here we go again." The former paladin rolled her eyes and grinned.

CHAPTER SIXTEEN

"I thought barbarians were better-known for their axes, clubs, and claymore swords. No one ever considered a barbarian and thought immediately about a bow."

Skharr scowled at the halfling. She had been full of questions from the outset and while it had been a pleasant change from the tedium of travel, it was a distraction when he attempted to focus on what they were doing.

"If you had ever traveled to the mountains his kin call home, you would know that DeathEaters are deadly archers, able to climb high in the rocks and rain death on those who travel the passes below."

One of the bright sides was that the halfling—a young adult by their standards at the age of thirty—had begun to grow on Cassandra. Or, at least, her incessant questioning had triggered something of a teaching instinct in the barbarian princess, and she now answered most of the questions while he was left with the work to locate the deserters' camp.

When they finally reached it, they stopped for a moment and stared at what was not so much a camp as a small fortress. The barbarian settled onto his haunches and studied the gate ahead of them to determine what their best course of action would be.

"They are good soldiers, these," he decided.

"Not if they deserted, they aren't." The former paladin scowled at him, then returned her focus to the structure they needed to gain entry to.

"They might have had trouble with discipline but they know how to build a fortress. We would need a fucking army to breach those godsbedammed gates."

The wall was made of wood, which was in abundance in the area, and that was merely the start of their problem. A platform had been constructed on the other side of the wall and patrols moved regularly across it. The trees had been cleared to almost forty paces out by his reckoning. The worst part—and one few folk building walls ever considered—was the moat that encircled it. There was no water to fill it, but the spikes pounded into the ground would be more than enough to deter any idiot from trying to walk through.

The gate itself was simple—split doors, probably held in place with a crossbeam on the other side. It was something easily done away with if they had a battering ram.

Since it was only the three of them, there would be no such option.

The biggest problem lay with the two flanking towers, both of which were manned by archers. There would be no cover in the open ground on the approach to the gate, and even a proper shield wouldn't withstand arrows from both archers who were most likely sharpshooters.

"They have to get water from somewhere," Skharr said thoughtfully. "A fortress like that doesn't survive long on water from a well."

Leahlu looked at him, her eyes narrowed, and he continued.

"Water from a well is necessary, but there must be some way for the piss, shit, and other waste to get beyond the walls without them having to leave to pour it out. They will have some way to dispose of it and use water from the well or rain to clear it if it won't flow on its own."

"Do you think you would be able to get in?" the halfling asked.

"I might if they have grates. From there, we would be able to climb inside and avoid the walls entirely."

"What if it's too small for you?"

It was a good question and he shook his head. "We will find another way. At worst, our princess here can raise some shields and I'll climb over the wall with a rope and a hook."

"Or I could find my way in, get rid of the archers in the towers, and open the gate for the two of you."

It was his turn to turn and look at her with narrowed eyes. "Are you sure?"

"We need this contract over with so I can be cooked to death by a fucking dragon, yes?"

"Aye. But you'll have to climb through shit, piss, and waste to get through to the gate."

"It would not be the first time."

It wasn't an offer they could honestly refuse. They circled to the rear but remained in the cover of the trees as he studied the structure intently and tried to locate the place they used for waste disposal. When he finally saw it, he wasn't at all surprised that it was on the opposite side of the gate and was too small for him to use.

"We go at night," Skharr said finally. "From the looks of the horses, the whole troop is there. All...I'll say two dozen of them. We cannot charge in like we own the fucking place."

"Have you a plan?"

"Aye."

They would not move until they had the cover of darkness. There was no moon and enough clouds to obscure them. He could tell there would be rain from the way the ache in his shoulder worsened, but they wouldn't wait until the time was perfect. Nothing ever was.

"How long until the halfling runs away, do you think?" Cassandra asked.

He shook his head. "If she runs, she dies. That is the benefit of the geas. She knows it and she would rather die in dragonfire than die by the geas, especially one tied to Theros."

"Oh. Well, I assumed that she didn't know any of that and was willing to run anyway."

The barbarian shook his head. Even in the darkness, he could discern movement in the towers. They had no fires lit as they were supposed to keep watch over the region, not get too comfortable. None of them, though, would have found a way to remain alert while the fires were out though and the temperatures dropped. He had a strong feeling they would wrap themselves in blankets, try to not fall asleep, and fail.

When the gate moved, so did he. Cassandra followed closely and immediately raised a shield over them in case one of the archers let loose on them from above.

No arrows fell and Skharr was fairly confident that none would. He pushed the gates open carefully only far enough for the two of them to pass through and left them open. There was no way to know if they would need to make a quick escape.

Now that they had gained entry without rousing the guard, his thoughts turned to what they would find inside.

The halfling was there, however, and remained low. She held the small blow flute in her hand as well as a handful of darts she'd taken from her belt.

"The archers?" he asked.

"Dead."

"The patrols on the walls?"

"I wasn't able to get to them. I would need to climb the walls."

The barbarian nodded and gestured for her and Cassandra to stay back as he hefted his bow and drew three arrows from the quiver he carried on his belt. Three men patrolled the walls at all times, even at night.

"And the rest of them?" the former paladin asked.

"Some are asleep," Leahlu whispered. "Most are in the mess hall drinking. From the looks of it, they raided a caravan that carried ale."

And a good thing too, Skharr decided. With the noise in the mess, none of them would hear him or his bow.

He dropped to a knee and nocked one of the arrows when he saw a patrolman on the wall. By now, he was used to the weight of the bow and while he could feel the strain in his back, it was the kind he knew he could bear fifty, sixty times in a day before he began to flag.

It was the kind of power an archer would have to carry in any military in the world, although he doubted there were many imperial longbowman who carried a weapon with a similar draw weight.

The bowstring hummed and the arrow streaked free and climbed smoothly in the cool night air for a moment before it descended. The guard on the wall snapped around with it jutting from the side of his neck, and the power of the strike pushed him over the stockade. A soft thud confirmed that he'd landed on the spikes in the moat.

The barbarian shifted to target the second and send him to a similar fate. The third followed soon after. The walls were now abandoned. If he'd had an army with him, he would have lit one of his arrows and launched it skyward to tell them that if there was ever going to be a time to attack, it would be now.

There was no army, of course. It was him, a former paladin, and a halfling—a formidable fighting force but not against twenty or so trained and armed soldiers. He could kill five, perhaps six. Cassandra could account for a similar number, and the halfling would be hard-pressed to deal with two and possibly less.

Of the three of them, Leahlu would be the most likely to survive. She would find a way to slip out when the battle started and he couldn't have blamed her. But Skharr had no intention to die and especially not at the hands of deserters. Desperate measures were therefore required.

"Wait here," he instructed as the two women joined him.

"Where are you going?"

He placed the bow and arrow quiver in Cassandra's hands. "I'm going to have a word with the ale-swilling dickheads who made this place their home. They'll need to adapt it to meet higher fucking standards."

"What?"

Before either of them could stop him, he strode to where he could hear the most noise, which was the largest building in the entire fortress. This would be the mess hall, where the group of men celebrated their ill-gotten gains.

Skharr had a sword and a dagger on his belt and his heart beat faster with every step he took toward the door. The more he thought about it, the more it seemed like a bad idea.

Well then, it was best to not think too much about it.

The barbarian pushed the door to the mess hall open, and the heat in the room and the smell of warm food and ale washed over him.

The sound of revelry came from within, which included one of the soldiers who played a lute. The musician stopped immediately when the intruder entered the room and the doors closed behind him as he approached the nearest table. All eyes were on the warrior as he studied the group. He could see no officers among them, only soldiers, although it was possible that the officers had already gone to sleep for the evening.

One of the men at the table closest to the door stood, his eyes narrowed, and moved his hand toward the mace he carried on his belt.

"Who the fuck are you, then?"

Skharr smirked and focused his attention on the man who had asked the question as he advanced toward him. "I'm the fucker who broke into this godsbedammed fortress of yours and who will burn it down. And unless you want to burn with it, you'll leave."

His warning wouldn't work the first time around. That much was a given at this point. The question was how many of them he would have to kill before the others decided they did not want to fight.

The one who had stood was the first aggressor and hefted his mace. Before the weapon could be raised, Skharr lunged forward with the dagger drawn from his belt and slashed his throat open.

He was already drawing his sword when the other four at the table pushed to their feet, ready for a fight. The first of these fell when his hand was severed cleanly at the wrist. The second staggered and dropped to his knees when the warrior planted his dagger in the deserter's chest. The last one tried to back away, not ready for the fight. She hadn't even reached for her sword yet.

If he let her live, however, the others would see that moment of weakness and pounce. Without a moment's thought, he closed the distance between them and buried his sword in her chest. It cut through her gambeson as though she hadn't worn anything at all.

In a smooth movement, he drew the sword out and hacked into the neck of the one man standing. He was missing a hand, probably lost in a battle somewhere, and his head dropped clear of his shoulders, thudded hard on the table, and rolled off almost immediately.

The other soldiers in the mess hall were already on their feet and some had even drawn their weapons by the time the final body fell.

Skharr ignored them. He planted his sword into the long

bench his opponents had been seated on, kicked off the first one who had fallen onto it, and took his place.

He could practically taste the confusion spreading through the room as he sniffed the nearest mug of ale and grunted softly before he took a sip.

"Good shit," he said appreciatively. Cassandra and Leahlu entered the room, their weapons drawn and ready for a fight, although they looked equally confused to see he had sat calmly and left his weapon in the bench while he faced a room full of armed deserters.

There was no point in giving them a quick explanation for his actions. Instead, Skharr paused long enough to drain the mug and pounded it on the table. None of the soldiers showed any willingness to inch forward yet.

It felt right to take a large bite of what he assumed was a leg of lamb before he stretched forward, yanked his dagger from the chest of one of the fallen, and pointed it at the deserter closest to him, a young man with a frizz of blond hair adorning his head like a halo.

"What's your name, boy?" Skharr asked around a mouthful of the freshly roasted lamb.

"Sa...Salazar," he answered and looked at his comrades like he was afraid the group would lynch him for answering. None of them moved and he returned his gaze to the barbarian, who took another bite from the meat.

"Do you know who I am, Salazar?"

"Aye."

The warrior waved his dagger at the rest of the room. "By all means, inform your comrades. They appear to lack your education."

"His...his name is Skharr, the DeathEater."

It was a gratifying moment to see that most of the eyes in the room suddenly widened. A few of them pointed at the sword with the silver hilt and the pommel of two intertwined snakes with emerald eyes.

"It's a surname," he informed them. "Not a title. Skharr Death-Eater. It means I'm from the barbarian clan known as the DeathEaters."

They all nodded and paid close attention.

"Are...are you taking over the fortress, Sir DeathEater?"

There truly was no point in correcting them. He was no knight but breaking the semantics down at this point would cost him their attention.

Instead, he laughed, snatched the mug of one of the other dead men, and washed down the mouthful of lamb he'd chewed on.

"This dung heap?" He laughed. "Not fucking likely. I'll burn it to the ground. All those who have no desire to be part of the ashes will leave immediately. Gather your possessions and go. But be warned that once I am finished with my meal—well, their meal, but they won't need it—I'll set fire to this godsbedammed swill pit, whether you are in it or not."

Skharr turned his back on the group and checked to make sure that neither Cassandra nor Leahlu were about to do anything stupid before he bit another chunk from the meat in front of him.

After a few whispered conversations between the deserters, he could hear the shuffling of steps behind him. One by one, the soldiers began to hasten out of the room. A few paused and bowed their heads at Cassandra before they left.

His heart still beat rapidly in his chest and it felt as if every eye in the room watched him, but he forced himself to continue to eat and drink like he didn't care if any of them remained or not.

The act had been the best he could think of but in a matter of minutes, the mess hall was empty except for him, Cassandra, and Leahlu.

The doors closed and he gestured for his two partners to join him. "Eat and drink. It'll require effort to burn this whole fucking fort to ash."

The halfling was the first to respond. She clambered into the seat across from him, pulled one of the jugs of ale closer, and poured the contents into a nearby mug. Cassandra sat next to her but did not partake in any of the food or drink.

"Was that your plan?" the former paladin asked. "Talk them into leaving and hope that they would listen?"

"In its entirety."

"And how did you know they would listen?"

"I didn't."

She sighed heavily and leaned forward over the table. "You fucking what? You left your sword on the godsbedammed bench and started to eat and drink when you didn't know if they would back down or not?"

"I still don't. But they had to think that I knew they had no intention to fight me. A little reputation goes a long way with a few men who are too drunk or too tired to fight. They could have killed me as a group but they knew that not all of them would survive. None of them wanted to die tonight. They all preferred to fuck off and continue with their lives once these four were dead."

The halfling took a piece of the lamb and a few slices of bread and ate ravenously. She didn't even look like she'd gone up the godsbedammed sewer. "How do you know they aren't simply waiting outside to kill us all?"

Skharr tilted his head and his brow furrowed.

"Aren't you going to answer her?" Cassandra asked.

He raised a finger and took a sip from his mug as the clattering of hooves could be heard outside when the group rode out of the gates.

"I know now."

"You are such a fucking…asshole." The former paladin shook

her head before she snatched the jug of ale and poured some for herself. "You risked it all on this harebrained scheme of yours and you were lucky that it worked. But one day, luck will not side with you and you will die."

The barbarian nodded. "Aye. It was a gamble but the odds were better than us surviving a pitched battle against them."

"We could have waited until they were in bed and slit their throats in their sleep."

"Not if they discovered the dead patrols and archers. An alarm would certainly have been raised and we would have had a battle anyway. This was the best option. And if it all went to shit, I could have killed enough of them to make the odds better for the two of you to win or at least fight your way out."

Cassandra had no answer to that and simply shook her head again before she took another gulp of the ale. "This is good shit."

"That is what I said."

"There is pitch in the towers," Leahlu told them once the clatter of hooves outside had ceased. "We can use that to set fire to the godsbedammed place."

Skharr nodded. "A sound idea. I might have considered the possibility of spending the night here but if they do not see the fire in the distance, they will be tempted to return. It's best to spend the night in the forest."

"On that, we can agree," the former paladin acknowledged. "After we've had some fucking food and drink. Then the two of you find a place for us to stay. I need to talk to someone about a book."

"As you say," he responded and took another bite of lamb. "I don't suppose Leahlu knows a decent inn around these parts?"

"I do, as a matter of fact."

"Do you intend to meet the elf in that?" Skharr raised an eyebrow at Cassandra's attire. "You know I approve but high elves are a stuffy bunch."

"I know, I know. I'll think of something. I'll leave in the morning."

Traveling alone with the godsbedammed barbarian was not quite what Leahlu expected it would be. She'd anticipated questions to come from him at a mile a minute but for the first few hours on the road, he did not say a word.

At least he didn't pester her to pick their pace up as most humans did. She walked quickly for one with short legs, which meant they made good time, and Skharr and his horse called Horse did not appear to be in too much of a hurry. The idea that they were heading off to find a place to stay while Cassandra attended to her business did not seem to worry the warrior, which meant she was not worried either.

The woman off on her own did imply that trouble would follow, of course, but it did not appear to be the kind she needed to pay attention to.

"Is that where we are going?" he asked as a handful of buildings came into view ahead of them.

She had assumed there would be lines of farms and towns being burned by the deserters who had left their fortress, but there was no sign of it. Perhaps things had gone as Skharr had hoped and they had dispersed, or perhaps they encountered an imperial patrol that could not be bought or intimidated.

Their base was in ashes and rebuilding it would take months. The area was safe from them for the moment.

"Aye. It's where most of the farmers and trappers spend their time when they are not working, so it is well-stocked with all manner of fresh food and drink. It will soon be a hub of this region, and I imagine a city will be built around it before too long."

It wasn't the kind of settlement that was generally accepting of halflings, but the fewer humans in the area, the safer it was for folk like her.

Skharr nodded. "I suppose you might be right. I wouldn't be surprised if it were a regular stop for the imperial patrols in the region if what you say is true."

He was not wrong about that. A number of horses with saddles bearing imperial seals were stationed around the area. The soldiers noticed them and studied them closely as they approached before they turned their attention to their work again.

Whether they knew who he was or not didn't matter much, and Skharr led Horse and Leahlu to the entrance of the inn. Fortunately, it had all the trappings of an establishment that was well-frequented, including a handful of young boys who worked for a little extra coin by caring for the horses of the patrons.

The attention of the two men who stood outside the inn was a little more worrying. Both were armed and had the look of mercenaries as they smoked their pipes away from the door, likely to prevent the smell from ruining appetites. Leahlu never understood why humans had acquired the habit, although from what she'd heard, most of them learned it from the dwarves. Folk didn't think there was much that separated dwarves from halflings, but she'd never known any of her kind who had the need to inhale smoke into their lungs.

That was not why Leahlu watched them closely, however. Something about the way their gazes had fastened on them as they approached the inn made her feel like her skin was crawling.

"What do you know?" one of the men taunted. "I guess all the pieces that went into him were chunked out of the little one."

She rolled her eyes. Humans somehow thought they were hilarious, no matter how stupid they sounded.

"Aye," the other agreed and laughed. "It's the start of a joke. A barbarian and a half-pint go into a bar—"

He stopped when Skharr stepped in front of him, prepared to

finish the joke. The barbarian in question twisted his body without warning and his fist collided with the man's jaw with enough power to knock him off his feet. He sprawled in the courtyard before his friend could pull his clay pipe from his lips.

"Remain seated," the warrior growled in warning. "Or join your friend."

Leahlu turned and moved her hand to the dagger at her belt. She expected to see the patrolmen and guards rushing to help but while a few watched curiously, those who had seen the punch laughed and made jokes with their comrades before they turned their attention to their horses.

Her large companion certainly had a way of intimidating folk from what little she had seen of him, but she was surprised that he would react to a man who made a joke about half-pints.

He could see the confusion on her face and a small smile played on his lips. "I'll take any insults directed at me well enough, but disrespect my friends and it will guarantee teeth lost."

She narrowed her eyes. There were questions about who he considered a friend, but she had a more pressing matter to discuss and quickly collected the unconscious man's coin purse before they entered the inn. "How do you handle insults directed your way well enough?"

"It could involve a battle of wits if the insult is good-spirited," he answered. "Or an honest brawl between gents. I'll allow them to get a few good blows in before I respond with what could end the fight immediately."

"That is interesting."

"What do you do when someone insults you?"

"I avoid them. Little folk are not the type to get themselves into fights that can be avoided."

"Hmm. I see. I have nothing against that, of course."

"Nor do you seem to have anything against any fight you can shove your fists into."

"Naturally. And yet there is some enjoyment to be gleaned from it."

"And what if someone draws a knife instead of merely using their fists?"

"They have."

"And?"

"They died."

Leahlu nodded, not sure what answer she had expected. Of course they died. If they hadn't, Skharr would not have been around to tell her the tale.

"Taking coin from the downed man is fine," he stated as they moved to one of the tables. "But try to not cause us trouble here, especially when you are no good at it."

"How do you know I was no good at it?"

"Because I caught your hand before you'd even found my purse. That's the kind of thing that will only avoid detection by someone so deep in his cups he might as well be unconscious. I had similar trouble with a dwarf with aspirations to be a master thief until I taught him that he aimed too low for his life."

"Too low. Because he was a dwarf?"

The barbarian grinned. "The double meaning might have been intentional, yes. Even for a dwarf, Brahgen was smaller and leaner than most of his kin. It caused a few issues to develop in his mind. All I can hope is that I helped him, although the means through which that help was provided might not have been orthodox."

"You put him through a variety of life-threatening situations, then?"

"Aye. A few too many. One of which resulted in him needing to save my life as I wandered stupidly into a situation I had no control over."

"Interesting. You don't seem to be the type to admit that you needed help. Ever."

"That should only tell you how badly I fucked up."

"It seems like you should abandon your life as a mercenary and spend it helping thieves find their true calling, wouldn't you think?"

"I godsbedammed well hope not," Skharr protested as one of the barmaids approached their table. "I did manage to talk to a real goddess about the thief who prayed to her, of course, so that proved to be time well-spent, at least."

"There is a goddess for thieves?" Leahlu frowned and seemed unimpressed. "She seems like the kind of goddess who simply lacks anything better to do."

He motioned for them to be brought two ales. "Are you saying you do not believe in anything?"

"Oy!" The shout came from the door. The man Skharr had knocked unconscious was now able to walk and was followed by a handful of his comrades. "You two thieving shits took something of mine."

The barbarian shook his head, took a gold piece from his pouch, and slid it across the table toward the halfling.

"And what am I supposed to do with this?" she asked as she picked it up quickly.

"Give it to the owner of the inn. He'll know what it's for."

He stood and walked to where the group still stood at the door and looked around as if to locate whoever they had come to inflict violence upon. How they had managed to miss the barbarian was beyond her.

With a shrug that suggested what she thought of their mental deficiency, Leahlu did as she was told. She hurried to where the owner was pouring their drinks and scrambled onto one of the seats.

"The barbarian told me to pay you," she said and handed him the gold. "He said you would know what it was for."

The man chuckled and pocketed the coin. "You'll want to watch the situation develop. It's good of him to pay for the damage before the fight starts, I suppose."

"Fight?"

She looked around as one of the men stepped forward with a haymaker that snapped hard into Skharr's jaw. The warrior barely budged from the impact and a grin settled on his face as he returned the blow with sufficient power to make the man stumble back but far from full strength. It was enough to get the fight started, however, and before long, he guffawed as loudly as the men who had joined the fray.

"Fucking barbarians," Leahlu whispered, grasped the mug with both hands, and took a long, slow sip.

It was a little difficult to find something appropriate for a barbarian princess. Cassandra had made good time traveling on her own. She also had a feeling Strider enjoyed being able to move at a good pace instead of laboring under the heat while they waited for Skharr to walk faster.

She respected the absolute hells out of the barbarian, but she wondered if he kept his pace slow simply to annoy her. Perhaps there were circumstances when a barbarian was allowed to ride his brother, but he was unlikely to acknowledge that to her, not when she'd nagged him about it already.

The former paladin drew a deep breath and decided she needed to stop allowing him to annoy her. The man was not even around, for fuck's sake.

The clothes she'd selected were coming along rather nicely and much better than she thought they would. She'd managed to find a seamstress who did not mind working quickly for the extra coin. Her time as Ytrea had taught her that there was likely some magic involved in how the woman used her thread and needles. The manipulation was more than welcome, however, as it paired her usual armor with the leathers that had been damaged. These came together with fabric in purple that seemed to make everything look a little more royal than it had before.

It wasn't likely to survive her first battle but hopefully, that would happen after she met with the godsbedammed elves.

Barbarian princesses did not exist. She was the very first of her kind, which meant she was allowed to be a pioneer in how they should dress from this point forward.

The seamstress did not so much as comment on what she created and merely took her coin and kept her eyes lowered to allow her customer to move on without delay.

The town still simmered with the presence of the elves, which made them fairly easy to find. Extra guards were stationed around the villa where they were housed for the duration of their visit, and it seemed like every effort was being made to ensure that the city of Calaser was more than welcoming to the elf ambassadors.

It was an unsettling thought. She did not like the idea of meeting the elf, although it was probably best that the warrior was not present. The man had a way about him that got under her skin and before she knew it, she would react with jealousy.

For no reason, she reminded herself. The last she'd heard, full-blooded high elves—especially those who had been removed from humans for so many years—did not find much to attract them to the short-lived humans. Of course, if there was ever a human elves would find appealing, it would be Skharr.

When she arrived at the villa, too many of the locals stood around the entrance. She brought Strider to a halt and scowled deeply as she studied the crowd before she finally dismounted and advanced on foot. A few didn't move and she pushed them aside physically. Those who saw her dress and the weapon she carried at her hip, however, were more than willing to allow her the space to proceed unhindered.

Before she could reach the gates, two guards stepped out in front of her. The long, flowing way the steel plates were formed around their bodies was enough to tell her that they were high elves as well, even if she couldn't see the way their eyes were shaped. Their ears—thought by some to be the most identifiable feature of elves—were hidden, but there was no mistaking them.

"Fucking shites who think they can push aside the folk who rightfully live in this town," one of the men in the crowd challenged. He rolled his eyes and refused to move out of the way as she approached the gates.

"Why are you here, then?" she retorted.

"We are here to see the elves. Now wait your fucking turn, bitch!"

She narrowed her eyes and turned toward him as he tried to grab her shoulder. A second before his fingers touched her, she caught them and twisted hard until his eyes bulged almost out of his head. A swift kick to the shins caught him off-balance and when he tried to back away, she swung her fist in a powerful arc to hammer it into the side of his head.

A cut appeared in his cheek and she grasped the base of his skull and shoved him headfirst into the ground.

"You fucking self-important snot-brained turd," she snapped and hissed her irritation when she realized that some of his blood had splattered onto her hand and her new clothes. "Does anybody else have a problem?"

None of them did and she turned away to advance toward the villa.

"Please do not approach farther until you have identified yourself and your reason for being here." The elf who spoke was male, and his soft voice and polite wording did little to assure her that the saber he carried would not be drawn if needed, especially in light of the scene they had witnessed.

"I have come to speak to the Lady Elanea Thaorore. I am told she will wish to help me read this." She held the journal up for the guard to see.

"And who told you this?" he asked as she handed him the

leather-bound book.

"The Lord High God Theros," she answered almost without thinking. There would be no telling how the elves would respond to hearing that someone claimed to have spoken directly to a lord high god.

"This is bullshit!"

Cassandra turned to the man she'd dealt with, who was on his feet again. He staggered toward her while the other townsfolk inched out of their way.

"Is it now?"

He ignored her and looked directly at the guards instead. "Will you seriously take the word of some barbarian whore—"

Whatever insult he'd intended to use was cut off immediately when she took a step forward and whipped her body at the hip, brought her right leg up, and snapped it down in a sharp kick that caught him on the side of the head. She smirked with satisfaction. It wasn't the kind of strike she would have been able to deliver while wearing full plate armor, no matter how light or well-fitted it was to her.

The kick was enough to silence the hooligan again and he fell heavily with a soft thud.

"That's barbarian princess to all of you," she instructed the townsfolk gathered, who had fallen into silence and watched the entire exchange while they backed away slowly.

No one voiced any dissent to her statement, and Cassandra turned to face the guards, neither of whom had their hands on their weapons. They did, however, look surprised by her actions.

"I'll not tolerate anyone speaking to me in such a manner," she offered by way of explanation.

Both smirked and shook their heads.

"Spoken like a true princess," one stated, although she was not entirely sure if he was the same one who had spoken to her before. "If you would follow me, I will escort you to the Lady Thaorore."

CHAPTER SEVENTEEN

"I 've seen you around here before, yes?" the proprietor asked.

Leahlu placed her mug down, wiped a foam mustache from her top lip, and uttered a mighty belch.

"You might have," she answered once she settled again. "A few of my kin frequent this establishment, so you might know them as well."

"Aye, a few. I trade with the colony nearby. They bring me some of the freshest venison I've ever seen and at decent prices as well. There is always a seat for any of your colony should they come for a drink or something to eat."

It was good of him to say so. Not many humans were so hospitable, at least not around these parts. She'd heard that those up north were more welcoming due to their regular interaction with dwarves, dark elves, and other races that enjoyed the colder climes.

Her attention was drawn to the fight when she noticed that three men still surrounded Skharr. From the power he had in him, she knew he was toying with them and simply threw enough punches to keep them engaged while he allowed them to land a few strikes as well.

Even so, two of the five lay on the floor. One groaned and clutched a mouth that was missing teeth. The other snored softly, face-down on the timber.

The barbarian certainly appeared to be enjoying himself. He laughed as one of the men hammered a hard punch into his ribs, then lifted the attacker and flung him into a nearby wall almost effortlessly. The impact made the whole inn shudder, and those who had not watched the fight unfold now gave it their full attention, without a doubt.

The one who had been thrown made no effort to stand. Skharr stepped forward and tripped one of the assailants who surged toward him. The man stumbled and flailed to maintain his balance before his head thunked on one of the nearby chairs and he slumped without so much as a whimper.

One of the patrons reached down idly to make sure he was still alive and looked satisfied with the result before he returned to his drink.

One of the other patrons immediately showed herself to be a little more willing to engage in the fight. She picked the chair up, screamed, and hammered it hard into the warrior's back.

There was enough force behind it to push him a step forward, but he spun and looked surprised that he had been attacked from behind. The woman realized somewhat belatedly how stupid she'd been and that she had irrevocably joined the fight.

"You wouldn't—"

Her voice cut off when the barbarian snapped his fist forward and drove it into her face. She staggered away and clutched her nose. Blood seeped from it, although Leahlu wasn't sure if it was broken or not. It didn't matter in the bigger scheme of things. The woman struggled to stay on her feet even from a light tap like that.

He twisted in time to catch a fist that had been aimed toward the back of his head. His hold was tight enough that the man who threw the punch was unable to pull himself free despite repeated attempts. Skharr lunged forward with his elbow extended to power it into his opponent's temple.

The last one fell leadenly, his eyes closed but hopefully still alive.

A half-hearted cheer issued from the crowd in the inn at the end of the fight, and Skharr offered them a smirk before he moved to where Leahlu and the barman waited for him.

"Have you had your fun, then?" she asked and regarded him with a half-amused, half-irritated expression.

"A good scrap," was all the barbarian had to say on the matter and used a piece of cloth to stop the bleeding from his cheek where one of the men had landed a hard hook. "What do we owe you?"

The question was directed toward the barman, who chuckled softly. "The gold coin will more than suffice for the damages caused."

"And for the work of cleaning the mess?" he asked. "Dealing with the rat-fucking gutter slime cluttering the floor? What say you—another gold piece, two more mugs of ale, and we'll be even?"

"You are generous." The statement was immediately followed by a clear look of greed in the barman's eyes as the warrior placed the coin on the table.

It disappeared quickly and the man went to work to pour them two more drinks, which Skharr collected—as well as the one remaining from their previous order—and nodded for Leahlu to follow him to the table.

"That was very generous," she stated once their drinks were in place and they were seated again. "Given that the cost of the broken furniture could not have been more than a silver. And the cost of cleaning it all will amount to a few coppers for the man."

"Aye. But what I purchased was not what I bought."

The halfling narrowed her eyes. "You were hit a little too hard on the head, weren't you?"

"No. The point is that the next group that inevitably arrives tends to be a little more official than the first." Skharr took a sip from one of the mugs before he pressed the cold ceramic to his cheek where it had begun to swell. "And it pays to ensure that the owner of the establishment has no gripe with you over how the fight finished."

It seemed to make a little more sense, but she couldn't think of exactly what he had meant before more shouts came from the entrance. They increased in volume when the doors were opened so the staff could remove the unconscious men from the floor inside the inn.

"Make way!" a harsh voice bellowed. "Make way for the guard!"

She nodded and the barbarian smirked.

"It would take more than a few knocks on the head to relieve me of my senses," he told her, still with the cool mug pressed to his cheek.

Of course. Of fucking godsbedammed all the hells course.

The elf was easy to identify. She stood under five feet tall and looked almost as young as a teenager, although something about the deep-green eyes defined her as a great deal older than she appeared, at least to Cassandra's human eyes. Elves likely had other determiners for age than wrinkles on the skin.

She possessed a delicate beauty, something foreign yet very feminine, especially in a flowing dress of deep purples and reds as she inspected a small rose bush. Her silver hair flowed well past the middle of her back, mostly unhindered aside from a handful of small braids fashioned to cover the long, pointed ears that stretched almost to the back of her head.

"The barbarian princess," she said softly with a brilliant smile.

"I was not aware that the barbarian clans had any sense of royalty."

Hells, even her voice was melodic and enticing at the same time, with the same oddly lilting accent displayed by the guards.

"I am the first of my kind."

"Your bearing...it is familiar to me although we have not met before. But you carry the mark of someone I have met—a barbarian as well. Skharr, the DeathEater, I believe he was called."

"Only DeathEater. It is a surname, not a title."

She couldn't imagine why she should suddenly focus on the semantics when she had other more urgent business.

"It can be both, I believe, especially for the members of The Clan, as they liked to call themselves."

"Of course. And how do you know Skharr?"

The elf regarded her with what might have been amusement. "We met twice. He is an odd creature, primal and yet civilized. The kind of being that most humans try to not be these days, yet he embraces it. It makes an oddly titillating combination."

Cassandra sighed softly. "Of...fucking course."

Elanea laughed with real amusement. "You misunderstand me. I know humans are confused by my appearance, but I was present when the high elves last mingled with humans."

"Decades ago."

"And I was over three centuries old by that time as well."

"Oh, no, I understand." She rolled her eyes. "You'll simply be flawlessly beautiful for centuries."

"I do not believe you do." A hint of annoyance threaded the elf's voice but it was well-hidden. "But that is not the reason you came to find me. Theros sent you here so I could read something written when I last stood on these shores, or so I was told."

"By Theros?"

Another laugh followed. "Unfortunately, I have not had words with the Ancients in a long while. No, my guards told me the reason for your visit. Might I see the journal?"

The former paladin drew a deep breath and tried to not lose her temper with the elf. It wasn't her fault and she knew that. She honestly needed to control herself a little better, she thought glumly as she retrieved the journal. When she handed it to Elanea, the elf brushed her fingers over the inscription in the leather on the front with a small smile.

"I thought all the old tomes were burned," she whispered and shook her head. "It is odd to see this preserved."

"Do you know who wrote it?"

"This inscription is a signature. Or it might as well be. Threasos Kavian, one of the scholars in the distant past who thought it would be a wise endeavor to study alongside humans for a few decades, both to discover what your minds are capable of as well as to advance his studies into the magical realm."

"So...his were the remains we found?"

"Possibly." She opened the cover and inclined her head as she read through the opening section of writing. "Do you read any elvish?"

"A little but mostly what the drow have written. There are some similarities so I was able to make out a few words, but Eladrin is far more complex, I think."

"Our drow cousins have a closer connection to the earth and find less need for verbal communication. Some say that makes them primitive, but I think they have developed better ways to exchange ideas with their surroundings than speech and writing."

"I...never thought of that."

Elanea chuckled and looked up. "My apologies. I can ramble on sometimes."

"So, this book was written by this...Kavian?"

"Yes, but it was dictated by someone else. There has been research spanning millennia about ways to control dragons and use them as weapons, but they are interestingly resistant to magic. This describes the history of the study. The half-elven emperor Tolan Keiran was in his waning years, and the humans in his city were greedy and delved into the depths of the mountain Ziammotienth. They woke a mighty dragon that tore the mountain asunder and broke it in two at the top. It is known that elf magic was critical to aid in the downfall of the beast."

Cassandra couldn't tell if the elf was translating the writings or if she simply gave her crucial context into understanding them. Either way, she kept her mouth shut and let her continue to speak without interruption.

"Thousands sought ways to kill the dragon, but more than a few wanted to bind it and force it to go and leave the lands it was tormenting alone." She placed her fingers on one of the pages and her eyebrows furrowed delicately. "There are methods in this journal—means to command the great wyrms— but...this is dangerous. The original writer of the journal did not complete his writings and if my suspicions are correct, he fled across the waters as well."

"Leaving Kavian to complete his work?"

"I do not believe so. It might be that Kavian simply decided to continue without his mentor. Here, you can see where the writing changes from him as the annotator to him recording his own musings."

She showed Cassandra a section of the book, and it took the elf a few seconds to remember that none of what she was looking at made any sense to the barbarian princess.

Elanea cleared her throat and found a small bench to sit on, and her visitor sat beside her.

The elf drew a breath and continued. "It would appear that they decided the best means of control was to capture the mind of the dragon. That is the point when the other elf must have left, and here we can see the theoretical musings of Kavian on how to do precisely that."

"So...we were right? They were trying to control a dragon using elvish magical schemes? I'd say they succeeded but the dragon didn't take too kindly to what they did."

"It wouldn't. Dragons are intelligent creatures in their own right and some are even said to have magic of their own. If it were able to overpower a spell or find a loophole, it would have been able to kill those who enslaved it, although if it did so before the binding agent that kept it restrained was destroyed, it would still be bound."

"That explains why it hates humans so much." Cassandra rubbed her chin. "Are there any spells that let us talk to the dragons? That might help us to determine how they captured it and how we can set it free."

"Hmm."

She studied the elf carefully. "What?"

"It is odd that humans speak of freeing a dragon instead of killing it. Even refreshing, to be frank."

"Aye, we're full of surprises. Is there a spell or not?"

"Not a spell but a potion. Dragons communicate using pheromones."

"Faro...what?"

"Oh...uh, chemicals they exude from their scales. The potion would allow you to communicate what you mean to say in the way the dragon is most familiar with and from there, it would be able to respond in like fashion."

"Ah." That seemed like it would be incredibly useful.

The elf looked through a pouch that she carried and produced a small vial with a pink liquid inside.

"You simply...happened to have one of those?"

"You never know when you might need to communicate with a creature that speaks through pheromones. At my age, you learn to always be prepared."

Of course. Her age was somewhere well past three hundred and fifty, after all.

"I don't suppose you might have two of those?" Cassandra asked. "Or...no, three. There are three members of our party."

"Yes. Well, I do not think you will need three. A single sip is enough for it to work, so you might only need one vial for two. Of course, if the barbarian will be with you, he might need a full vial so two might be required."

The barbarian princess nodded as Elanea took another vial from her pouch.

"I assume you're not doing any of this for free, right?"

"There is a great deal we can learn from each other on this subject. If you do not trust my motives, I would ask that you leave the book with me for a while so I can read it for myself. Not only would that allow me to learn more of the contents should you need help in the future, but it would also be a sound way for me to reconnect with those who were here before my kin left."

And there was the simple truth that it didn't look like she would be able to get any more out of it, but Cassandra couldn't help wondering if it wasn't somehow dangerous to leave it in someone else's hands. She merely wasn't sure whether her reluctance was because Skharr's biases had begun to spread to her or because of Theros' warning about the dangers of the magic in the tomes if they fell into the wrong hands.

Either way, she could see no way to avoid it, not unless they planned to fail in their quest and leave the dragon where it was.

"The journal is yours," she answered, took the vials, and inspected them quickly. There was no sign that they were not what she claimed them to be. "How long do the effects last?"

"Until you next sleep," the elf answered with a small smile. "Or...until you are eaten. Whichever one comes first. I suggest not coming too close to the teeth."

It was sound advice, although Cassandra had long since reached the same conclusion herself.

"Out of curiosity," Elanea interjected before she could move away, "what did Skharr use the dagger I gave him for?"

She paused and regarded the elf calmly as she tried to determine the reasons behind the unexpected question. It wasn't that she was arrogant enough to think she could understand what went through the mind of a high elf in the span of a single conversation. Then again, she hadn't told her about what happened. It seemed like she was intuitive as well as utterly beautiful and practically immortal.

"We were battling an elder god," she answered. "A beast from the depths was summoned by those who worshipped it. I was mortally wounded and Skharr told me he knew he would not be able to kill the creature on his own, so he used the dagger to save me. How did you know it had been used?"

"I cannot claim to have crafted the weapon myself, but I traveled with it for many years. It becomes…intertwined, somehow. I'm not sure I know how to explain it but I sensed when it was used. It is odd that he would have used it for you and odder still that he survived. As you say, humans are full of surprises."

"It's what we're best known for." Cassandra bowed—not quite sure why—and turned away to where the guards waited to escort her from the premises.

They paused when they approached the gates, and it took her a few seconds to realize why. The man she'd beaten—twice—still stood at the entrance and appeared to be waiting for her to appear again.

"Would you prefer that we exit through another way?" the guard asked.

"No," Cassandra answered and rolled her shoulders. "I have tension I need to expel from my body and this is as good a way as any to accomplish that."

"As you wish."

The gate was opened and the man straightened and his eyes widened.

"The bitch has returned!" he shouted. "No doubt to run off before she realizes that catching me unawares would not be enough to defeat me forever."

She smiled as the odd, crazy energy filled her body and advanced on him. For a moment, he flinched and inched away as if he regretted his decision. But he seemed to recall the words he'd spoken and knew that he would forever be remembered as a coward if he ran now.

Skharr always did or talked about doing something when he wanted a brawl. Engage but do not obliterate. It was difficult to put this into practice but she barely managed to avoid attacking the man outright.

Instead, the small square outside the villa rang with the sound of the back of her hand when it smacked into his cheek. She had put enough force behind the strike to make him stumble back and looked at her in shock as he touched the growing bruise on his cheek.

"I assume you've said a great deal about me while I was inside." She snarled her belligerence as she approached him to ensure there would be no escape from her in the crowd. "Prove it to yourself and to them. Give me a real fight this time."

He roared, pushed his fear aside, and rushed toward her. A punch connected with the side of her face. It was backed by fury but not properly grounded. She twisted out of the way as he tried to throw another, brought her knee up into his gut, and knocked the breath from his lungs.

Her assailant made another wild lunge, this time out of desperation as he struggled to breathe. Cassandra grasped the sides of his head with both hands to hold him in place as her head jerked forward.

The resulting crack was met by a gasp from the crowd as he staggered, stunned and still struggling to breathe, with blood streaming from his broken nose. She closed the distance between them again, lifted the man off his feet with an unrelenting hold on his neck, and swung him hard onto the cobbles.

"Do you have anything else to say?" She all but hissed the question.

"Please..."

"Barbarian princess." She straightened and spat on him. "Not bitch."

She took a moment to make sure their scuffle hadn't damaged the potions she carried and with her head held high, strode silently through the crowd. Strider followed at her heels as the people parted willingly before her.

The men had all been removed and the guards now spoke to those present. One of them who bore all the markings of a captain spoke to the barman and the owner of the inn before he turned to look at the two teammates who were still at their table.

Skharr had managed to finish one of the mugs of ale while he pressed his other hand to his cheek. There was no way to improve his brutish features, although it seemed there were some humans who would find those features attractive.

They honestly weren't quite to her taste. Cassandra was closer to what she found attractive, although not many women were interested in sharing pleasure with a halfling female.

The captain walked to where they were seated and pulled a chair closer, although it was curious that he turned it to put the back in front of him as he straddled the seat.

"I have five men outside," the man stated, rested his arms on top of his chair, and leaned forward. "They are in varying states of consciousness but they all tell a similar story. A story of a barbarian who hit one, a halfling who stole from him while he was unconscious, and the barbarian again who beat those that came to reclaim what was stolen."

"Five men who were beaten by one?" Leahlu asked and raised an eyebrow. "This must be a mighty barbarian indeed."

"True enough," the captain answered. "But these men insist that I place both of you in jail cells for what was done to them."

"The barbarian must pay for the crime of defending himself." Skharr shook his head. "Nothing changes in the world."

"That is what crossed my mind. The barkeep tells me that you were seated when the men came in and caused a ruckus, and you even paid for any damages that might be caused although he tried to quiet the men. There are far too many bar fights in which everyone wants the other to be flung behind bars."

A few jeers and cheers came from the entrance as well as a few rude remarks which were quickly silenced when the guards snapped that they did not want any more disturbances for the day or arrests would be made.

She didn't need to look to know that Cassandra was among them again. The woman looked flushed and a little annoyed like she had pushed her horse hard on the road to meet them.

"I can see the effects you have on the local populace already, Skharr," the former paladin commented as she sat and relieved Skharr of the mug he had pressed to his face. "Half the male populace is already sporting trophies from your fight."

"Skharr?" the captain asked and narrowed his eyes. "Skharr DeathEater?"

"The very same." She took a long draught from her drink. "Who the fuck are you?"

"Captain Soren Tavar. I apologize for bothering the Barbarian of Theros. Have a good day."

He stood quickly and shouted at his men to take the men involved in the brawl to the local prison.

"You didn't boast about being the Barbarian of Theros, then." Cassandra grinned. "Good for you."

Skharr nodded. "We'll spend the night here, I think. Then, assuming you found something we can use, we can leave in the morning again once a plan has been formulated."

Her grin widened. "I found something. But...uh, I'm not sure you'll like it."

"I didn't think I would. Now for something to eat, then some rest. Hopefully, none of the fucking bastards comes around after they are released to taste what the barbarian princess has to show them."

Leahlu looked warily at each of them in turn. "As long as we have separate rooms, I will be a happy halfling."

"Two rooms. You can share one with the princess."

"What?" Cassandra asked.

"Rest is the idea. We would have precious little of it if you and I were to rest in the same room."

The halfling coughed and shook her head. Sharing a room with the princess was not a guarantee that she would rest well but they didn't seem to care about that—or simply hadn't considered the possibility.

CHAPTER EIGHTEEN

L eaving a coin with the owner of the inn had felt like a sound idea at the time. There was always the possibility that the bone-headed piss-bags who had bothered them before would make another attempt, probably in the middle of the night. Skharr knew he had no intention to treat them as gently as he had in the brawl, and there was the possibility that things would turn messy if they lost all reason and decided to seek revenge.

Thankfully, there had been no sign of the assholes all night, and he woke when the sun began to peek through the slats on his window.

He lay in silence for a moment and allowed himself to be pleasantly surprised. Perhaps they had learned their lesson, even though he had a feeling the halfling had nabbed a couple more purses during the fight.

Or perhaps the guards hadn't released the group from their prison cells yet. Hopefully, their small party would be long gone by the time they saw the light of day.

Then again, a part of him had hoped for a rematch where he

did not have to hold himself back. Perhaps it was an opportunity to spread the legend of Skharr DeathEater a little in these parts.

Instead, he had been granted a good rest although he felt a little sore from the fight the day before. The sense of peace he woke to was somewhat unsettling, but he knew he could get used to it.

His reflection in the water left for him in a nearby bucket revealed his injuries. Overnight, his cheek had swollen to the size of a peach and if it got any worse, he decided he would make use of a healing potion before they headed out. There was no point in allowing himself to endure the throbbing lump for longer than was necessary.

It was tender as well, to the point that every step he took felt like a jolt to the bruised flesh.

Skharr sighed, retrieved one of the small vials from his pouch, and swallowed the contents. He winced as the effects took hold quickly and a stinging sensation touched each injury and began to work on the bruising. He was left with nothing to do but take another deep breath as he pulled his clothes on.

The potion had almost completed its effects by the time he reached the bottom of the steps, where three tables were already filled. A familiar barbarian princess and a halfling were already seated at one of them and sipped from cups that steamed between mouthfuls of bread, dried fruits, butter, and cheese served on dark platters.

Most places generally made use of the meat cooked the night before to provide cold cuts for the morning after. None appeared to have been left from the evening meal, however. Skharr dropped into the seat and the barman approached them immediately with another mug of the hot liquid and a platter of food for him.

"We would have paid for it," Leahlu commented once the man was out of earshot again, "but he said you had left him a gold piece in case there was trouble and he wouldn't return it."

"He might discover that he is taking advantage of my generosity," the barbarian replied. "But it is a good thing that he considers our debt for the night paid."

Cassandra shrugged as he sniffed the steaming liquid in his cup.

"It is not koffe," she said with a sad shake of her head. "It's black tea that the innkeep said would have the same effect."

He snorted derisively but still tried the liquid. It was a little bitter with a hint of honey and something else mixed in he couldn't quite place.

"It isn't quite koffe but it is better than only water," the former paladin conceded and took another sip.

"Fascinating." Leahlu rolled her eyes and her voice dripped with sarcasm. "Do you think we should have a word about the dragon we will face rather than focus on the merits of fucking tea?"

"There is little chance that we will battle a dragon and walk away," Skharr commented. "Not without an army, which is why we attempted to stay away from the godsbedammed beast the first time we visited the temple."

"Do you think the dragon might not attack below?" Cassandra shook her head. "When I spoke to the elf, she mentioned that it might be held in there by something. She suggested we speak to it and try to find out what has trapped it and allow it to break free."

That appeared to catch the immediate attention of their halfling comrade.

"Why would you want to release a dragon?" she asked and looked around in consternation. "Given that it might decide to turn an entire godsbedammed city to ash, that might not be the finest of choices."

"Dragons don't like to be around people."

"And you've spoken to many of them, have you?"

That was a fair point. "No, but the fact that they avoid human settlements even though they could turn them to ash if they wanted to is an indication that they are not mindless, bloodthirsty beasts."

"Some might be. You never know. What if the one that was caught was imprisoned because it was a mindless, bloodthirsty beast?"

Again, she made another fair point. Skharr had no answer for it but she shook her head firmly, which assured him that he didn't have to search for a reply.

"It doesn't matter. The three of us would not pose much more of a threat to the dragon than the odd sniffle would to a human. Finding a solution that encourages it to leave an area where it can threaten folk might involve a way to leave the dragon alive as well, and I have made my peace with that. How do you suppose we should approach?"

The barbarian shook his head and took a mouthful of food and another sip of the tea. The effects were certainly not as powerful as he remembered with koffe but he could still feel the last traces of sleepiness slip away with each sip. It was certainly an alternative, if inferior.

"From below worked for us before," he replied. "As long as those godsbedammed ass-ugly goblin-spawned lizards leave us alone for the most part. It might be that the path we used in and out of the area is not where the dragon attacks."

"I am still trying to understand the fact that we are intentionally attacking a dragon—a live one that breathes fire," Leahlu stated. "Why are we attacking the dragon?"

Cassandra's face twitched and Skharr knew she hadn't reacted well to the questions. Shades of what had happened to her already had begun to make an appearance and he leaned forward quickly.

"It's because that is the contract. Nothing more and nothing less. We have an opportunity to ensure that it poses as little risk to others as possible."

"Right. And how exactly do you plan to chat to the godsbe-dammed beast? Over a nice piece of roast boar?"

"It might not be a terrible idea."

"It is," Cassandra interrupted and an odd calmness in her voice sent a chill down his spine. "But the elf I visited gave us a way to speak to it if we are so inclined."

"And we will simply take the word of some drow about how to speak to dragons?" The halfling snorted and looked unimpressed

"A high elf," Skharr corrected. "And the last magical bauble she gave me worked as she had promised, so I assume that whatever she gave Cassandra to allow us to communicate with the dragon will work as well."

"In fact, she gave me something that will allow any and all of the three of us to speak to it." The former paladin withdrew two vials, both containing an opaque pink liquid. "She explained that dragons speak through...chemicals released by their scales or something. This will allow us to communicate with it in a similar manner."

"I cannot help but count two vials for the three of us," Leahlu pointed out.

"You and I can share one," she replied. "It's the big one who needs a full vial for himself. Do you know that the fucking elf described you as...what was the word? Titilating?"

The barbarian regarded her warily. While he wasn't quite sure what the word meant, if it was something that had annoyed her, he could only assume it was a compliment of some kind.

"Right then." He nodded, having decided it was safer to not pursue that particular line of conversation. "We'll have a chat with the dragon. It is as good a plan as any. I say we finish our breakfast and ride out."

"Are you in a hurry?"

"I have no plans to encounter the slime suckers Leahlu robbed again. I doubt the town guard will be as understanding this time around and we do not want to be delayed."

"Wait, she did what?"

The halfling nodded. "I agree with the giant. We might as well get an early start to the day."

"Well, as long as we are spending someone else's coin, I don't suppose you two are too eager to leave to remember that we need to resupply first?" Cassandra raised an eyebrow.

Skharr nodded reluctantly. "She has a point, unfortunately."

"Fuck you." She rolled her eyes. "But unfortunately, my left ass cheek says it's too soon for that."

"What the hell do I need charms for?"

"Do you want to be poisoned or caught in a magical trap?" Cassandra stood over the halfling with a scowl on her face.

"What the hell do you think the charms I wear are for?"

The former paladin pulled them out again and flipped through them one by one. "Flawed, broken, and never was a magical charm to begin with."

"That's a locket, not a charm—personal shit. I assume you are familiar with the concept."

She ignored her and focused on the last item. "Oh, this one is effective. I assume it is what helps you move around without being heard if you want to do so."

"That and personal talent. You need to have the latter for it to work. That concept, I imagine, is one that you are not familiar with."

The two had bickered from the moment they left the inn, although it seemed to be good-natured for the most part, at least as far as Skharr could tell from Cassandra. He knew her mannerisms well enough, he thought, to be able to make a good judgment.

"You talk a pile of shit for someone I could hurl through the nearest wall with one hand."

"The way I understand it, I die by a barbarian's hand or by a dragon's flame. What the hell is the difference?"

The halfling made a good point there but Skharr knew that if he joined the debate, all he would do was escalate things. It was best to leave them to their argument while he selected the food they would need from one of the local merchants.

"Having a charm that silences your steps is a good start," Cassandra said at last and moved to the other side of the mage's stall.

"Aye, the best start unless you happen to have something that makes me invisible."

The former paladin turned her attention to the mage, who appeared to have recently finished college and now sold charms and trinkets to pay for the debt his studies had incurred. "Do you have anything that makes one invisible? A ring or something like that?"

"A ring that makes you invisible?" The mage scoffed. "That is preposterous. What would happen if it fell off? I do have an earring that can be bound to the person wearing it, however. Here…"

He pulled out a small silver ring designed to be clasped on the ear. A small mechanism attached to it would lock it in place when it was worn to prevent it from slipping off.

"It will meld together when you wear it, so you would have to rip the whole godsbedammed ear off to remove it," the mage explained and passed it to Cassandra, who pushed Leahlu's unruly hair up to see if it would fit her ear. "There is a small amethyst on the back that the owner can touch to release it. A touch to the Kyanite there will make the effects active."

"How long will the effects last?" the halfling asked as she took it and held it at the hole already present in her ear. It immediately settled firmly into place.

"As long as you do not touch either gemstone."

"She meant how much power does it contain, moron," Cassandra snapped. "I would say...four to five hours before it needs to be replenished. How does one do that?"

The mage's eyebrows raised as he tried to account for where her magical knowledge could have come from before he decided it was probably best if he did not know.

"It takes its power from the sea," he explained. "Waves and movement caused by the moon. One night left in shallow waters and lapped by the waves is enough to refill it. Even less time is required if it is in the light of the moon—the fuller, the better."

It was the former paladin's turn to look surprised, and even Skharr knew why. Magical items that could absorb power from their environments were incredibly difficult to create and even more difficult to control. There would have been no point in mentioning that, though, and he simply paid the food vendor and moved to rejoin his partners.

"Why would you want to be invisible?" he asked. "I thought halflings didn't need much help to go about unseen. You should be proud of your personal abilities. Be proud of who you are."

"That is what we want people to think." Leahlu grinned at him. "And if I'm invisible, I can stab folk before they can make fun of my size."

"Imagine, if you will," he replied, "punching someone hard enough in front of you—"

"I'd hit them in the codpiece." She tilted her head and nodded. "It would have to be one hell of a punch."

"Agreed."

"I'd have to reach up a little to punch you in the balls, though."

"Why would you punch me?"

"Aside from your threats to use me as a club and relocate my teeth, and tying me into a contract that forced me to climb through shit and piss, while that is somehow not the most dangerous contract of the two?"

The barbarian scratched at his chin. "Aye. Aside from that."

"Well, you would have to be a godsbedammed soulless bastard for me to try to injure you in that particular place."

He nodded. "If I was a godsbedammed soulless bastard, I would have to try to bear it somehow."

"You wouldn't retaliate?"

"Not if I deserved it."

"What if I punched someone and they didn't fall?"

"Aim better next time," he suggested. "Or…grow stronger."

"Ah, yes, grow stronger, as if it were simply that easy."

Skharr shrugged. "It can be. Of course, not beyond what you are capable of, but always seek to improve yourself."

He became a little distracted when he realized that more than a few gazes had settled on them. With a scowl, he looked suspiciously at the guilty parties and noticed that the attention was not on them but Cassandra. Most of the men in the city seemed to be present and talked about the barbarian princess. The fact that she knew they were watching and appeared to enjoy the attention was even more of a distraction.

"I don't suppose you might have koffe in your stores?" she asked a merchant who sold a variety of tea from her stall.

"Oh…yes," the young woman replied. "I had a recent arrival of stock in the past few weeks. It was one of the few caravans that managed to reach here despite all the deserters. How much will you need?"

"I think…two pounds should be sufficient."

"Of course." The woman pulled a scale out, weighed what they needed, and secured it in a pouch. "If you don't mind me asking… what is it like to be a barbarian princess?"

Cassandra paused and seemed to consider it for a moment. "Folk think you're an oddity and that you're below them. I tend to use that against them and let them think what they want to until I can use the advantage. It does help that most men are distracted by what they can see. For a woman, you will more often have to prove the adage of look but do not touch."

"Does that bother you?" the young merchant asked and handed her the pouch of koffe. "Them trying to touch?"

"Not if I'm in the mood for a fight."

"And what if you are not?"

The former paladin smiled. "I'll let you know when it happens."

The woman had nothing to say to that and Cassandra slipped the pouch of koffe in with the rest of their supplies and handed the packs to Skharr.

It appeared it was his responsibility to put the packs on the horses. All he could hope for was that Strider didn't still hate him for whatever reason.

"Oy, halflings don't have to pay half here, right?" one of the men asked as they moved toward the gate. A few of the other men laughed.

"I guess all I can hope for is half a fuck from that one," another stated as the group approached where the hecklers stood. "I bet you my cock looks huge compared to her—"

Leahlu closed the distance between them with a quick leap and hammered her fist into his groin. The blow seemed to draw all the power out of the man and he dropped to his knees as his hands clutched the injured area while he sank slowly into the fetal position.

The other three seemed ready to punish the halfling for striking their friend but they stopped when Skharr stepped forward to stand behind her, his eyes narrowed.

"I wouldn't." He growled a warning and folded his arms in front of his chest.

The message was simple but more than effective and they helped their friend to stand shakily before they dragged him away and out of sight.

"It's all in the hips," the barbarian said as she moved away.

"Hmm?"

"Power the strike from your legs and pivot your hips."

"Doesn't that take longer?"

"Not particularly and it is more difficult to see. Most of these half-brained street crawlers throw their punches from the shoulders. It feels more powerful but it reveals precisely what they plan to do in advance. If you pivot from the hips, they will not see the strike until they are on their asses."

Retracing their steps to the ruins took a fair amount of time and effort. Thankfully, while the flying creatures continued to glare balefully at them and screeched loudly, there was no sign of the larger, ground-based monsters. With the tide already out, they were able to reach the entrance area where they'd killed the snake with no mishap.

From there, it was easy to follow the route toward the mountain where the greater part of the temple was situated.

"I don't like it," Skharr muttered as he sat on a rock and studied their surroundings. "I see no sign of the godsbedammed dragon anywhere. You would think it would have heard the noise those flying goblin-spawned lizards made."

Cassandra shook her head. "Perhaps someone has sent more paladins to deal with it and they hold the beast's attention."

"Another group of paladins?" Leahlu settled on a nearby rock and used a leather strap to tie her curly hair away from her face. "You mean there was one before?"

"Aye." She nodded. "Neither of the paladins who traveled with me was the finest but they were available. I cannot say the same about too many others. Jacen was not a pleasant person overall but he was one of the most skilled, at least when it came to battle magic. Yazek was a little more tolerable. He'd only been a paladin for a few years and I think he was a little intimidated to travel with the two of us."

The halfling's eyes narrowed as she took a sip of water from her skin. "Why were two paladins traveling with a barbarian princess in the first place?"

"They might have been celibate but they would have had to be blind to not appreciate an ass like that," Skharr interjected quickly. If the woman wanted to explain to the halfling that she was once a paladin herself, she would have the opportunity to do so on her own terms.

Cassandra laughed at the comment. "I cannot argue with that. This is an ass built for riding, after all."

"I should say so," he agreed before he realized that both women were watching him.

"One might say the barbarian speaks from experience," Leahlu commented and glanced at Cassandra, who nodded.

"Aye. And he was both ridden and the one riding. It is odd how I was the one left sore both times."

"That seems unfair," the halfling agreed. "He should be left sore at least once. Did you try to ride him from behind?"

The barbarian scowled and immediately changed the subject. "The temple sanctuary is directly ahead, although I imagine that if we race directly up those rocks, it will not end well for us."

"Do you have any alternative routes?" the former paladin asked. She seemed inclined to spend more time pestering him but had accepted that they were there for a far more important reason.

"If I recall the map correctly, there should be a small town about four days away. If the settlement has not been burned, folk there might know of another way into the temple. We could ask them, although it will mean another detour."

"We might not need one, not if the dragon needs our help and we are able to explain that we can assist. The elf said it was bound by something similar to a geas. It would have had a serious magical effect and it would not be able to break it without aid."

"It might also be royally pissed off and will kill anyone no matter what their intentions are," Leahlu noted. "But given that it is bound by a geas, I can relate."

CHAPTER NINETEEN

"**W**hy?" Skharr asked. "Why does she always attack them in the cock?"

He directed the question to himself since Cassandra was dealing with a group of the creatures on her own. She pushed them back with blasts from her shield and sliced them open with her sword before they could retaliate.

A handful had already fallen to arrows from his bow, but the attack had moved too close for him to use the weapon effectively. The close quarters forced him back to attack those that were in range with his sword.

They looked like wolves, at least from the shapes of their jaws, but they were completely hairless, tall, and painfully slim. Their ribs protruded from their chests like they had not eaten in years. They attacked in a pack, which suggested that there was some relation to real wolves although they were something else entirely.

Leahlu had vanished almost immediately when the battle started. Skharr had no time to wonder if she would take the opportunity to run, but her purpose became clear when two of the creatures stopped suddenly in mid-assault. They looked between their elongated hind legs where heavy gashes had appeared and bled profusely.

It had been a snippet of advice he'd always passed on to the younger, less-experienced fighters whenever they faced a battle —protect your groin and strike theirs. Not only did it have the possibility to disable any man who was struck, but any deep incision in the area would also cause the victim to bleed out within minutes.

It seemed the halfling had taken the advice to heart and used her newly acquired charm to go invisible. While the creatures were occupied in the fight with the larger humans, she took the opportunity to strike while they did not expect her. He assumed that the wolf-like creatures would have been able to track her by scent alone as they had already with him and the former paladin, but perhaps it was difficult for them in the middle of a battle.

He had honestly thought they had avoided their den without too much trouble, but the incessant howls warned him that they were far from successful.

At least the racket had not summoned the dragon to their location, and given that he could see the effects of it on the landscape with the scorched tree lines, they were godsbedammed lucky that was the case.

Another of the wolves doubled over as blood gushed from a deep wound between its legs, and he couldn't help a shudder. He could see the signs of the halfling running away in the tracks she left on the ground before she vaulted over some rocks to avoid the attention of the monsters.

A faint silhouette was discernible in the sunlight, which begged the question of how effective the charm was when the sun was shining. In darkness or at night, however, he knew it would be practically impossible to see her before her dagger hacked his cock off.

Another shudder rippled through him and the barbarian took a moment to clean his blade when the pack began to retreat before them toward the den. None of them paused to retrieve their dead, not even those that were far enough away that it was safe to do so. At least it meant that the creatures did not indulge in cannibalism.

The halfling materialized a few paces to his left, cleaned her dagger, and grinned at the expression on his face.

"No male of any species likes the thought of any other creature's groin cut into," she quipped.

"I would assume females are not particularly fond of the strike either," Cassandra commented. "How many of those fuckers did she take?"

"Three that I counted." Skharr waited for the halfling to nod in agreement.

"I wonder how the pack avoided being torched by the dragon," the former paladin said thoughtfully and her gaze swept the same scorched areas he had noticed before.

"They probably use their den and the surrounding foliage for protection," he surmised and sheathed his blade. "I suppose we should not have pushed directly to the temple sanctuary after all."

"I didn't mind it," Leahlu responded as he collected his arrows from the corpses. "Besides, if the dragon is trapped by an elf geas, it would be best to see to it that it's freed without delay."

"Death by dragon was never my preferred way to die."

"What is your preferred way to die?" the halfling asked as they continued and the horses rejoined them.

"Either my heart giving out while I fuck or in battle," Skharr answered after a moment of silence. "They seem like the most fitting ways for a warrior to die, wouldn't you say?"

"I would have thought a barbarian would prefer to die while fighting some god or beast that cannot be killed," Cassandra interjected.

"Aye. Dying while fighting or fucking. It's the finest dream."

"Wouldn't you want to…" The halfling frowned. "I don't know, not die at all?"

"Who would want to live forever?" he asked and raised an eyebrow. "There is a saying from…I forget from where but they say 'may all your dreams but one come true.' What worse hell is there than living with nothing to live for?"

The halfling shrugged. "Hells, I'd want to live forever. I'd find myself something to do once I ran out."

"You're still young."

"Or perhaps you're still…boring."

The former paladin snickered softly at the exchange, although her attention returned to the temple sanctuary they now approached. It appeared to be a fortress of some kind built directly into the mountains. The most telling part, he thought, was the fact that chunks of the walls appeared to have been melted from the intensity of the dragonfire that burned through it.

As far as he had heard, rock melted like that revealed the intensity of the fire as well as the age of the dragon. The story was that the older the dragon, the hotter its flame.

"We have to make plans for what will happen if our attempt to speak to it does not work."

Skharr turned to look at Cassandra, who stared at what the beast had done and for the first time, he saw genuine terror in her eyes. He knew, of course, that it came from seeing and feeling firsthand what the fire could do.

"What did you have in mind?" he asked.

"Defensive positions," she replied sharply. "Along the walls. We can designate a location to retreat to if it all goes wrong."

"So you…still mean to have a chat with a dragon over how we can unleash it on the world." Leahlu nodded. "That sounds entirely logical."

"I'm glad you think so," the barbarian answered.

"I could not have been more sarcastic."

"And I could not have cared less. Cassandra?"

She still studied their surroundings and after a moment, she pointed at a small enclave that had been mostly torn apart and burned by the dragon, except for a corner that appeared to have withstood the fire.

"If we were ever to find a place that would survive, I think that one is it."

Skharr nodded. "The horses and supplies remain there, then. We take what we can carry in and see if...talking to the dragon works."

"Even you cannot say that with a straight face," the halfling muttered.

"That does not mean it will not work."

They found the small enclave and the way it hugged the mountain made it the most defensible position possible. There were even murder holes that would allow him to shoot through. It would be one hell of a nod to the makers of his bow if it was able to shoot an arrow through dragon scales but he held no high hopes. If they reached the location, it would be a last resort and he fully expected them to be dead within minutes.

But there was no need to tell them that. Leahlu already looked terrified enough and Cassandra was only too aware of what the dragon was capable of.

"Who owned this fortress?" the halfling asked.

"I assume the dragon priests," he replied and raised an eyebrow.

"Yes, I know about that. I meant before them."

"Wouldn't your colony have records since you remained in these parts?" Cassandra asked.

"Halfling colonies move around regularly. We are nomads but avoid the mountains where there is little to hunt and too many predators. Like dragons."

"I would imagine a decent-sized eagle would be able to carry you off." Cassandra raised an eyebrow and grinned teasingly at her.

"If it weren't distracted by your tits."

Skharr wondered if he would have to intervene before fists were thrown, but a silence fell over them as they approached the fortress and entered through one of the gaps in the wall to see what was mostly hidden on the other side.

The effects were only too clear. The former paladin's expression turned to stone and even Leahlu was suddenly subdued as they looked at what appeared to be a small town, no doubt the living quarters for those who served in the sanctuary. Not much of it was left and everything appeared to have been burned to the ground. The stonework had melted and some sections had been turned to pure glass by the intensity of the flames.

"Gods," the halfling whispered. "That is one angry dragon."

They could only agree and Skharr noticed something green and acrid-smelling spread over most of the open ground. It was, without a doubt, a warning.

"That is how a dragon marks its territory," he said and pointed to some of the sections where it had practically soaked into the soil. "And it burns equally as hot as whatever comes from the beast's mouth."

"Noted," Cassandra snapped and grasped her sword a little tighter as she drew a deep breath. "We continue."

The lack of a snide retort from Leahlu wasn't at all surprising. Something steely in the woman's voice did not invite dispute.

CHAPTER TWENTY

The smell grew stronger as they reached a place where the town appeared to be carved directly from the mountain. If he had to guess, Skharr would have said dwarves were responsible for building it since it was reminiscent of the other dwarf city he'd seen. When he studied it though, there were a handful of indicators that suggested other influencers as well.

Elf, likely as not as they certainly weren't human.

The bile substance was spread thickly across the ground and it appeared to be much fresher as well. Actual puddles had formed where it couldn't soak into the dirt. It formed an unpleasant blanket over most of the area, although it appeared as though the dragon did not like to walk through it as a wide path directly through the center allowed them to avoid it.

"All this catches fire, did you say?" Leahlu asked and covered her nose.

"Aye, from the smallest spark. I would advise against using torches here."

"That is the brightest thing you've said all day."

There was no doubt that if it caught fire, they would not even need to be in the flames to be cooked alive.

Which did beg the question of how they would be able to escape if it went badly.

As they approached what looked like gates leading into the castle of a king, less of the goop was spread about them to the point where there was none up to ten paces around the entrance.

"I guess even it cannot stand the smell," Cassandra whispered as they passed through the doors. The heat of the day was immediately soothed and a pleasant cool settled around them and made it surprisingly pleasant inside.

As their eyes adjusted, Leahlu gasped softly and it was quickly followed by an unsubtle giggle.

"I thought dragon hoards were myths," the former paladin whispered and despite her attempt to speak softly, her voice echoed through the chamber.

Skharr was willing to admit that he had also thought that no dragon would collect gold and shiny things when it had other more pressing matters to attend to. It was somewhat disconcerting to see evidence to the contrary staring him in the face. A massive pile of gold, silver, jewels, and a variety of armors, weapons, and charms waited to be collected.

"You could fucking swim in that," the halfling whispered with an eager grin on her face.

"Not one copper," he warned her sharply. "If the tales about dragon hoards are true, it'll have counted every last piece and will not stand for thievery."

"Are you shitting me?"

"We deal with the dragon first." His voice was firm and he glared to emphasize the order. "Do you want to fight a dragon when you're laden with too much treasure to walk?"

That appeared to get through to her and she mumbled something in her own tongue that he assumed was some kind of insult.

He was fine with that as he'd heard any number of insults

before. But he did not want to engage in a battle without one member of his party.

"You know, there might be an advantage to taking a little of the hoard," Cassandra whispered, unable to tear her gaze from the mound.

"You're mad."

"This is well-known. My point is that if the dragon treasures all this, it might be worthwhile to find ourselves something to hold in front of us so it does not kill us outright. It will possibly buy us a moment to speak to it."

Skharr opened his mouth to argue but it made some degree of sense. Especially if it were some kind of shield that could be used to protect them from an initial blast if things did go awry.

"Fine," he conceded. "But not too much. We do not want to be overladen."

"Thank the gods." Leahlu hissed in a breath and shook her fists in victory as she rushed to the pile.

"Remember, if you try to carry too much, you won't be able to dodge the flames and you'll fucking die."

His voice still carried, even though he had whispered, and he winced when she reached the treasure, sifted through it, and finally selected one of the charms. It looked like an eye with a massive black diamond in the center as the pupil.

"This has to be worth something," she commented and hung it around her neck.

The barbarian noticed a suit of plate armor in silver and black that appeared to be his size, but as tempted as he was, he moved past it, content for the moment with his gambeson. There were few things less pleasant in his mind than being cooked inside a suit of armor. He would claim it once the battle was over.

Instead, he collected a tower shield large enough to cover him from neck to shin. Four jewels were embedded at each corner of the rectangular barrier, and while it was made almost entirely of plate metal, there appeared to be some kind of a silver mirror in the very center where a boss should have been. The bottom had a pair of steel spikes, likely to be dug into the earth when it was necessary to stand one's ground.

He had no idea what or who it was for but it was certainly eye-catching, the kind of thing the dragon might not want to melt outright.

Not that he expected it to be much of a deterrent, but they could hope.

Cassandra finally found a spear that appealed to her. It was as long as she was tall and the blade extended about a foot and a half beyond the haft as well. Overall, it was almost as long as a short sword.

She swished it from side to side and displayed some skill with it.

All things considered, they would need as much help as they could find so perhaps their selections might have more practical use beyond dragon taming.

He paused suddenly and inclined his head as he sifted through a few stacks of coins. They had been pushed up to support what looked like a doll.

It was larger than most dolls he had seen and it was an odd thing to find in a dragon hoard. Although there was no sign of damage or scorch marks on the outside, it looked threadbare as if it had been there since the beginning. The dress was similarly worn but large buttons were attached where the eyes would be and a smile was worked in black thread into the pale-gray face.

It looked like it had been cleaned—obsessively so—and a handful of tears repaired over the years. As far as he was aware, no dragon in the world was capable of sewing, which meant a human had been allowed to approach and patch the rips.

That was extremely odd. He lifted the toy, which he guessed was stuffed with down, and noticed that the treasure around it had been arranged into what he could only describe as a bed.

It seemed increasingly like the dragon had cared for the doll, which was about Leahlu's size although considerably lighter given that it was filled with goose down. He wondered if it would have more value to the beast than anything else in the room.

"You're…uh, going to battle the dragon with a doll," Leahlu pointed out with a frown of disbelief. "That is an interesting tactic and I can honestly say the dragon will not suspect it."

Cassandra seemed similarly surprised that he had picked a doll up.

"I've never thought to find something like this in a dragon hoard," the barbarian explained. "It's been kept clean and there is no sign of dust. It has even been repaired over the years. I would say it is a clear indicator that the dragon, for some reason, cares for it. I found it in a bed of gold coins—one much like a green dragon might set up for itself but smaller."

"Do you think it might hold that doll dear to its heart?" Leahlu asked.

"I hope so." Skharr looked at it and shrugged. "I can't say I want to die holding it in my hand, though."

"It would be the kind of end that legends are made of," Cassandra pointed out.

Before anything else could be said, all three turned to look deeper inside the temple sanctuary. They could hear heavy steps approaching through one of the tunnels, which meant the dragon was coming.

The barbarian inched away from the treasure pile and Cassandra motioned for them to move into a small alcove at the side of the room and out of sight of the hoard. They hurried within and realized that a small window allowed them to observe what was happening with the hoard while they remained hidden.

He grasped both his new shield and the doll a little tighter. After a moment, he scowled and handed the toy to Leahlu. Her unasked question was answered when he strung his bow quickly as the footsteps drew even closer. If she wanted to be the one to draw the fucking bow, she was more than welcome to try.

The women understood and offered no protest, and he stood ready with the bow when the footsteps were finally close enough that they could see what made them.

An old dragon emerged, vastly older than any other he had seen—although admittedly, he hadn't encountered all that many. It must have been centuries old by the time it came to the temple and it felt like there was something decrepit about the way it walked.

Most dragons were able to move along the ground with only their four limbs, but this one used its wings as an extra pair to pull it forward while the lower legs moved closer. The scales gleamed in the light, which was the clearest indicator of a healthy dragon, but something else was wrong with it.

If Skharr had to guess, he'd happily bet that something was wrong in its mind—like a mental exhaustion it couldn't quite shake. He almost felt sorry for the beast.

But it was the dragon that had almost killed Cassandra, which was something to keep in mind. It was more than capable of flying and breathing fire on anything that approached it.

The massive beast pushed into the pile of treasure and appeared to enjoy the touch of the cool metals as it moved its tail to pull more over its back. It almost seemed to swim through to where the doll had been.

The barbarian tensed when the beast snorted softly as it reached the place and pawed through the jewels around the bed the doll had rested on. The tail flicked aggressively to fling coins and gold across the room as it searched again before it snorted a little more impatiently.

Cassandra looked surprised like she was willing to admit that he had made a good call with the doll. Having had no success in its search, the dragon now looked and seemed considerably more agitated.

She handed him one of the vials while she sipped the contents of the other before she passed it to Leahlu when she had finished.

Skharr pulled the stopper and immediately recoiled from the sour, bitter smell of it. He swallowed it quickly before he started to gag.

The liquid seared his mouth but seemed to take effect immediately. He was suddenly aware of something in the air that did not come from any of the three of them.

The feeling he sensed made him extremely nervous. The dragon was looking for something and it grew angrier by the second.

CHAPTER TWENTY-ONE

"**W**here is she?"

The voice struck her like a hammer and knocked the breath from her lungs for a moment until she realized that she felt it now more than heard it. What she heard with her physical ears was a roar, but the voice was suddenly clear in her head.

The elf hadn't swindled her after all. Still, she had the feeling that the elf had come away richer for the bargain. The book held the kind of power mages would kill for—provided one could read it—but in the end, while it was certainly valuable, it didn't profit her anything and there was little point in resenting Elanea because she could make sense of it.

All she could consider was what she was looking at now. If the potions earned her a way to keep the treasure they almost stood in, perhaps it was a godsbedammed good bargain for her as well.

She held the doll in her hand—having taken it from Leahlu who had thrust it at her when she received it from Skharr—and grimaced when another roar preceded the raving from the creature in the next room. For a moment only, she closed her eyes and drew a deep breath as she fought the need to run.

Memories of what awaited them outside were enough to freeze her in place and overcome the urge to escape. If she ran, the dragon would not need to do much to make sure she was nothing but ash in minutes.

Instead, she would stand her ground against a godsbedammed dragon. It didn't help that it looked like it was large enough to eat her whole, although it was probably smaller than that. Her mind no doubt made it look far larger than it truly was.

The beast stopped in its raving, turned, and grasped the piles of gold with its wings. Its legs, which had moved sluggishly before, were suddenly infused with energy when it sensed the intruders.

"Are you looking for something?" the former paladin shouted and stepped into full view. She felt like her voice impacted the rest of her body somehow and made it carry through the chamber with unnatural force.

The dragon looked at her and pushed a little higher with its wings as the massive red eyes, slitted like a cat's, caught sight of the doll in her hands.

"Not...something," it hissed, although she could not see the mouth move in anything other than a deep, rumbling growl. "Someone. Return Satar to me. Now!"

"Satar—is that her name?" Cassandra looked at the doll and tilted her head speculatively. "You know, she does look like a Satar to me now that you mention it."

"Do not patronize me, human. Your life is insignificant compared to mine, and all that an immortal will remember of you is an annoyance to be slapped aside."

"I would say you'll want to do a little more than that to me," Cassandra said and after a moment of consideration, tossed the doll forward to land on a stack of coins. She did not appear to be any the worse for wear, but the dragon rushed forward. Instead of attacking her outright, she was a little surprised to see that it moved directly toward the toy and balanced itself with its wings while it cradled it with its forelimbs.

Skharr and Leahlu stepped out from the enclave and the beast noticed them too.

"A whole troop of thieves," it grumbled and continued to stroke the doll tenderly. "Yet you approach me openly. It is odd but thieves must still die."

"I wondered if you needed more humans to fix...Satar," she answered and ignored how dry her mouth had become as she took a bold step forward. Intense heat radiated from the beast and sparks issued from its mouth as well. All it had to do to incinerate her was to press the liquid out of the sac in its neck and the whole space would go up in flames.

Which begged the question of why it hadn't done so already.

"We are here to free you from what has bound you to this place," she stated and took another step closer to the creature. It stared at her but now had to arc its neck to keep her in view with both eyes.

"Elves bound us here," it hissed softly, slithered across the gold, and placed the doll where Skharr had found it. "They smell different. They smell of the fucking elves—burn them! Burn them! Silence, Satar!"

The exchange made her study the dragon curiously. It sounded like it was addressing the doll and spoke in what she assumed was the toy's voice as well.

The former paladin took a step back and noticed that Leahlu was already invisible while Skharr stood motionless with his shield. She wouldn't back down but it had become increasingly clear that being bound to the location had not had a pleasant effect on the dragon.

"They will release us." The beast crawled to the doll again and looked at it. "After what we did to them? Never. They want to lower our guard and kill us once the geas is broken. One has disappeared and it will be there to stab us in the back. You watch and see."

"What did you do to us?" Cassandra asked.

"It acts like it has not heard of the destruction we wreaked on the city."

"Which city?"

The dragon turned to look at her and she could have sworn that she could see a gleam in its eyes and a smirk on its mouth, although that was possibly the effect of the potion.

"It has not heard."

She grasped her spear a little tighter and tried to keep her breathing even and stance relaxed.

"Which city?"

"All of them. All those they put in our path!"

That explained something. The dragon, whatever it had been before, was utterly livid. This was no innocent creature caught up in the greed of those who had bound it there. This place was meant to be its prison while the elves studied it, and she assumed it had made those who bound it pay with their lives.

"Cassandra, look out!"

The former paladin had already begun to turn a split second before the warning. The monster's tail slithered under the treasure and whipped around to catch her. She flung herself aside and a shower of coins and jewels hammered into her back as she rolled away from the strike.

Before it could press its advantage, Skharr had an arrow nocked to his bow. It whistled across the space but it didn't look like he hoped it would kill the beast on its own.

Surprisingly, the projectile impacted with sufficient force to pierce the dragon's shoulder and bury the head deep in the flesh, but not deeply enough. It had powered through the scales enough to injure it but achieved nothing more.

The roar that emerged in response had no words Cassandra could understand, and their adversary shifted on the treasure to assume a menacing posture that suggested an attack. Sparks flurried on its tongue as its entire neck contracted.

She could feel the heat from across the room as the flames lit the whole area when they were launched at Skharr. It was extremely odd to see the barbarian truly afraid as he rushed to where he had placed his shield.

"Godsbedammed scaly bag of rancid troll snot—fuck!"

In all honesty, she was as unconvinced as he looked that the large barrier would be of much help against dragonfire. It was aesthetically appealing but seemed puny when compared to the sheer fury of a dragon's flame. Expecting the worst, she gaped when the silver plate at the center glowed suddenly as the flames touched it. The blaze lost all power and extinguished immediately. The barbarian looked at the shield, his expression as shocked as she felt.

He hefted it and held it a little tighter when a flash of white light burst from the jewels on each corner. They streaked across the chamber and blasted a chunk of stone from the wall. Unprepared, he was thrown back three paces before he landed heavily, rolled across the stones, and lost his hold on the shield.

"Fucking hells—you're supposed to injure that thrice godsbedammed devil spawn, not me."

The shield had more to it than merely the impressive metalwork, that much was obvious, although from the shocked look on the warrior's face, it appeared that he had no idea what had happened or how it was done. A new expression slid into place that suggested the beginnings of an idea in his mind, but the dragon was not deterred by his unintended attack. It gave him no time to explore any possibilities and forced him into a sprint to evade another stream of flames cast at him.

The barbarian had saved her life with his warning, but if she allowed the beast to continue as it was, he would die and their adversary would set the whole room on fire in retaliation. Cassandra hefted her new spear and raced forward when the beast was distracted by Skharr. She vaulted over what looked like an ivory throne and stabbed her weapon into the creature's wing.

"I told you! They'll stab us in the back at the first opportunity. Burn them all. Turn them to ash."

She couldn't tell if it was the dragon or the doll speaking. Both clearly held an equal share of the creature's mind. She had heard of dark magic being used to turn dolls into sentient beings in their own right but it did not appear to be the case in this instance.

The beast had gone mad. It did not see humans as equals enough to satisfy its craving for company, so it pressed its madness into the doll it had collected. This inevitably created a link between them, to the point where it would bring captured humans to mend it and keep it company.

The former paladin could almost feel sorry for it if it weren't for how it had gleefully spoken of destroying whole cities. That was a matter for another time, however. Skharr was on his feet again and tried to scramble to reach the shield when the dragon turned its attention to Cassandra. She left her spear in its wing to pin it down and hold it in place as she rushed away and drew her sword, although she wasn't sure what she would do with it. The beast turned to locate her and she dove aside and its jaw snapped the air where she had stood only a moment before.

"Fuck!" A jeweled goblet dug into her hip as she stood quickly and tried to maintain her balance. She frowned when she caught a hint of movement. It appeared to be a shadow cast by the flames and it moved quickly. In the next moment, a dagger flicked out of nowhere, aimed at the dragon.

It was an impossible throw but the blade followed a perfect arc to bury itself between the scales of the monster. It sank in deeper than Skharr's arrow had, certainly deep enough to draw blood.

The monster roared again but the shadow continued to move

and vaulted onto the dragon. In a second, the dagger vanished again as Leahlu pulled it free.

"We see you, rat!" their adversary hissed and launched a shower of sparks in the direction of the shadow, quickly followed by a burst of dragonfire.

"Now see this, lard lizard."

Skharr was already on the move and leapt in front of the flames with the shield in hand. Once again, it absorbed the power of the flames and they disappeared almost instantly before the jewels glowed and he was launched back by the power of the resultant blast. The trajectory of the assault was thrown wide by his inability to stand firm and it pounded into a nearby pillar.

The blast was powerful enough to sear through the stone and the rocks it supported crumbled alarmingly. Cassandra had a feeling it would take more than that to bring the temple sanctuary to the ground but the shield was certainly an oddity. It seemed to have been created specifically to battle a dragon by turning the power of its flames against it and this suggested it was no coincidence that it was in the beast's hoard.

"A mighty throw, little one." Skharr grunted and pushed to his feet. He'd lost his hold on the shield again and limped forward carefully to retrieve it.

"Next time, remind me to throw you," Leahlu answered and must have touched her earring because she appeared again. "Did you have to fall on top of me?"

"It wasn't like I had time to plan every step."

The former paladin rushed to where they stood. The crumbling rocks were enough to distract the dragon for the moment but they were far from safe. It moved away from the rocks and hissed in pain before it ripped the spear out of its wing and flung the weapon aside.

"We need to get out of here," the halfling suggested.

"The outside area is coated by the liquid." Skharr shook his head and winced when he touched his side. "The moment we reach the doors, this whole place will go up in flames and we'll cook with it."

"What do you suggest then?" Cassandra asked.

"That shield is designed to fight dragons. If there was ever a way for us to defeat it, I'd say that will help."

"It is a great pity that it knocks you on your ass every time you try to use it."

"I'll find a way. We have to find a way to remain protected from the flames. Go!"

She knew what he planned. Separating their team would divide the dragon's attention. The fact that they hadn't been standing together was the only reason why they were still alive, but it wouldn't take long for their adversary to kill them one by one.

"You'd best turn invisible again," she told Leahlu, drew a deep breath, and summoned as much power as she could store in her body at the same time.

The armor would help to protect her but not from the ferocity of a dragon. She needed more. A magical shield would be enough to deflect the flames if she used it cunningly.

"I assume a dragon like you has a name," she shouted as it began to move a little closer. "Will you tell it to us before we die?"

"I have many names." It hissed, rose on its six limbs, and twisted its neck to look at her from above. "Those given to me by elves were soft and gentle, as sickening as rotten fucking flesh. Humans, in their simple tongue, gave me names that were abrasive and reflective of their fear. Of these, I prefer Gyrsun, the Winged Dread. All those who saw the sun glint on my glorious scales knew their death had come."

"I saw you once." She took a step forward and thrummed as the magic burned hot in her. "I lived and I've come to make sure nothing like that happens again. I was willing to let you find a place in the mountains where you could live in peace, but the Winged Dread is not a name for a creature that avoids conflict."

"Why would I avoid it? I am a god to you puny snot-nosed shits, and I'll revel in destroying everything you think elevates you from the mud you rose from. Why are we speaking to it? Kill them all! Now! This one survived me once. Not many can say the same."

It was talking to the doll again and the former paladin was surprised that its madness was intrusive to the point that it would interrupt itself while speaking.

"I'm not as insignificant as you might think I am. I met an actual god once."

"Then you will die with the memory." The dragon returned its attention to her. "What is your name? Perhaps you will be remembered when you die."

"I am Cassandra, the Barbarian Princess, and I will be remembered when I die." She grasped her sword firmly and met the beast's gaze. "But it will not be this day."

She could see the fire building the moment she said her name, and the heat touched her face while they were still ten paces apart. All the power she had surged forward to deflect the flames away from her and where she could see the rest of her group.

It was the least she could do. The dragon couldn't see her through the blaze and she gritted her teeth as she pushed into motion. The heat made it a genuinely painful endeavor but she managed to retrieve the spear the creature had discarded and ran on to where she could hopefully find cover.

And where, hopefully, her partner had some kind of plan brewing in his crazed barbarian mind.

CHAPTER TWENTY-TWO

A mad dragon, he thought with a sense of inevitability. He had always known that when he died, it would be by something out of the ordinary and this certainly qualified. Not many dragons were left in the world and of course, he would have to battle the one that had lost its mind.

Then again, he had no idea how many of them were truly sane by the human definition of the word. Perhaps they were all self-aggrandizing bloodthirsty maniacs that had conversations with dolls.

His opinion on the matter had little relevance, however. He had long since moved past a need to understand and besides, it was time to fight—especially if he hoped to avoid this utterly weird end to his life.

Skharr had no idea how to use the shield. He was certain that the blast it produced when it encountered the dragonfire would be capable of at least wounding the beast, but there was no way to aim it. And even then, there was no way to tell if it could die. It was said that a geas of particular power could keep the subject alive to hold it to what it was bound to.

He looked above them at the top of the chamber, which was

supported by numerous pillars, all of which showed signs of dwarf work. Perhaps he would not be able to aim at the dragon, but if he could bury the monster beneath the ceiling, it might not matter.

It was a possibility, but not one he could fully entertain while running for his life. Breathing deeply was painful and his ribs protested with every step. He wasn't sure if the next blast would be enough to kill him but it would certainly leave him less able to fight. The barbarian wasn't sure which and was not anxious to find out until he was certain that it was a blast that would end the fight.

He could see Leahlu moving about the chamber. She was fast for a halfling, and while he was certain that the dragon could see her, it was more concerned with easier targets. Hells, if they weren't able to fight their way out, there was a chance that she would at least be able to leave there alive.

It wasn't the most pleasant thought but fighting a dragon would never be a pleasant situation.

He dove behind a group of rocks when another blast of fire filled the room. Cassandra was running as well but the dragon had turned its attention to him now and the flames began to heat the rock he huddled behind. If it continued its assault, it would start to cook him too.

"Oy, you there, you winged bag of stinking hot air!" Cassandra's voice was not difficult to hear, even with the blazing fire around him. She was on her feet with the spear in her hand and she steadied it and threw with the kind of precision he had never been able to summon with spears. Not that he was unable to use them but it was still difficult and he'd not attained anything close to mastery of the weapon. Bows and arrows came more naturally to him.

The spear flew true and buried itself deep in the creature's body. There was something magical to it like his sword, and it sliced smoothly through the scales to dig deep and dragged another wordless roar from their adversary. The injury wasn't enough to kill it but it was a significant wound nonetheless and turned its attention to her again.

"I think I like that new name for you," the former paladin shouted, rolled her neck, and flexed her fingers. "It's human and abrasive, certainly, but I don't think it has the kind of fear that gets you hard, now does it?"

It launched a blast of fire toward her but she raised her shield in time, deflected it, and thrust it away and into the wall behind her, although the force knocked her onto her side.

Skharr rushed to where his bow had fallen when he first took the brunt of his shield's blast. He skidded across the floor as he snatched both bow and quiver, nocked an arrow quickly, and drew and loosed it in a smooth motion without a pause or even regaining his feet.

The shot was compromised by his haste. He had aimed for the creature's eye but the projectile sailed well to the right and drove into its neck instead. Unfortunately, it didn't penetrate enough to kill it either.

"I have to get enchanted arrowheads, I fucking swear," he promised himself as the massive creature spun with remarkable ease to engage him instead of his partner. He didn't mean the words but they sounded encouraging. Given the rate at which he lost arrows, he would have to pay a godsbedammed fortune every time he needed to restock. Besides, he wasn't even sure if there was such a thing as enchanted arrowheads.

Still, his attack achieved what it was intended to, which was to buy them time. There would be no sudden killing of the beast and they needed to outlast it and wear it down.

His partners, fortunately, seemed to have the same idea although they hadn't discussed it. As the large, slitted eyes turned to him, the dagger launched at the beast and sank home, this time in the monster's tail to pin it in place. it roared and twisted to see where it was being attacked. The shadow Leahlu scrambled away from where the massive teeth snapped toward her and yanked the spear from where it was buried in the creature.

Blood flowed from the open wound and the spear vanished until it appeared in the air when she threw it to Cassandra.

"Get up," the halfling shouted. "I don't want to find out what the barbarian princess smells like while she's being cooked alive."

Skharr was partial to her being alive as well. He retrieved another two arrows, planted both in a crack between the flag-stones in front of him, and selected another and aimed as the dragon tracked Leahlu. It couldn't see her, not entirely, but it was able to follow her movements as he could through the shadows cast by the flames around them.

He wasn't about to let the halfling be killed while helping them. Another arrow released from his bow and sank into the creature's shoulder to force its attention onto him again. He stretched to pull one of the arrows free, paused, and gaped for a moment.

"Son of a motherfucking vermin-infested stinking cock-sucking whore," he whispered, yanked both arrows out, and raced away but a burst of flame followed him. He could feel it blistering his heels and his back and his gambeson caught fire when it came too close. The barbarian flung himself prone and rolled to extinguish the flames when he reached the shield. He picked it up smoothly as he regained his feet and ignored the agony that rushed through his body as he sprinted farther from the flames.

An idea penetrated his somewhat panicked thoughts. It would probably not end well for him but if it killed the snake-eyed, death-breathing fucking overgrown lizard, he didn't much care beyond that.

"What are you doing?" Cassandra called as the little shadow rushed toward the dragon. Leahlu didn't appear to tire and the other woman raced forward as well since their adversary appeared to be busy with him for the moment.

He was too out of breath to explain but circled quickly and drew their adversary's attention as far away from his comrades as he could. It came as no surprise to feel more heat behind him.

"Run all you want, little humans." The dragon cackled with appropriately insane laughter. "You will all burn!"

"I'll pass on that, thank you!" Skharr retorted and skidded into an alcove that was deep enough to keep the flames away from him for a moment. He tucked his arrows into their quiver and placed both it and his bow in the safest corner, hoping he would be alive to retrieve them again.

Leahlu yanked her dagger from where it had stuck in the beast. There was no magic to it, but he had a feeling there was something in the amulet with the eye that guided her throws and enabled her to strike the monster repeatedly in the perfect places. It now bled from a dozen wounds but didn't appear to have slowed in the slightest. He had hoped to land an arrow in the sac with the liquid it spat out and which burned so hot when it did, but it was too well-protected.

"Why do I always think of these things?" he wondered aloud. "I honestly will fucking die."

It was a fate that was inevitable for all men, and dying while killing a dragon was the kind of tale he would want people to tell about him.

Still, he'd prefer it if it was well in the future and wished he had a better idea than this.

Skharr drew his sword and studied the beast while it tried to determine a target. It grew increasingly annoyed with the small shadow creature who injured it repeatedly with unerring throws of her dagger. Cassandra, however, proved to be a threat as well with her spear. She slashed a deep gash on the creature's forelimb before she retreated to a safer distance, only to attack again when it was distracted by Leahlu.

Without thinking too hard about what he intended, the

barbarian rushed from his cover, hefted his sword, and threw it at the beast as hard as he could.

It spun and as if guided by the magic in it, the blade burrowed into the dragon's chest all the way to the hilt.

Unfortunately, it was far from deep enough. The dragon paused in its attack, hissed, and growled in pain as it focused its attention only on him.

"Get back!" he roared and stared into the unsettling red eyes. "This godsbedammed hell-spawned scaly fucking lizard wyrm is mine."

"You would kill us with a shield?" The dragon growled, took a step forward, and pulled the blade from its body to toss it carelessly to the side. "Are all barbarians this brave? This foolish?"

"I assume you haven't fought many of us." Skharr stood his ground and steeled himself as their adversary approached. "But yes."

"You think to use my power against me exactly as the elves did when they forged that shield. They, however, are dead. At least you put up more of a fight than they did."

The barbarian grinned, planted the shield into the ground, and nodded when the two spikes dug into the rock to lock it in place as the dragon's mouth opened. Its tongue snapped and crackled with sparks and the fluid surged first. It was immediately engulfed in the fire that streaked toward him.

It was, he decided, an incredibly bad idea. His gambeson was singed while the flames still approached and he closed his eyes and simply prepared himself for the worst.

In the next moment, the blaze disappeared when the mirror in the center absorbed all the heat and the power from it—power, he now realized, that belonged to the dragon in the first place. In that moment, he tightened his hold on the shield and twisted while it remained locked into the stone to aim it away from his enemy.

The blast battered his shoulder painfully and he didn't realize that he had fallen until he stared at the effects of the power from the gemstones on the shield when it pounded through the pillars that arched into the ceiling.

He hadn't been able to see if Cassandra and Leahlu had heeded his warning and all he could do was roll away as the ceiling started to collapse. Boulders the size of houses began to plummet onto the dragon in the center of the room.

Skharr covered his face and coughed as the entire chamber was suddenly filled with dust but the falling ceiling immediately extinguished most of the fires.

Finally, when it appeared that the worst of the destruction was over, he stood warily and probed his shoulder carefully. The impact of the shield had left it very tender—and even worse, he realized, the arm had been pulled from the socket and even the slightest movement triggered a searing pain through his body. He sank to his knees again and gritted his teeth.

A deep breath was all he could manage. It had been a while since he'd taught himself to heal these kinds of injuries or at least treat them to the point where he could continue to fight. He closed his eyes and used his good arm to brace the other as he twisted it into place. Another surge of pain burned through his body and he grimaced as he drew deep breaths until it eased.

"Sonofagodsbedammedbutt-fuckingtroglodyte."

The ache remained as a dull throb but he could move his arm again. That, at least, was a boon given the overall dismal outlook to their predicament.

He turned his attention to where the shield was still planted in the rock. The blast had affected it as well and had, in fact, cracked it in half and almost blasted it apart. The mirror and gems appeared intact, at least, but the shield would certainly not be of any use.

Hells, if it took that kind of punishment again, it would likely explode and hurl pieces of shrapnel indiscriminately to kill all those in the vicinity.

Thankfully, it would not need to be used again. He patted the top of it and grinned when it wobbled in place.

"Skharr, get down!"

Something struck him from behind. It was a little too low to be Cassandra but still had enough power to upend him as something bright and blue crackled over his head. It moved too quickly to be seen but was very clearly reminiscent of lightning and carved a blue streak through the area as it struck the walls instead of him.

He looked around and his gaze settled on Leahlu. She was covered in dust but otherwise none the worse for wear as she handed him his sword.

"So you aren't dead yet?" the barbarian asked as he took the weapon. She grinned and shook her head.

"Close, but we have work to do yet."

Skharr nodded and turned to where the dragon was pinned under dozens of boulders far larger than it was. It was buried under the weight but it twisted and tried to yank itself free. While it hissed in fury and pain, it attempted to summon more fire but the sac in its neck was crushed as well and did not respond to the call.

"Crushed," it screeched, "but not dead. I'll burn you all with my last breath."

"It's time to prove the nutty wyrm wrong," Leahlu whispered, touched her earring, and vanished. The warrior ducked as another flash of lightning coursed through the empty air above him.

"Aye," he agreed and adjusted his hold on his sword. "It's time to put an end to this."

CHAPTER TWENTY-THREE

S kharr certainly did have a way with plans, even impromptu ones that redefined the accepted levels of insanity. There had been no way to kill the dragon, so all he could do was bring the whole place down on them. Cassandra had no idea if he intended to kill the fucker and did not expect to live through the attack but somehow, they had all survived.

The disadvantage, of course, was that the beast had survived as well.

"Son of a godsbedammed sheep fucker," she whispered. It was surely in its death throes as nothing could survive having that much rock plummet onto it from such a height. When the sparks of lightning filled the room, however, she realized that it was as deadly now as it had been before. It jerked in fury and tried to pull itself free, even though all it seemed to accomplish was to exacerbate the wounds in its body.

But it could still kill them while it thrashed wildly. She had to put it out of its suffering. Perhaps she could find a way to let it go peacefully.

She grasped her new spear, watched the blood drip from it as it usually did from Skharr's sword, and smiled as she shook her head.

"Barbarians with magical weapons," she whispered. "How very odd."

The former paladin wouldn't look that particular gift horse in the mouth—not yet, at least. The fact that most of the treasure was now buried under tons of rock was another problem they would have to deal with later.

Skharr kept himself low as the dragon's attention was focused on him, and she pushed closer and made sure to remain behind the massive boulders. Any thought that they would keep her safe if the dragon turned its mind toward her disappeared as she saw another streak of lightning leap across the room to touch one of the boulders. It shattered it and scattered the hundreds of pieces across the floor.

All she could hope for was to remain unseen. Cassandra studied her spear for a moment and wondered what it was capable of. There was always a possibility that they could retreat and return when the dragon was dead, but it felt wrong—the kind of decision she would regret. She abhorred the cowardice of injuring an animal and letting it die in agony. It simply wasn't in her and she doubted that it was in Skharr either.

There was no way to tell if Leahlu felt the same, but she was willing to bet that the halfling, having remained to this point and even saved the barbarian's life, would see things through until the end.

She calmed her mind and closed her eyes for a moment of silent prayer. While she wasn't sure why she was praying or what for, it was something that came from too much time spent as a paladin.

It calmed her, nevertheless, and she rushed out from behind the boulder she had been hiding behind and moved as quickly as she could. Skharr noticed her and a hint of panic touched his face when he realized what she was about to do. He looked desperate to keep the dragon focused on him.

In all honesty, it wasn't the decision she had hoped he would take. Cassandra raised her hands and pushed a shield up to block a moment before another bolt of lightning lashed out, caught the barrier, and deflected into one of the walls and thankfully collapsed a section of it as she had suspected it would. Something prevented them from falling and she had a feeling it was the same power that kept the dragon contained in the fucking temple sanctuary.

The binding was obviously weakening if it was able to scour the Seastones, but it was still tied to the place where it would die.

Her shield drew the dragon's attention to her, and she realized that she had to make another attack as it twisted and rolled its neck beneath the rocks that trapped it. The slitted eyes fixed on her immediately and lightning crackled from its tongue, and she knew it would be unleashed to kill her in a moment.

A flash of steel caught the meager light and Leahlu's blade buried itself in the monster's eye. The attack diverted its attention for a brief moment and she vaulted onto the closest boulder and lunged forward. A scream erupted from her throat as she powered the spear in a thrust driven by all the power she could manage.

The long head cut cleanly through the dragon scales and sliced through to the other side. The monster's blood splashed across her skin, impossibly warm and almost painfully hot as she drove it down far enough that the spear tip pierced the stone beneath.

Pinned, bleeding, and dying, she could see the fight suddenly leave the beast. It was tired and it sagged as it heaved a deep, shuddering breath.

Panting and out of breath, Cassandra dropped to a knee beside it. "I'm sorry it had to come to this. I...I truly am."

Oddly enough, she meant it too. The potion still maintained

its effect and as the fight ended, she could almost feel the pain radiating from the dragon. The worst part was that the agony of its wounds was dull compared to something deeper within, a pain that had drained the strength from its body for decades.

"The geas..." the dragon called and heaved as she ran her fingers lightly over its scales. "Please. Only one moment without it before I die...please."

"How?"

"Reach for it."

The instruction seemed simple but a little strange. Still, the former paladin felt around her with a magical touch and found it easily. The sensation it gave off was very much like a leash. She raised a hand and pushed a hint of power into a shield but only enough to cut the geas. It dissipated immediately once the line was severed.

For a moment, it looked like the creature would rise again but all she could see was a sudden relaxation accompanied by something like a long, slow sigh as it sank into the rubble. She extended her hand to touch the scales again. There was no way to heal the wounds they had inflicted but for a moment, at least, she could ease its pain and let it live its last moments without agony.

"Your touch is kind, unlike most humans. Are all barbarians like you?"

She looked as Skharr and Leahlu approached. They studied her closely, confused by her actions.

She saw no need to explain it. The potion had revealed the madness the beast had felt and while she couldn't allow it to unleash its fury and insanity on the world, it seemed only fair to let its last moments be peaceful.

"I cannot speak for all of my kin," Cassandra answered as the dragon's eye shifted to look at her. "But what I have learned was from those I knew. Fight with all you have but show no viciousness. The need to inflict pain is a base thing left to base folk."

"Those are wise words. I might have...followed them one day."

It was close to death and she closed her eyes and tried to help it to drift into sleep and dreams.

"I cannot say I ever taught you that," Skharr commented. "I'm quite fond of unleashing pain on those who deserve it."

"That's what separates you from barbarian royalty." The former paladin stood, took hold of her spear, and yanked it free. There was no reaction from the neck when she drew it out.

Her words were meant to be a joke but they felt empty even to her ears. She shook her head and drew a deep breath as she looked at the fallen dragon.

"Are you hurt?" he asked.

Cassandra looked at a few bumps and scrapes across her body. Nothing seemed serious, although she could see he had taken more of a beating. His gambeson had caught fire a couple of times and a few of the marks had burned deeply enough to scorch the skin as well. She could tell that he tried to hide it, but he was injured and in need of some time to recover.

"We should start a fire," she suggested and looked at Leahlu, who nodded. "See that you take some healing potions and perhaps have some koffe before we decide what to do with the coin you didn't manage to bury under the mountain."

"It saved our lives but yes, I suppose it did result in a fair amount of inconvenience."

He turned to move to where their horses had been left but she placed a hand on his shoulder.

"Sit your ass down and take some potions."

She would not allow him to disagree and he groaned softly as he settled on a rock while the halfling proceeded to build a small fire. By the time the former paladin returned with Horse and Strider in tow, it blazed happily. He winced from the effects of the potions he had taken while seated beside it.

Leahlu wandered around the cavern. It was no longer protected and the halfling couldn't restrain herself from exploring the riches that remained.

"You'll need some real armor," Cassandra said as she sat next to the fire and filled a pot with water, added the koffe, and placed it on the blaze. "That gambeson has seen the last of its days."

Skharr nodded, removed it with a grimace of pain, and inspected it closely. "I fear that no amount of patching will make it whole again."

"Why didn't you find better armor before? You would think the Barbarian of Theros would have the time and the money to find something more suitable."

"Knights walk around in plate armor," he answered and shook his head. "Mercenaries parade about in their chainmail hauberks. A gambeson suits me well enough. It's good enough to travel in and good enough to fight in. All I need is a helm and I'm ready for battle."

Cassandra raised an eyebrow and he shook his head.

"I lost mine."

"We're in a room full of armor, weapons, and gold. You might as well choose something from what is available."

"I already have." He held up the silver mirror and the gemstones from the ruined shield. "There's still magic left in them. The shield is ruined, but I know a dwarf who might be able to make something of the pieces. A weapon that can withstand a dragon attack would be of great interest to those in the mountains."

The former paladin pulled the pot off the fire and poured the black liquid through a mesh that kept the ground koffe inside while it allowed the water infused with it out. She poured two cups and handed one to him.

"To Abirat," she whispered.

"To that godsbedammed fucking madman." Skharr agreed and took a sip.

She grinned and shook her head as she shifted her focus to where Leahlu approached them. The halfling had filled her purse with coins and jewels but she wore a pair of bracers that looked like they had been taken from the hoard as well.

"What do you think?" she asked.

"Are they magical?" The former paladin stood to inspect them.

"I would say so." Leahlu looked at Skharr. "Come on, I'd like to see what they can do to you."

He raised his hand. "Thank you, but I'm still recovering from my bout with a dragon."

The halfling grinned and turned. Her gaze finally selected a boulder about her size to attack and she threw a hard punch into it.

Cassandra grinned at Skharr's surprise when their partner's fist shattered a chunk of the boulder's corner with no sign of injury to her hand.

"See, that is why I do not volunteer my body for experimentation." The warrior laughed.

"Aye." Leahlu smirked. "I pity the fool who calls me half-pint when their dick is at my eye level and my uppercut can—"

"I can imagine the result," he stated quickly and moved his hands instinctively to protect his groin.

The other woman laughed. "I'm glad you found something that appeals to you."

"You don't care if I leave?" the halfling asked.

"We would be sad to see you leave," she answered. "But you've proven your worth ten times over. You've fulfilled your oath to the geas and it's severed. If that is what you wish, you're free to go with as much treasure as you can carry."

"I have already seen to that." Leahlu patted her bulging coin purse. "As much as I hate to leave the rest of it to you, I am rich now. I think I'll wander to that city four days away and from there, return home."

Cassandra smiled as the halfling embraced her warmly. "Travel safely. And take shit from no man. You have the means to make them pay now."

"I will. And I do." She moved to where Skharr now stood and embraced him too.

A moment later, his eyes widened and he snatched at the hand that pinched his ass and lunged forward in an attempt to retaliate. The halfling was already out of his reach, however, and laughed wickedly as she ran toward the doors.

The barbarian shook his head and sat again as his partner sat beside him.

"I'm a little worried about her, to be honest," she admitted after a few minutes had passed.

"She's capable enough," he reminded her. "Plus, she has an earring that turns her invisible and bracers that make her about as strong as I am. She'll be fine. But if she changes her mind, we will not leave here immediately. She can find us here or on the path if she needs to."

"That is true enough."

A little sadness tugged at her heartstrings as she left the two behind. She had been dragged into the situation by them, of course, but if nothing else, she now knew she could battle a dragon if she wanted to.

To remind herself of this and move past the surprising sense of what might be called nostalgia, she drew her dagger from her belt and twisted it a few times between her fingers before she thrust it into its sheath again.

The sound of a donkey braying almost made her miss the sheath the first time, and Leahlu looked up as it slid home on her second attempt, ready to draw it again if trouble approached.

An elderly human who leaned heavily on his walking stick and who was followed closely by an ass that had grown long in the tooth did not suggest much of a threat. Still, her hand remained on her dagger although she did not bother to touch the jewel in her earring.

The old man's eyes narrowed when she approached and he straightened his back. He continued to lean on the walking stick, although it was considerably less convincing now.

"Hello again, sister," he said cheerfully as she approached. "Fancy seeing you here."

The world shifted as she approached him. The earth was suddenly a little farther away, and her legs moved her forward with a little more speed and efficiency.

By the time she was within arm's reach of the man, she stood at his height. Her hair had gone from curly and brown to straight and black, and her ruddy skin had paled considerably.

"What are you doing here, brother?" she asked and regarded him with her head tilted speculatively.

"I came to see what you were playing at."

"I have been helping, no thanks to you," Ahverna replied with a small smile. "I'll never understand why you rely on humans to kill the godsbedammed dragons for you."

"There are rules."

"Fuck the rules," she retorted. "That barbarian of yours has earned me a mountain full of followers."

"Skharr is anything but my barbarian." Theros chuckled and his form began to change as well. In seconds, his thinning beard was thick and full and his hair long, and the stick in his hand had transformed into a spear. "If you knew anything about barbarians, DeathEaters in particular and that one specifically, you would know that possessing them is a futile exercise and not worth the effort."

Ahverna shook her head as he plucked his donkey up when the beast diminished in size and he placed it in his pocket.

"Well, you're probably right about that," she conceded.

"As a half-god, you have a little more leniency, I suppose. I did not notice any fluctuations in our reality due to your meddling."

"I didn't meddle."

"Oh? You did not avail yourself of the barbarian's dragon?"

Ahverna's face contorted into something close to disgust. "I will never understand referring to one's genitals in that fashion. Besides, do you know how large a halfling is? It would take a miracle for that to work."

"Hmm." Theros tugged thoughtfully at his beard. "So no miracles occurred?"

"Not that it is any of your business as you do not claim him as your barbarian, but no. I did not want to feel the steel of your paladin. I was led to understand that she was not the sharing type."

"But you would have?"

"What the hell does it matter to you? Do you and my asshole of a half-brother Janus have some kind of wager in place?"

The god coughed and looked away. "Whatever your intentions, I do appreciate your assistance. Cassandra is special to me and without your help, I fear a very different result would have come to pass."

"I would not be too sure of that." She patted him on the shoulder. "They are utterly mad and insanely skilled at creating mayhem. You should have a little more faith in them both."

Theros grunted in response. "Well, I must tell them that I need Cassandra on another quest for me."

"And Skharr?"

"I am afraid not." He sighed deeply. "She needs to continue to heal and the scrying suggests that having him present will interfere with that."

"Why?" Ahverna scoffed. "Will she be too focused on his—ugh —his dragon?"

Another cough from the high god indicated, as it had already, that there was some truth to what she had said.

"The scrying did not suggest the why," he finally said but it sounded weak. "Only that the augury did not bode well."

"Hmm. It seems she will not lay claim to all his attention then."

Theros' eyes narrowed. "What?"

She smiled and waggled her fingers at him in farewell. "I said I wonder where all her attention will focus instead."

CHAPTER TWENTY-FOUR

"You could do whatever you want in life," Skharr said softly. "You have enough coin to open a shop of your own, create dresses, and have others sell them and make them for you without ever needing to stab someone again. Even if some of it is lost under the rubble."

"Most of it," Cassandra pointed out but he did have a point. "Still…you're right. I can hardly believe it. There's more wealth in here than most dukes or even kings can boast of. Hells, I think even your friend the emperor would be hard-pressed to find this much wealth in his vaults."

He nodded and sat beside her. "That's true enough."

She turned to look at him. "Doesn't it tempt you? This kind of wealth?"

The barbarian stared directly ahead for a few moments before he sighed softly. "I would be lying if I said no. But I've learned to take what is needed along with a little extra as a cushion. Otherwise…well, my life will be shackled. I'm not a barbarian who would do well shackled."

The former paladin stood and looked at him. "So to you, wealth is…"

"A shackle, yes."

"And a relationship? Would you find that similarly binding?"

He paused before he answered. "It can be, depending on who and when. I am not against such things but I'll admit that I fear the responsibility."

"You?" She turned away and drew a deep breath before she focused on him again. "You fear something?"

Skharr laughed at the question, which wasn't the kind of reaction she had expected. "There is much in the world that I fear. That dragon is the latest but certainly not the last."

"Why would you fear a relationship?"

"Not a relationship." His expression turned more serious. "But the responsibility implied. If I am to be with one person, what if that person decided their life needs a change? What if I am changed?"

"What? That you might retire and settle as the owner of some tavern?"

"No, but it is a thought. At least if I owned a tavern, I would enjoy a fight or two at every moon or so."

She shook her head. "Honestly? If you were to settle down, the decision would not be guided by hiring tempting wenches to serve food but to fight?"

"If a woman were to guide my mind like that, she would always have my heart," the barbarian answered, his voice softer than he perhaps intended it to be. "At that point, there will be only one cave for my dragon."

Cassandra sat again and smiled. "I…well, that is…"

"An odd thing for a man to describe his cock as, wouldn't you say?" said a voice behind them. They both pushed hurriedly to their feet and turned to a familiar face, although his younger features made it a little more difficult to identify. "Covered in scales and breathing fire. I suppose that might be an apt analogy for a barbarian but perhaps not others."

"Theros." The warrior showed no sign of the kind of deference most men would have when faced with a god.

She didn't bow either but drew herself tall before Theros despite his godlier appearance.

He didn't appear to mind and approached the rubble the dragon was buried under and dropped to his haunches to inspect the dead beast a little more closely.

"You killed it," he said and looked at the barbarian.

"No," Skharr responded and shifted his gaze to his partner. "She tried to talk to it and to convince it to let us release it from this place. As it turned out, that would have proven an even larger threat. It was completely mad so it was a choice between killing the demented creature or dying. She chose the higher calling."

"I see." Theros chuckled softly. "My brother the ass did wonder how you would explain it."

"I couldn't spare either a shit or a piss over what your brother the ass thinks."

The god nodded before he turned to his erstwhile paladin. "Are you still wearing this armor?"

"I'm still on sabbatical," she reminded him. "I'll fight the good fight as I always have but until I am willing to accept the requirements of being your paladin again, my mind leans toward a life as a barbarian instead."

"My...second barbarian?" He raised an eyebrow.

"Fuck that. I'll be your barbarian princess, the first of my kind." She smiled and decided she liked the sound of that even more now that there was no fight to distract her from her consideration of it. "Except this princess might desire to kill a few of the unholy shits. What was done to this creature was beyond horrifying. It might have been a selfish dragon but not evil."

"It does suggest that one should be careful what type of creature you try to form a geas with," Theros agreed.

"I wouldn't say the halfling was a creature," Skharr responded and shook his head. "There is much that we could discuss about her need to pilfer and steal everything she laid eyes on, yes, but she saved my life while we fought that dragon and she did not need to. I'll not stand for anyone calling her a creature."

"No indeed. I would treat her as though she were my kin."

The barbarian's eyes narrowed and even Cassandra turned to look at the god, who laughed softly.

"She has always been fond of the oddest disguises."

"You're one to talk," Skharr responded.

"The appearance of an old man traveling the world has served me well and for a variety of purposes. But my half-sister finds the oddest forms to take."

"Your half-sister?"

"You remember Ahverna, do you not? Goddess of Thieves—the one your dwarf prayed to when you traveled with him. What was his name?"

"Brahgen. You…do you mean to say that Leahlu…"

"Was Ahverna, yes. And the halfling is one of her less odd faces. She took the form of a warhorse once, many years ago. At another time, she took the face of a half-troll, half-man beast and assumed the position of a king over a small, uncivilized plot of land."

"Ahverna was Kharos the Mad?" the former paladin asked.

"You have heard the tales then?"

Skharr shook his head. "I've never heard them."

"In that form, she was as mad as a spring hare," the god explained and sat. "She led her armies to burn and pillage anything they encountered. I suppose, as the goddess of thieves, this was the finest way to show her appreciation. It was when she sacked the city of Moranis that action needed to be taken. Paladins were raised and stories of how Kharos was a demon in human form were spread. An army stormed her fortress in the mountains and hundreds died in the assault."

"Three paladins reached the inner keep," Cassandra continued. "Maelus, Saran, and Teluv. The story is that they battled the demon into the night until they almost succumbed to exhaustion. Then, Theros showed his power and gave them strength, even though only Maelus was his paladin, and this enabled them to overcome the demon's power and take the victory."

The barbarian sighed and rubbed his temples. "I assume you have a better idea of what happened that day?"

Theros shrugged. "I did appear to the three paladins that day, and to my sister. A few words convinced her that if the attack failed, a real invasion would happen—one powered by the wills of the combined gods. It would involve the kind of power even she would not be able to protect herself against. I convinced her that if she faked her death and found other means to occupy her time, there would be no need for it."

"Why were you alone?" Skharr asked. "Why was Janus not with you?"

"It…might have been my brother's suggestion that led her to assume the form of the giant," he admitted and refused to meet his gaze. "If he had made an appearance, it would have only made matters worse. Once Ahverna agreed, I infused the paladins with a little more power and allowed them to defeat the demon very convincingly. The illusion was easy to perpetrate as the three were exhausted and the fire spread quickly."

"I learned at the feet of Maelus." Cassandra shook her head. "He taught me almost everything I know about being a paladin. Although he was almost a hundred years old at the time, his legend was such that it elevated him in the ranks of the paladins."

"He was certainly a loyal paladin but perhaps not my best." Theros shook his head. "And now you see why I consider Ahverna taking a halfling's face was the least concerning disguise she has assumed. I don't need to tell you that she's wandered about and stolen from kings, fucked lords, and made them steal for her instead. I truly was curious about her interest in you, Skharr."

The woman narrowed her eyes as she turned to face him. "Yes. Her interest in you is interesting."

"Not particularly. I helped one of her few followers. I assume there are few enough who would be willing to do so and she was therefore curious."

"You are an atrocious liar," she challenged. "Why would you fuck a goddess?"

"More importantly, why would the goddess be so interested in you thereafter?" Theros shook his head. "It does not matter but it does beg the question—should I fuck you to find out what the appeal is?"

Skharr turned to look at the god and even Cassandra couldn't tell if he was joking.

"What?"

"I could turn myself into a woman if I wanted to. The concept never appealed to me, however. My consciousness in that regard is considerably less…fluid you might say. And yet—"

"No." The barbarian shook his head. "No. Do not— You would not be—"

"Well, it does have its advantages," Cassandra pointed out.

He turned to look at her with utter confusion.

She stared at him before she cleared her throat. "You…shouldn't."

Theros shrugged. "Either way, certain questions need answers. And fear not, I have no real interest in you either, Skharr."

"Is that why you follow me around the fucking world?" he asked. "Because you are not interested in me?"

"That is not…you…" The god shook his head.

It was odd how two men could make the conversation of sex so uncomfortable. She could only imagine how uncomfortable they were although the reason escaped her entirely. Cassandra shook her head.

"It does beg the question," Theros said and changed the subject, "of what you will do with the riches you now possess."

The barbarian shrugged. "I will do as I always have—take what Horse and I can carry and be on our way. There might be a few interesting trinkets to be acquired here and there as well, but mostly for curiosity's sake."

"You could buy a farm," the god suggested. "And live a life of peace."

"I've tried that. Old men with maps of treasure and danger tend to find me regardless."

"Indeed, and yet this…" Theros gestured to the wealth around them. "This is the ultimate treasure. You could become royalty again if you wished it."

"Again?" Cassandra asked. "You never told me that particular tale."

"Apologies." The god smirked and shook his head. "Did I say that aloud?"

"Aye." Skharr fixed a glare on him before he turned to Cassandra. "It was but a season before I realized that being a monarch was…"

He struggled to find the correct word but she knew what it was.

"Constricting," she agreed. "As a great deal of wealth would be as well."

"It is not a barbarian's way."

"So, you merely take what you can carry along with those interesting baubles?" Theros asked.

Skharr nodded.

The god turned his gaze to his former paladin. "And you, Barbarian Princess?"

"The same, I suppose." She nodded. "Skharr might grunt considerably—both horizontally and often when vertical." She winked at him. "But I feel his answer is the wise one, nonetheless. To take on more shackles is not what will save me. Freedom might."

"Then what should I do with the rest of this?" Theros asked, looked around, and gestured at the treasure strewn through the room. "I can't simply leave it lying around for any dumb shit to find."

The barbarian shook his head. "You might find another dragon that would be willing to accept it. Not only would you earn yourself a little goodwill with the dragon, but any dumb shit would have to earn the treasure through clever thievery or impressive battle skills."

"Well, that is a rather clever solution," the god agreed. "There might be problems if the wrong hands take possession of some of the items here, though. Aside from that, it would not be wise to simply leave it and hope it remains undiscovered."

Cassandra leaned a little closer and bumped Skharr with her hip. "Is he talking about the economic problems that come with large treasure hoards?"

"Yes," he agreed. "Although I am not sure of the implications myself. Thinking about them hurts my head."

"Here." She pulled his head down and placed a light kiss on his cheek. "Is that better?"

Skharr nodded. "And I might add that it was not the only place where I was injured."

"Oh, for the love of—" Theros shook his head. "I can tell that my presence is an intrusion here and so I will not dawdle. As my first and…only Barbarian Princess Cassandra, do you promise to see to it that others are helped in my name?"

"I do."

"Will you be true to yourself, forever considering that others might need a little forgiveness?"

"I'll consider it, but I have to tell you that some of those assholes deserve more than a kick to their cock."

"A kick is better than a punch, between you and me." Skharr covered his instinctively. "Why did she always punch them in the cock?"

"She was short and it was convenient," Cassandra answered with a shrug. "It seems logical to me."

"She might have wished for one of her own and took it out on others," Theros muttered and shook his head. "But now you have me speaking what should be left in the gutters. I know your heart, Cassandra. Be true to it and unless you fail yourself and me, I will leave you with your paladin's gifts. At some point, however, I do hope that you will take that mantle again."

"I make no promises."

He turned to her companion. "And you, Skharr DeathEater, first Barbarian of Theros, you have supported me when I have failed. Now, I owe you in return."

"I wouldn't say that," Skharr answered with a chuckle. "I would cross land, sea, mountains, and even the odd swamp to help my friends, and Cassandra is my friend. And you told me of her pain. I do owe you for that, which would make us about even by my reckoning."

He winced as she took a firm hold of his shoulder and twisted him to face her. "What in the hells are you doing? Are you insane? Theros is offering you a gift. That doesn't simply happen at any time. There are rules for when he can do so."

The god nodded. "She is right, you know."

Skharr pursed his lips and rubbed his shoulder when she released him. "But if I accept, will her heart know that I came for her? For my friend? I am not so sure. This way, there will never be any doubt that she was the driving force behind my actions. So while I appreciate the gesture, I will surely have to decline."

Theros studied him carefully before he turned to Cassandra, his eyebrows knitted. Finally, he rolled his eyes and shook his head. "Barbarians, both of you."

"Why does he say that like it's an insult?" Skharr asked.

But the god was already fading from view and a moment later, he was gone. The warrior looked around, a little startled when he realized that most of the treasure had gone with him.

He cleared his throat and nodded. "I think that went well, don't you?"

It was her turn to roll her eyes. "Come one. Let's gather up what he left for us and be on our way."

CHAPTER TWENTY-FIVE

Cassandra shifted in her saddle and looked somewhat uncomfortable. Strider did not show any sign that the additional weight of the treasure in his saddlebags bothered him, although Skharr could tell that she wasn't sure if she had added too much weight.

"What do you think, Horse?" he asked. "Is too much treasure weighing you down? Would you be able to carry me if I needed the help even though you have this burden?"

The stallion merely looked at him, tossed his mane, and stretched his neck to take a mouthful of grass before they began their journey into the open.

"I thought so. You would take the coin for yourself, leave me to die, and live like a king of horses for the rest of your days like a traitor."

"It would be nice if you rode for once," Cassandra commented. "Even if he is carrying an unusually heavy burden. As long as he walks at a comfortable pace—which is faster than you can walk anyway—we'll escape this fucking heat faster. He would thank you for that."

Skharr turned curious to the beast. "Would you thank me for that?"

Horse merely snorted.

"I thought not."

"That's not what he said," she protested. "You're only keeping his answer to yourself because you prefer walking to riding. I would imagine it makes your cock uncomfortable."

"Do you understand what horses are saying now too?"

"No, but I can see through your bullshit. I think better than most others." Cassandra looked at the temple they had left behind. It had been a difficult decision to set everything aflame, but it was best to burn everything the dragon had used to mark its territory before someone else did accidentally.

Or intentionally. The last he had heard, a dragon's fire fetched a mighty price and was frequently used as a weapon of war when it could be found. The particular properties of it were demanded by most generals and battle engineers who searched for ways to get through gates and walls. He would be godsbedammed before he allowed them to get their hands on such weapons.

Even at a young age, he knew the allure and dangers of dragonfire. While he couldn't exactly claim that many things he had done when he was younger were wise, that was one thing he could be proud of.

The conflagration would probably burn for a few days and would destroy most of the temple simply by the sheer heat of it, but there would be nothing left for anyone to use to the detriment of others—he hoped so, at least, but it did seem fairly certain that it wasn't wishful thinking.

Skharr patted Horse gently on the neck, shook his head, and turned away. Cassandra realized that his mood had changed and ceased her pestering. There would be time for that later, she decided.

They moved slowly and cautiously to make sure they didn't wander into another monster pit. Finally, as the heat of the day began to dissipate, they emerged into a safer area away from the monsters that would have been closer to the dragon's lair.

Not much was said as they set up camp for the night, and there was no need to decide on whether a watch was needed. Even with only what they and the horses could carry, there was enough treasure to make any bandit's mouth water. While they might be farther from danger than they could have been, it was still no reason to lower their guard.

At the end of the day, it was always best to be safe rather than sorry.

"It's odd, isn't it?"

Skharr had sat in silence and stared into the fire but he now looked at her and raised an eyebrow. "What?"

"We should be celebrating a job well done. We have the treasure and we'll make more once we collect on the contract. And you can say you've killed a dragon. We should be celebrating, yes?"

"There is time for that later, I suppose," he answered and tossed a twig into the fire. "The heat of battle has dissipated and we are left feeling somewhat empty without it. I've seen it turn even the most exuberant of warriors sullen. You learn to accept that as a fact of life."

Cassandra chuckled softly. "You kill a dragon and the hoard simply disappears? We didn't even have the chance to let it roll through our fingers. Hells, we could have swum in it, Imagine the stories—I was swimming in a hoard of gold. Haven't you always wanted to say you did that?"

The barbarian looked at her and narrowed his eyes with a frown. "I cannot say the idea has ever appealed to me. Has it to you?"

"Yes." She studied him carefully. "You're an odd man."

"An odd man who has no intention to swim in gold? I cannot think it is a common fantasy among men."

"It's more common than you might think," she answered. "How do you think Theros calculated how much we could carry?"

"I'm fucked if I know."

"He might have gotten it wrong and Horse and Strider will both be angry with us over making them carry too much."

"That is true."

"You'll have to provide him with a healthy number of apples. Bribery generally works when it comes to horses."

Skharr nodded. "There is that."

"Do we still have to tithe on all of this?"

They exchanged a look, and both shrugged at the same time.

Cassandra laughed. "I admit that was a silly question. Gods always demand the nominal coin passed on to their temples. Greedy bastards."

"Godsbedammed avaricious fuckers." He leaned back, stretched, and groaned softly. "So much for my plans to buy a farm and live out my days in peace and harmony with nature."

"You never seriously planned to do that, right?" She shifted closer to him. "I have a story where you said yourself that isn't what you want at the moment."

"You're right." He sighed. "I do not. I still feel like I have more to accomplish before I can settle down and do nothing for the rest of my life. Someday, however, I think I might want to own that tavern, along with a few horses out back for Horse to frolic with in his later years. Provided that is what he wants."

"I think what Horse wants is to be with his friend," she suggested.

There was no answer from the beast, who pretended to be asleep already.

"Did you notice that Theros took the dragon as well?" She glanced at him. "That was nice of him."

"Many powerful spells require pieces of a dragon. I doubt it was done out of the kindness of his heart."

"I've heard stories about sacs being used to burn holes in walls and gates during sieges. You don't believe he might have taken it for something like that, do you?"

Skharr sighed. "Even if he did, would there be anything that we could do to stop him?"

"You make a good point."

"The disadvantage, of course, is that we now have no real proof that we killed a dragon."

"Who cares? The story spread that you killed one when you hadn't."

"With a little help from the emperor. There will be no such help this time."

Cassandra smiled and inched even closer. "A paladin's word is not one to be doubted. Theros himself would have to take action if I were to lie when telling the tale."

He studied her for a moment. "You seem to be…hot?"

"No." She pulled some of her clothes free and nudged them from her shoulders as she moved again. "One dragon is gone, yes, but one is still left and I intend to battle it like a true barbarian princess."

"Well, I could argue that you should probably respect my—"

She cut him off when she touched her lips lightly to his neck first, then pushed onto her knees so she was high enough to press them to his. Her soft touch lasted only a moment before she took hold of his cheeks with both hands and pressed against him as her tongue slipped past his lips. She tasted him hungrily before she dragged herself back with a soft gasp.

"What were you saying?" she asked, her voice a soft, breathy whisper as her fingers caressed his cheek lightly.

"I forget," he answered in a whisper as well. She was right. Something was most certainly rising that she was particularly skilled at handling.

Without a thought, he lifted her carefully and positioned her to straddle his lap facing him. She giggled as her fingers worked to pull his shirt off.

There was no gambeson between the two of them now, which made it easier. She leaned forward to press her lips lightly to his collarbone, then let her tongue flick out and dance down his chest.

Skharr couldn't help a soft groan when her hands moved faster than her lips and she curled her fingers around him to stroke him gently and carefully through his trousers. She seemed anxious to battle the dragon in person as quickly as possible, and it was not long before he undid his belt and pushed the breeches down.

It seemed unchivalrous of him to not explore when she did so with such skill. He lowered the straps of the sparse garments she wore and his fingers caressed her nipples lightly. She nibbled his hips teasingly before she moved her mouth to where her hands were already hard at work.

"You..." His train of thought was lost again when her tongue teased expertly for a moment before her mouth slid around him. He shuddered as he grasped her ass and pulled her closer to him while her fingers, lips, and tongue continued their ministrations.

Without a doubt, he knew her intentions were only to rile the dragon up to ensure a more challenging battle to come.

Finally, the words he had searched for returned to him. "You'll probably want to remove your clothes. It might prove painful if I have to remove them myself—and expensive to replace as well."

Her mouth was occupied but her gaze turned to meet his and a playful, daring expression played across her features.

"Very well, but you cannot say I did not warn you." The barbarian growled and threaded the fingers of his free hand through her hair to hold the back of her head and guide her a little closer.

It would most certainly be a mighty battle but he knew who would come away the victor.

AUTHOR NOTES - MICHAEL ANDERLE
JUNE 7, 2021

Thank you for reading both this story and these author notes at the end.

We are finished with book 07 of a larger story arc about this world. Below, I will share with you a cover and explanation where we are going next.

BUT WHAT ABOUT SKHARR?

Oh, we have more Skharr coming. Skharr DeathEater - *The Assassin's Trial* Book 08 is now on pre-order, so if you want to make sure that the 'Zon brings you all the goodness, feel free to grab the pre-order now.

MY FIRST (SOMEWHAT) EPIC FANTASY

Skharr 08 will be released AFTER the Axe-Wed stories and the Barbarian Princess stories. The next release (late in the year) for book 08 will be right about the time of the release of our first fantasy series (not swords & sorcery) in this world.

Here is the cover:

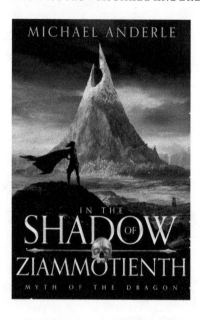

To give you some idea of the size and scope of the *Myth of the Dragon* series, we are almost done with the first book, yet we won't be releasing it until either November or December of this year in hardback.

We have a LOT of work to do for our first release.

We are looking to do something cool with the hardback, including the jacket sleeve artwork (above) and an embossed inside cover with additional artwork inside the edition by Jeff Brown, the artist doing the covers for the *Myth of the Dragon* series.

We have monster images being done by the same artist doing the covers for Skharr DeathEater, The Barbarian Princess, and Axe-Wed stories.

We are now at a total of twenty (20) books planned for this world. I'm hoping you are as excited as I am with fantasy stories and will give them a chance!

GOT THROUGH THE GRADUATION

For those who remember that Judith and I were heading towards Texas in my last author notes, the graduation went off without a hitch.

That son (Joey) is presently driving his way from Texas to California to start his journey into the future. Like his twin brother Jacob, he doesn't shy from driving far. I will admit I'm not sure if I would have made that trip at their age.

I'd like to say I had something to do with encouraging the guys to be willing to "go out there and do it" with the long drive.

But to be honest (and not taking anything away from them for having made the trips), it was probably more their mother encouraging them to get out on the road and make it happen. I have to admit I'm the overly protective person here. It doesn't help them, and I have to bite down on my natural inclination. Otherwise, I'd just stress the hell out.

I remember when Jacob was last driving from California to Texas. He told me, "Don't worry, it will all be fine."

It helped a lot.

2021

It is almost halfway through 2021, and I must admit this year has flown by. It will be the end of the year before I know it, and I'm going to think, "Where did it all go?"

I hope you and your family (whether by birth or choice) are doing fantastic, and I wish you the best summer (or future summer if you are reading this in the future) you can have!

Ad Aeternitatem,

Michael Anderle

CONNECT WITH THE AUTHOR

Connect with Michael Anderle

Website: http://lmbpn.com

Email List: http://lmbpn.com/email/

Social Media:

https://www.facebook.com/LMBPNPublishing

https://twitter.com/MichaelAnderle

https://www.instagram.com/lmbpn_publishing/

https://www.bookbub.com/authors/michael-anderle

BOOKS BY MICHAEL ANDERLE

Sign up for the LMBPN email list to be notified of new releases and special deals!

https://lmbpn.com/email/

For a complete list of books by Michael Anderle, please visit:

www.lmbpn.com/ma-books/